TERA LY....

Eye
Candy

Eye Candy
a City Chicks novel

Tera Lynn Childs
2232 South Nellis Boulevard, Suite 112
Las Vegas, NV 89104

teralynnchilds.com

Second Edition

♥

ISBN 978-0-9904605-0-3 (ebook)
ISBN 978-0-9904605-2-7 (trade paperback)

For Mom, because everything

ONE

MY LOWER LEFT desk drawer holds a secret.

Looking at the rest of my office you'd never guess. The pristine mahogany surface of the desk is unspoiled by dust or clutter. Every office tool has a place and every file is appropriately color coded. Rows of sales data binders are neatly aligned and in chronological order. The flat-panel monitor is oriented at the perfect ergonomic angle to minimize eye strain and glare.

But that drawer—securely locked if I'm out of the office for even a second—is the exception to my immaculately professional appearance.

That drawer is loaded with candy.

A sweet-tooth soup of peppermints, lemon drops, butterscotches, caramels, lollipops, and atomic fireballs. A treasure trove of red vines, gummy bears, licorice whips, fruit slices, red hots, and tropical dots stacked in disorderly piles.

My name is Lydia Vanderwalk, and I'm a candy-holic.

I've known this for a long time and freely confess my dependency. I know I couldn't stop, even if I wanted to.

I would never, ever want to.

I live for the sugar rush of a one-pound bag of M&Ms. Sour apple tape got me through my college all-nighters. Every great idea I ever had was Lifesavers-induced.

When I was four years old, my mom dressed me as Jo from *Facts of Life* and took me trick-or-treating. Everyone thought I was Michael J. Fox. I was traumatized. When we got home I dumped my booty onto the carpet and started consuming. Amongst the Smarties and fun-size Snickers, I found comfort for my costume identity crisis. Candy soothed my pain. And has ever since.

Next Halloween I was a gumdrop. Not one nearsighted neighbor mistook me for a pink mountain.

Candy is my coping mechanism, and it's less destructive than other addictions I could have. As far as vices go, it's a harmless one.

In my industry, though, it's the eighth mortal sin. People in fashion—correction, *women* in fashion don't eat anything, let alone candy by the bucketful. That's why my secret could never get out.

Thankfully, I am skilled at maintaining the appearance of normalcy.

So when Janice, junior VP of Marketing for Ferrero Couture and my direct superior (otherwise mentally known as Jawbreaker—hard on the outside hard on the inside) barged into my office without so much as a knock on the closed door, I slipped open the drawer, pulled out a Werther's, and popped it in my mouth.

She was dressed, as usual, like an aging Vegas cigarette girl. Shoulder-padded silver blazer with a deep-v neckline, tight black pants, and eye makeup that made Cleopatra look like a bare-faced virgin. She thinks she's the Donatella Versace of Ferrero Couture. She's an executive, for Good&Plenty's sake —a design diva she is not.

In my grey, summer wool pantsuit and lilac cashmere shell I felt deliciously like Belgian chocolate next to a bag of carob chips.

"Have you seen the new *GQ*?" she asked.

"*Uh-uh*," I hummed around the toffee. The buttery sweetness melted into my tongue and improved my overall sense of well-being.

She plunked the magazine on my desk and smirked. I flicked my eyes to the cover and back to her, trying to maintain an air of nonchalance and disguise my annoyance at her intrusion. My gaze flew immediately back to the slick image on the glossy cover. *Gavin!*

Now Jawbreaker's smirk made sense.

Here came conversation #3,524—not that I'm counting— about the Lamentable Loss of Gavin the Great.

"Isn't this your fiancé, Lydia?" she said, gloating. "Oops, I mean your *ex*-fiancé."

Right, that was a slip-up.

If I could manage to scalp her hip-length platinum tresses and braid them into a fashionable tiara without getting fired, I would. That might even become the next hot trend from Ferrero Couture. But as that was a remote possibility, I held my tongue and started mentally ranking my favorite Jelly Belly flavors.

Toasted Marshmallow, Cotton Candy, Buttered Popcorn...

I smiled politely.

...Green Apple, Juicy Pear, Strawberry Cheesecake...

"Imagine all the women chasing after him now."

My smile fake-brightened.

...Crushed Pineapple, Watermelon, Grape Jelly...

"Have you tried to get in touch with him? Maybe there's still a chance—"

I had to stop her before my head exploded and a rainbow of Skittles drizzled down over my immaculate office. "Haven't I told you,"—Jawbreaker—"Janice, about the new guy I've been seeing?"

I regretted those words almost before they left my mouth. Lying was not my strength, but when Jawbreaker started down the Gavin path, I couldn't help myself. So I came up with the one thing sure to stop her in her tracks: a boyfriend.

Unfortunately, she was a seasoned social veteran and her path changed faster than you can say Reese's Pieces.

"How wonderful," she cried, not meaning it at all. "You simply must bring him to the Summer Sail Away next weekend."

Summer Sail Away, my mind echoed. The end of summer gala at Jawbreaker's Southampton *tres* posh estate—her husband owns a ridiculously successful import/export business. *The* fashion industry event of the season. All the senior VPs will be there. All the board members will be there. Ferrero will be there. Half the fashion world will be there.

Never before had I been graced with an invitation.

As senior account exec, my social profile never ranked high enough to warrant an invite. And, since my status had not recently changed, I had to assume Jawbreaker thought she was pulling one over on me.

Show up stag after the whole extremely small world of fashion heard about this new beau? It would be poor, pitiful Lydia. And a liar to boot.

I could always not show up.

But I wanted a promotion. A rumor had been circling that Jawbreaker was about to be promoted to senior VP of Marketing. And I would do anything to get her current job. The gala would give me the chance to prove I was more than a brain with a knack for numbers. A chance to show Ferrero that I was VP material and could schmooze with the best of them.

A chance I couldn't pass up.

With the KY Clique—my trio of nemeses at Ferrero—out to get my current job I had to seize opportunities where I could.

"Wonderful," I replied, knowing my farce was worth it just to see the scowl crease Jawbreaker's brow. Botox can't fix everything. "What time should we be there?"

♥

KELLY SHOWED UP FIRST. She was the most aggressive of the three KY girls—the team leader—and Jawbreaker probably ran to her with the gossip of my previously unheard of boyfriend the moment she left my office.

The KY Clique came on board at Ferrero as marketing interns in May following their Barnyard—er, Barnard graduation. From the start, they settled for nothing less than full control of the house. I have an under-the-table wager with Marlene in accessories that the house will be Ferrero, Kelly, Kathryn & Karyn within five years. Three if they stumbled onto a stroke of luck or juicy gossip.

And I might have just handed them that lucky gossip on a jewel-encrusted silver platter.

Kelly knocked—the simple courtesy the first sign she was up to something—and entered on the pretense of needing my opinion on an overseas marketing campaign. A blatant ruse as my region covers the western United States.

"Oh," she squealed as I tried to not-so-subtly urge her out of my office. "Janice told me about your new boyfriend. He sounds like a prince."

That's funny, because I don't remember telling Jawbreaker anything about him. Because I don't know anything about him. Because he doesn't exist.

"I mean, it's not as if just *anyone* can measure up to Gavin, but a girl's gotta try, right?"

"Mmm-hmm." Hopefully a vague enough response to derail conversation #3,525—not that I'm counting.

I'm never that lucky.

"It's about time you moved on to someone new. Two years is far too long for someone your age to stay single. You need to do your hunting before all the big game is shot."

Like I need relationship advice from a preschooler.

Her monologue didn't warrant any input on my part, so I contented myself with neatening up a stack of papers on my desk while she talked on.

"I can't believe you never mentioned this new guy before. He must be something special if you've been keeping him all to yourself," she cooed. "And we all get to meet him at the Summer Sail Away."

Suppressing the sudden and overwhelming urge to scream, I lunged for my candy drawer. Within seconds I had a Meltaway in my mouth. The sweet sugary goodness could almost make up for the news that the KYs—low chicks in the hen house—were already invited to the Summer Sail Away. It took me a fabricated boyfriend and an ex on the cover of *GQ* to earn one.

Clearly I should have gone to Barnard. Maybe if I changed my name to Kydia...

"Hi Kelly," twin high-pitched voices squealed.

Kathryn and Karyn bounded into my office. I was surrounded by KYs with no means of escape.

They looked so similar. They could be triplets, with their matching golden highlights, colorful wrap dresses, and stiletto slingbacks. I could usually tell them apart by their nails— Kathryn was natural and unpolished, Karyn was French-mani-cured, while Kelly was all-acrylic and more than a little scary around ripe fruit.

"We heard about the new boyfriend,"—I checked the nails —Karyn exclaimed.

"Shame on you for keeping him a secret,"—unpolished— Kathryn chastised.

"But," Kelly interrupted, "he'll be at the Summer Sail Away."

"Ooh, I can't wait."

"We can evaluate his TIP for you."

His what? I needed a KY-to-English dictionary.

"His Total Income Potential. Maybe his TIP will be almost as high as Gavin's."

"Not likely!"

I gave up trying to figure out which one spoke. Dizzy, I desperately grabbed for another Meltaway.

I felt like a spectator at my own execution. Only I had handed the man in the black hood the axe and pulled my hair out of the way as I laid my head on the block.

Mental Post-It: Stop making up non-existent boyfriends.

"*THAT'S* YOUR EX?"

I looked up from the engrossing occupation of swirling ice in my Lemon Drop to find Fiona clutching *GQ* to her chest. One grape-lacquered finger stabbing at the cover.

Next to Fiona I always felt like the worst sort of invisible person. No style. No flair. No taste.

Tonight she wore a dark-washed denim pencil skirt over Limeade green fishnets with a silver sequined tank and metallic silver gladiator sandals. With her exotic looks and flair for fashion, everyone noticed when she enters a room.

"Nice to see you, too," I replied, thinking it's not really so nice if the conversation was heading where I thought it was heading.

Not in the mood to launch into conversation #3,527—not that I'm counting—I downed the remains of my drink and signaled Bartender Barbie to bring another. Conversation #3,524 had gotten me into enough trouble today and I didn't need any more bad JuJu.

"No, really," Fiona exclaimed, dropping her corduroy satchel next to the bar stool and lifting herself up onto the seat. "*This* is the man who broke your heart?"

I turned my best Westchester glare on her, but Fiona is a force of nature and proceeded without pause.

"He's gorgeous, babe. And rich. And successful. And—"

Gee, all things I didn't already know about him, having been engaged to the man for nearly six years. "Thanks, Fi. That makes me feel much better."

Bartender Barbie set another Lemon Drop in front of me and gave me a look resembling pity. Great, my life was complete.

"The article gushes on about how he's this hotshot investment banker at Castile and Tatum, the youngest ever to make upper management."

Didn't Fiona notice my head banging desperately against the polished wood surface of the bar? Too engrossed in the details of my former—though I prefer to call him my late—fiancé, she didn't even care that I lost several strands of light brown hair to the sticky surface.

And, typical of the way my day had gone, I was not even lucky enough to knock myself unconscious.

"Why is Lydia already passed out?" a lilting Southern voice asked.

Bethany! Thank you Mr. Goodbar, I was saved.

Fiona peered over the magazine, surprised to see my face stuck to the bar. "Don't know," she mused, returning her attention to GQ.

Some girlfriend.

"I'm stuck," I managed to say, sounding even more pathetic than I felt, if possible.

"Let me help you, honey." Beth set her purse carefully on a stool before grabbing me by the shoulders and yanking.

That girl is stronger than she looks.

"Thanks." Cheek burning, I was now the only woman in the history of skin care to be exfoliated by a sticky bar counter. But at least I was upright.

Beth smiled before climbing gingerly onto the stool and smoothing out the wrinkles in her floral sundress. "What's the matter, sugar?"

Bartender Barbie brought her a Mojito before she had a chance to order. I tried to forget that Barbie never remembered my drink order, even after two years of Friday nights.

Bethany looked like the typical southern belle. Tasteful

but flirty floral sundress, sweet high heel Mary Janes, hose. Her long blonde hair meticulously curled and sprayed yet touchably soft. Guys jumped to be chivalrous for her. Everywhere she went doors opened before her, chairs got pulled out beneath her, and men fell to their knees begging for marriage.

But she did have that steel magnolia edge. She owned and operated a very successful shop in SoHo, and a sweet gal didn't last long in the city without learning to bite back.

"Oh my heavens," Beth exclaimed as she got a good look at the magazine in Fiona's clutches, "that's Gavin!"

"Yeah," Fiona answered, dropping the magazine to her lap. "Hot, huh?"

Beth will defend me. We've been friends since freshman year at Columbia, since before Gavin and I started dating. She knew his true nature—the sour, sticky core at his center.

I was wrong.

Beth nodded, taking a sip of her mojito. "Grade A Prime."

"I wouldn't mind rolling over to that the morning after." Fiona got a dreamy look, glitter-glossed lips grinning, that reminded me how much steamier her love life was than mine.

The conversation turned dangerous. In my experience, no woman is safe even fantasizing about Gavin Fairchild. I had to interject before someone got hurt. "Too bad he's such a Sour Apple Blow Pop."

Fiona was undeterred. "Does he have an agent?"

"An agent? Fi, he's a stockbroker."

"Yes, but he's a stockbroker on the cover of *GQ*."

I really shouldn't have been surprised. Fiona was a talent agent at Famous Faces, after all. Representing the most delicious hunks on the planet was her daily duty. Which was great, so long as this was one delicious hunk she stayed far, far away from. For all our sakes.

Just as I opened my mouth to say as much, a realization struck: What did I care if Fiona represented Gavin to super-model stardom? I didn't care about him. He was nothing but an anomaly in my otherwise normal dating record. He was the past. Good riddance to stale candy.

What I did care about was how everyone still treated me like I'd lost the winning lottery ticket. Gavin Fairchild was not my one and only chance at happily ever after.

Too bad I didn't realize this sooner. Like this afternoon. Like before Jawbreaker brought him up in conversation and I freaked. I freaked and now I was in such a tight fix that conversation #3,527—not that I'm counting—seemed like a shopping spree at Dylan's Candy Bar.

My groan, followed by the loud thunk as my head hit the bar again, must have caught Fiona and Beth's attention because each grabbed a shoulder and hauled me back up.

"What's wrong, sugar?"

"Tell us," Fiona urged.

"We can help," Beth promised.

"No," I said, recalling every appalling word of the conversations #3,524—not that I'm counting—and #3,525—not that I'm—oh, who was I kidding, I'm counting, "you can't."

Beth smiled. "Try us."

Resigned to the fate of relating every horrifying detail, I began my tale. As the words came out they picked up speed, and soon I was babbling about Jawbreakers, KYs, Southampton, and my desire to be a barnyard animal.

Fiona and Beth smiled and nodded and I could tell they wondered what in Hershey's name I was talking about.

The vodka in my Lemon Drops—plural—must have been getting to me. But confection was good for the soul and I couldn't stop.

"I had to shut her up," I continued between gulps of lemon-flavored alcohol. "I mean there's only so much ex-hashing a girl can take." Closing my eyes I pictured Jawbreaker, hip-length platinum hair twisting around one finger as she fantasized about Gavin right before my eyes. "So I told her I had a new guy."

Without looking, I felt them both shrug.

"I told her I had been dating this guy for several months and we're really getting serious. Seemed like a good idea at the time. Shows Gavin is forgotten and I'm moving on with my life, love and all. Until the unthinkable happened. Jawbreaker insists I bring him to the Summer Sail Away next weekend."

"Summer Sail Away?" Fiona's brow crinkled.

"*The* company function of the season at her mansion in Southampton." I groaned at the thought of losing my coveted promotion to a KY. "If I show up without this dream guy, my career is history."

"Why?" Beth inquired. "It's just a date."

"Jawbreaker would relish any excuse to humiliate me." And promote one of the KY Clique in my place. The bonds of Barnyard sisterhood are hard to break.

"We can find you a guy, no problem," Fiona announced.

"Oh yes," Beth added. I heard the excitement in her voice as my datelessness became her new project. "There's a guy in my building, Harvard grad, gorgeous to boot. He's perfect for you."

"No," I interjected adamantly. "I don't want a smart, gorgeous, lovable guy. No one interested in a relationship."

I was one busy Marshmallow Peep. My life was too full and too complicated already, without the added attachment of a guy.

Unfortunately, everyone in my life interpreted this independent streak as evidence of my pining for Gavin.

Beth smiled sadly. "It's been two years, sugar. Time to move on."

"I know. And I am," I insisted. "I have. But not right now. I have too much going on at work to get emotionally involved with anyone. I don't *need* a relationship."

Somehow, I couldn't bring myself to say that I didn't *want* a relationship. Rotten emotional longing. Stay under cover where you belong.

A look passed between my friends that I chose to interpret as concern, and I also chose to ignore it.

"Forget it. I'll just show up stag and weather Jawbreaker's interrogation."

"No, no, let us help." Resolve hardened Fiona's exotic features and I knew argument was futile.

I turned to Bethany, the face of a true steel magnolia.

"We'll find you the perfect guy," Beth promised.

"A trophy date."

"A date without a relationship."

"A man without opinions."

"Without emotions."

"Without baggage."

"Without a brain."

Coming to the bottom of my—third—Lemon Drop, I began to see possibilities. A guy for show. One that looks good and thinks little. Easy on the eyes and short on the intellect.

I grinned. "Eye candy."

We three stared at our drinks, deep in thought. Fiona finally spoke. "I know a guy."

"You know a guy?" I asked.

"From the agency, one of the models." Fiona paused. "He's looking for some extra cash, and..."

"And...?" I prodded.

"He's gorgeous and sweet. A little light in the attic but heavy in the basement, if you know what I mean." Fiona waggled her eyebrows.

I had no idea what she meant. But that might have been due to the Lemon Drops, so I gave her a shrug-nod and signaled for another drink.

"I'm sure he'd be willing to help you out," she continued. "For adequate compensation."

Whoa! Compensation? Have I reached the lowest of the low? Do I have to buy a date? And Fiona was selling me one. "You're pimping your models."

She shook her head, taking a sip of her Slow Comfortable Screw Up Against A Wall before continuing. "Just one model. Singular. And I'm not pimping, just arranging. Like a dating service where money changes hands."

"Sounds like pimping to me," I grumbled.

"Sounds like the perfect plan," Beth countered.

Had I thought earlier my day couldn't get any worse? Mental Post-It: Always anticipate something even more horrific happening.

"Sugar, this is everything you need," she persisted. "One gorgeous, boss-impressing hottie to get everyone off your back about Gavin and yourself out of the hole you've dug. One stringless guy who will accept your money at the end of the day and leave your heart intact."

Barbie set the fresh Lemon Drop before me, but I decided I had enough. This plan was starting to sound like a good idea —that had to be an alcohol-induced opinion.

"Look, give him a shot." Fiona dragged her satchel off the floor and pulled out her hot pink phone. A few taps of the screen and she announced, "He's doing an in-house shoot tomorrow. I'll talk to him and make all the arrangements. If he doesn't take, you can always publicly break up with him at the Sailboat Saga."

"Summer Sail Away," I corrected.

"Everyone will think you're hot stuff if you're too good for the likes of him." She shoved her phone back in her satchel.

"I don't think..."

"You're desperate. Take a chance."

Tired and fed up with feeling like a spectator in my own life, I took a stand.

"No."

Fiona and Beth peered at each other, brows raised. Maybe it was the vodka talking. Maybe it was the culmination of my horrendous day. Maybe it was me finally deciding to have a say in my own life. Whatever the case, they looked surprised.

But remained determined.

"You'll change your mind," Fiona stated.

With a groan, my forehead plunked to the bar.

REEHN, reehn, reehn!

"Uungh." I rolled over and slapped the alarm clock into silence. How dare it wake me up at 8:00 on a Saturday morning? Nine minutes later it started screaming again. Another slap. Another nine minutes later it started screaming again. This time, I pried open one desert dry eye and managed to find the off switch.

Ring, ring, ring.

"Nooo," I moaned.

There was no way I was prepared to speak. I let voicemail pick up.

My head felt like someone stuffed it full of gumballs— every movement sent the throbbing pain thundering to another side of my brain. My eyelids were stuck to my eyeballs, something that should have been medically impossible. And my stomach—well, let's just say my stomach was seriously rethinking everything I had consumed in the last twelve hours.

Having no desire to see any of that again, I sank into the softness of my feather-top and held a white downy pillow over my face.

Ring, ring, ring.

Even through the sound-baffling pillow I heard the phone.

I ignored it, ready to drift peacefully back to sleep. But as I started to doze my phone dinged. A message. Without opening my eyes, I played it.

There were actually two.

First message, Friday, 7:07 p.m.: "Hi, Lydia." Holy Hot Tamales. I jolted upright in bed. "It's Gavin. We need to talk. I know this is out of the blue, but can we get together this week? Call me, I can make time whenever you're available."

I replayed the message.

"Hi, Lydia. It's Gavin. We need to talk." What could we possibly have to talk about after two years of communication blackout? "I know this is out of the blue—" No, I totally expected this. "But can we get together this week?" Gee, my week was pretty full... "Call me, I can make time whenever you're available." Well that's different. He never had time for me when we were engaged.

As I recalled, he only had time for a certain redheaded secretary named Rhonda who wore high heels and short skirts —not that I noticed, but a girl is bound to retain a few details about the woman she finds her significant other of six years balling on his desk when she shows up to surprise him with Chinese food.

Delete or save? Delete or save? Hmmm... I jabbed the delete button with an exuberance usually reserved for a candy spree.

Second message, Saturday, 8:19 a.m.: "Lydia, this is Janice." Jawbreaker called on a Saturday morning? "I'm calling to let you know I e-mailed you directions to the Summer Sail Away. Remember, it's a weekend retreat so pack your jammies and your bikini. And make sure that new hunk of yours packs his too, unless he sleeps in the buff and skinny dips." Yesterday's farce—blissfully forgotten in vodka-rendered memory loss— came crashing back into my aching brain. "Oh, one more thing." I could hear Jawbreaker's smirk. The hair rose on the back of my neck. "Do you have Gavin's email address? I need to zap him the directions, as well. He can't make it Friday, so he's meeting Kelly there on Saturday. Ta-ta, see you Monday."

I sat there, blinking like a hummingbird on Pixy Stix. I finally found the capacity to press delete before letting the phone fall to the floor.

If my brain worked, I would probably have tried to figure out how my life had swirled around the bowl so quickly. I reached for the bag of candy in my nightstand drawer before dragging myself, clothed in my candy hearts-covered pajamas, into my workroom. Closing the door behind me, secure in the knowledge that there was no phone, no internet, and no outside distraction in this room, I crossed to the workbench and climbed onto the stool.

I chewed passively on some Swedish Fish.

The workroom was my sanctuary, where I left the outside world and turned inward. It was my stress relief. Some people tried yoga, others skydiving. I made jewelry. It had started when I took jewelry-making as an elective in college, and it just kind of stuck.

What had started as pure hobby became part business when my friend Bethany wanted to stock my designs in her SoHo boutique.

LIV Jewelry was selling like penny candy. For much more than a penny.

Beth couldn't keep it on the shelves. She kept pushing me to hire an assistant, to produce more and take my distribution wider. But that would mean taking my hobby seriously and that might take the fun out the process. For now I just enjoyed working on pieces when the inspiration struck. Like today.

I had a feeling today's sketches would result in some very scary jewelry.

Mentally checking my frustrations at the door, I pulled out a sketch pad and went to work. Dark swirling shapes decorated with spiked starbursts. Heavy lines. Black, midnight blue, and tarnished silver.

The doodles developed into a fine swirl of silver wire with dark sapphire beads and black onyx stars. I proudly titled the sketch, "Midnight sky."

Setting down my pencil, I pronounced the sketch finished. I

glanced up at the clock on the wall to find I had been working for almost two hours.

I produced one sketch and came to one conclusion.

If Gavin was gracing us with his presence at the Summer Sail Away, I was definitely not going singular. Even if it meant a degrading humiliation.

After safely closing all my creativity behind the workroom door, I retrieved my cell. I fidgeted as I waited for her to pick up.

"Yo," she greeted.

This was the moment of no return. I knew I could still back out. And I knew I wouldn't.

"All right, Fi," I said, twirling a candy necklace around my finger, "set me up."

TWO

I EASED my silver Passat into a parking spot and pulled the post-it from my purse to check the Brooklyn address. Yep, this was the right place.

When Fiona called to tell me her guy was booked solid all week, but I could pick him up from a Friday afternoon shoot, I had doubts. How could I drive a guy out to the Hamptons, on the pretense of being my long-term boyfriend, without having ever met him before?

What had she gotten me into?

What had I gotten me into?

This place was a dump, D-U-M-P. Once it might have been a thriving pier-side warehouse, but all that remained was a weathered shell. Of the twenty windows in the crumbling red brick façade, three had glass in them. The remaining seventeen were either boarded up or broken out. The kind of place where nightmares were born.

Desperate for a sugar fix, I popped open the glove box and dug around for a Jolly Rancher. Watermelon. Exactly what I needed.

Never underestimate the therapeutic sounds of crinkling cellophane.

I had just popped the block of heaven into my mouth when someone tapped on my passenger side window. I screamed— like a horror movie heroine—and spat my Jolly Rancher onto the dashboard.

My heart pounded in sugar-rush-heavy thumps. Short black hair. Tanned olive skin. Bright blue eyes that shone like a blue raspberry Dum-Dum after it'd been sucked on for a while. All blended into a face of breathtaking proportion. He motioned with his hand to roll down the window. Half a life-time of New York-learned safety melted away like wet cotton candy, and I complied.

"You Lydia?" he asked when the window lowered enough for his head to fit through.

"Y-yes." I reached for the Jolly Rancher. Freeing the sticky pink block from the charcoal gray dashboard, I eyed it care-fully before deeming it too grubby to eat.

"I'm Phelps." He smiled—a broad, white-toothed smile that belonged in toothpaste commercials. And before I could remember that he was a model and might very well have *been* in countless toothpaste commercials, he lifted the handle and opened the passenger door. He settled into the leather seat and pulled the door shut, dropping a well-worn duffle bag on the floor. "Sorry I'm late."

I got my first look beyond his beautiful, chiseled face. While he might be beyond reproach above the neck, the rest of him was another story. Clothed in some space-age silver body-suit, he looked like a Star Wars reject.

"What are you wearing?" I demanded.

Not the picture perfect boyfriend date I was paying for. He

21

belonged at a Trekkie convention, not a Southampton soiree.

My Jolly Rancher and my career, both ruined.

"What?" He looked confused and glanced down at himself. "Oh yeah, I was working."

"On what? A remake of Lost in Space?" I was beginning to think Fiona had overestimated his intellect.

But I didn't have time to care. We were late already, so I put the car in gear.

"A cologne shoot," he laughed, the kind that slipped in beneath your skin to tickle every feminine nerve ending. The kind that almost made me grin stupidly in return, despite the fact that Captain Kirk was my escort to the most important business function of my career.

I scowled. Men should not be allowed to use that kind of laugh on unsuspecting women.

"Don't worry." Phelps unzipped the duffel and produced a rolled up shirt. "I have plenty of time to get changed."

"Get ch—" Managing to drive between the lines, I caught sight of him tugging the silver spandex wonder over his head, revealing a chest as chiseled as his face. Holy Hot Tamales, this guy should be a Calvin Klein undies hottie. Which in no way explained why he was getting naked in my car. "What are you doing?"

"Getting dressed," he answered, buttoning the sedate blue oxford shirt over his impressive chest. "You might want to look the other way for a minute. In this getup I had to go commando."

I felt my cheeks erupt in flames. Surely this man was not about to— A zipper roared and I kept my eyes glued to the road.

Suppressing my feminine curiosity, I remembered my interrupted sugar fix. Maybe that explained my weak thoughts. Withdrawal.

With Phelps' current state of undress the glove box was out. Instead, I groped behind the seat, blindly rummaging through the seat pocket until I found my open package of Sugar Babies.

I tore into that tiny caramel ball like it was my first drop of water after a week in the desert.

"Hey, got another one of those?" Phelps held out his hand.

"No," I lied. No one shares my candy stash, least of all a Clone Wars reject sure to earn me a demotion.

Clearly he did not understand the gravity of the situation.

Keeping my eyes on the road, I said, "I don't know how much Fiona explai—"

"You need a token boyfriend to impress your hard-ass boss."

He arched forward in the seat and I caught a glimpse of tan line-free, naked flesh from the corner of my eye. Fiona's comment about his basement came rushing back as I saw exactly what she meant. My breath caught, and I concentrated on navigating my way onto the Brooklyn-Queens Expressway.

"Right," I answered. "I accidentally told her I had a boyfriend, and—"

"How do you accidentally tell someone you have a boyfriend?" Another rasp of a zipper and Phelps was fully clothed.

Was I relieved or disappointed? Relieved, I told myself.

"It's a long, long story, but the bottom line is she thinks we've been dating for six months and we need to make her believe that this weekend."

"No worries." He folded his arms behind his head and

relaxed back into the seat. "With Friday afternoon traffic, we have three hours to make up for six months of intimacy."

Steering the Passat onto the Long Island Expressway, I swallowed my retort to his smart comment. "My job dep—"

"Wait, we have been intimate, haven't we?"

My fingers tightened around the steering wheel.

"Listen, this may be just a game to you. A way to make some easy cash," I bit out through clenched teeth. "But my future rides on this weekend, and if you can't help that happen then I'll just drop you at the next train station."

"Relax, Lyd. I can play the part." He turned in his seat, facing me. "Tell me everything I need to know about you."

"I NEED A REST STOP," I announced as we drove through Massapequa.

More than a bathroom, I needed a minute away from sharing a confined space with Phelps. That man had a personality that would try the forgiving patience of a monk.

I pulled into a Shell station and shut off the engine.

"Want me to pump?" he asked.

Did I ever. Holy Hot Tamales, where did that thought come from? Sugar. I needed sugar.

"Sure," I said, anything to get away from him sooner. "I'll just pop inside."

"Grab me a Fiji water, will ya?"

He smiled that cocky smile I had fast become familiar with during the past hour, and I fled the scene. I didn't really have to use the restroom, but I thought I had better go for appearance's sake. In the cramped but thankfully clean ladies room, I splashed cold water on my face and touched up my flagging makeup. I needed more than some eyeliner and lip gloss to boost my flagging spirit.

My problem was more than just his overbearing attitude. In the car—my baby—he had to control the radio, the a/c, and even the driving. I was tempted to let him drive, just to stop his incessant directions. You'd think I'd asked the man to pilot the U.S.S. Enterprise into the Delta Quadrant, not navigate the Passat to Southampton.

"Speed up, it's sixty-five here," I mimicked. "Get in the fast lane. Pass that wagon."

We weren't even out of Brooklyn before I wanted to gag the man.

Sure, he was attractive—okay, he could make a girl drop her panties with a single wink—but that didn't mean he would get his way every time.

"Could ya find a radio station not playing bubblegum pop?" he had asked.

Who made him the arbiter of what counted as good music? Besides, I had to stay current on all things pop culture. Books. Movies. Music. They all fed the fashion.

I walked out of the ladies' room mimicking his complaints. "Damn, it's cold in here," he had said. "What are you, a penguin?"

Yep, that's me. Lydia "the Penguin" Vanderwalk.

Sugar, my mind called.

Like a piglet sniffing out truffles, I followed my nose to the candy section. So many choices. I was instantly soothed. I grabbed a Bit-o-Honey and a bag of Peach Os—and an Oh Henry, just to complete the "O" theme and just in case I needed the extra pick-me-up.

Glancing out the plate glass windows to see Phelps gyrating around my car in a dance frighteningly reminiscent of the Macarena, I grabbed a Rolo, too.

This was going to be the longest weekend of my life.

♥

BY THE TIME we got to the first exit for Westhampton—only thirty miles left to go—I knew more about Phelps Elliot than I ever cared to. As the dense urbanization of the city gave way to the more natural landscape of the far reaches of the island, his inhibitions—if he had any to begin with—melted away. The man did not have a problem with sharing.

"And this scar," he boasted, indicating the back of his right elbow, "I got mountaineering in Patagonia. The Andes can be a bitch."

I stared blankly down the road, concentrating on the car in front of me so I didn't give in to the temptation to drive my baby into a ditch and end it right there.

"And this one," he continued, scooting forward in the seat and reaching for his waistband, "I got—"

"Enough!" I shouted.

Phelps froze, thumbs tucked into the waistband of his black trousers, mouth open, about to detail yet another dangerous adventure. The man was a walking wonder of Emergency Room medicine.

"I think," I said more calmly, toning down my voice from the hysteria that threatened, "I know about enough scars. No one is going to ask me for a detailed accounting of your physical flaws."

"Hey, these aren't flaws, babe." He smiled that smile that made me cringe. "They're character."

The man leaned back into the corner between the seat and the door. I hit the door locks. As much as I might relish Phelps being splattered across the Route 27, there would be a lot of questions and police reports and paperwork if he fell out of my car doing sixty-five—as I'd been told several times was the speed limit.

On second thought... I hit the locks again, smiling smugly at the unlocking click.

With a casual grace, he stretched his legs out and folded his arms behind his head. He was the picture of relaxed elegance. Like an old-time movie star. Rock Hudson. Without the disappointing homosexuality.

Or maybe not.

I eyed him carefully. Neat hair and appearance. Nice taste in clothes. He had yet to mention show tunes or Liza Minnelli or a roommate named Kyle, but still...

"Are you gay?" I asked.

I expected him to be insulted, or to get defensive, or to say yes. Instead, he waggled his brows. "Wanna find out?"

His bright blue eyes raked over my three-hours-in-a-car wrinkled self in appraisal. I don't know what he imagined he saw beneath my khaki slacks and navy and white striped boatneck tee—let me tell you, there were no curves to ogle—but the sexy look he gave me was undeniable.

My mouth dropped open and I gasped for breath.

Before I could answer vehemently in the negative, he added, "Thought not." He rested his head on the pillow of his folded arms and closed his eyes. "Wake me when we get there."

♥

"WE'RE ALMOST THERE," I announced, giving him a sharp poke in the belly.

I could have enjoyed the sight of him jerking awake in surprise if I hadn't felt his firm, muscular abs beneath my finger. That single touch sent a shiver of sensation up my arm in a wave of goosebumps.

Unacceptable reaction. This was a business relationship. Supply and demand. Buyer and seller.

Which reminded me...

"We need to talk about money."

We hadn't had a chance to discuss his fee. With our busy work schedules, it was a miracle Fiona found time to talk to both of us and get us together at all. And Fi was not a money kind of girl—she was lucky to keep all her utilities paid. So it was no wonder she didn't think to talk with Phelps about it.

"What about money?" he asked.

"How much are you charging for this weekend?"

He sleepily rubbed at his eyes. "Shouldn't we have talked about this before we left the city?"

"Maybe," I said, irritated because he was right, "but we're here now."

"Okay. My usual fee is $200."

"$200 a day, that's not too bad."

"$200 an hour."

"An hour!" No wonder he wore designer clothes. "I can't afford that."

Though my salary at Ferrero is more than enough to pay my bills, support my jewelry-making hobby, and keep me in name brands, I couldn't afford to throw away ten grand on a weekend date. Someday I wanted to actually *buy* an apartment. And somehow I didn't think the IRS would consider a male escort a business expense.

Mental Post-It: Consult accountant about possible deduction.

"That's my usual fee, but this is a unique case." He considered for a moment. "How about $750 for the weekend?"

"$250," I countered.

"$500?" he offered.

"Sold." I felt like a top-notch negotiator. Dragging down the asking price by 95% was pretty impressive. "Hand me my purse."

"You don't have to pay me now."

"I want this part behind us."

"Fine." He handed me my purse and waited impatiently as I grabbed my checkbook, set it against the horn so I could make out a check.

I smiled, certain he was ready to grab the wheel the moment I started to veer off the road, but I was an accomplished vehicular multi-tasker.

"Oh, Double Bubble damn," I exclaimed as I handed him the check, "that was our exit."

Phelps grabbed the handle on the dash with white knuckles as I dove across three lanes of traffic and two sets of solid white lines.

I smiled—the Andes, my ass. Welcome to the Lydias. The weekend was starting to look better already.

♥

THE VALET at Jawbreaker's mansion took my keys and called

his partner to take our luggage. Well, my luggage and Phelps's duffle bag.

But Phelps waved him off. "I got this," he said, grabbing my over-packed suitcase with one hand and slinging his duffle over the same shoulder.

The valet shrugged, as if to say "Whatever, man," then climbed into the car and revved the engine.

Remembering my earlier mishap with the Jolly Rancher, I called out, "Oh, and could you wipe off the dashboard? I got something sticky on it."

Oh no, did that sound as bad as it sounded?

The valet threw Phelps a look that said, "Way to go, man."

Before I could explain, he closed the door and drove my baby away. I hated seeing her vanish in the hands of a stranger, professional or not. She was my urban tank. My escape from the concrete jungle when I needed to be far, far away. And after nearly 100,000 miles, she had never had any major injuries.

I scowled after the cocky valet.

She'd better not get any now.

Turning back to Phelps, I found him pulling a sport coat from his duffle. He unrolled it with a brisk snap and dropped the luggage to put it on. Compared to the space-age catsuit he had been wearing, the man sure cleaned up nice. Dark blue button-down shirt, casual-yet-sophisticated grey houndstooth sport coat, flat-front black trousers, black alligator belt, and shiny black oxfords. The setting sun casting a warm glow around him. He looked right at home on the porch of a Southampton mansion that looked like it belonged to a Kennedy or a Vanderbilt. Ready to take the Summer Sail Away by the stern.

He was only missing one tiny piece of information.

"There's one thing I, um, forgot to tell you."

"What's that?" he asked unconcerned, smoothing down the collar of his coat.

"Well," I began, "in addition to my colleagues from work and some industry professionals, there's one person on the guest list you should be aware of."

"Who?" He grabbed up the luggage with his right arm and turned to me. "Some celebrity?"

"No." Truth time. "My ex-fiancé."

He let out a low whistle. "That should shake things up at this squares-fest. Want me to sock him one in the jaw?"

"No! That's not what I wa—"

"Cause that'd be no trouble," he persisted. "Wouldn't even charge you extra."

"No, no, no. I don't want you to punch Gav—"

"Are you sure? Because it's been my experience that ex-fiancés usually deserve a punch or two. Otherwise they'd be husbands by now."

"No!" I shouted. Mr. Goodbar, this man was incorrigible. And made no sense. "Leave Gavin alone!"

The door swung open soundlessly as I ranted, revealing Jawbreaker with a beaming smile on her Botoxed mug.

"Now, you two aren't having a lovers' spat already are you?" Her smug expression indicating she would love nothing more. "The weekend has only just begun."

I started to answer defensively. "N—"

"Just a little debate over who loves whom more," Phelps said. He wrapped an arm around my shoulders and tugged me close. "But I think we both know who won."

He looked into my eyes for just a second. Just long enough

to let me know what he was going to do before he did it. Then, his mouth descended and I forgot Jawbreaker and the safety of Gavin's jaw and all the reasons I had to dislike this man. All I knew was the sensation of his hard, hot mouth and the tickling sweep of his tongue over my lips.

Sweet Saltwater Taffy, the man knew how to kiss!

His broad hand cupped my head and held me firm against his mouth. I grabbed blindly at his lapels, searching for even more connection.

"Ah-hem!"

Phelps pulled away at Jawbreaker's interruption. "Sorry," he said, still holding me close and not looking the least bit apologetic, "I get a little carried away when Lyd is around. Could you take these for me?"

He tossed her the luggage and pulled me back in for another kiss. Just before his mouth landed on mine I saw Jawbreaker scowl and turn away, carrying our luggage into the house like a bellhop and leaving us alone on the porch.

"That was masterful," I exclaimed, pulling out of the kiss before I got too involved to stop.

He grinned, and this time I didn't cringe. "Now, if you're ready to release me from your romance-cover clinch, are you ready to start this party right?"

I was too elated over besting Jawbreaker to even resent his cocky comment. Instead, I slipped my arm around his waist and said, "Into the spider's web."

We walked arm-in-arm through the front door, and I hoped that little quease in my belly was from sugar overload and not ominous premonition.

THREE

THE SUMMER SAIL AWAY was not just any party. It was an all-out, all weekend, all of society swank that put other bashes—Hamptons and otherwise—to shame.

Now I had been to plenty of society functions before. Growing up, my neighbors had been Getty and Kennedy cousins, for Good&Plenty's sake. But nothing had prepared me for the extravaganza that awaited me in Jawbreaker's mansion.

She hosted over 200 guests. And provided a guest room for anyone who didn't already have a residence somewhere between Westhampton and East Hampton.

That was where the trouble began.

Jawbreaker's butler showed us to our room—singular, of course, since we were so very in love—and dumped our luggage on the double bed. Again singular.

"If we weren't intimate before," Phelps boasted, "we will be now."

Counting to ten in all seven languages at my disposal, I

managed to keep from telling him to shove it. But it was a near thing.

"We will just have to deal with this later." I yanked my suitcase to the edge and unzipped it. Sixteen layers of carefully folded weekend wear bounced up like towels in a Downy commercial. "Right now we have to get ready for dinner."

At the top of one pile was my gunmetal-gray halter dress that I adore because the swishy matte jersey accentuates my less-than-generous curves. It ties behind the neck so I could adjust the height of the v-neck depending on my courage level. Tonight it was going to be tied up tight.

I grabbed the matching pair of strappy sandals—the ones with the dangly Swarovski crystals that made them sparkle when I walked.

Phelps meandered over to the window, drawing open the ivory jacquard drapes in a manly survey of the new environment.

"Wow, you must really rate."

I tried to turn off my hearing, I really did. But that didn't stop him.

"Who'd you piss off to get this view?"

Succumbing to curiosity of the purely idle sort, I looked up to follow his gaze out the window. At a brick wall.

My shoulders slumped and I dropped the dream dress back onto the pile. "My boss," I replied, darn tired of trying so hard for zero results. "If you hadn't already guessed, she hates me."

I braced myself for the smart-ass comment.

He crossed the room to my side and placed his hand gently on my shoulder. "She's just jealous." Then, before I had a chance to even consider a response, he added, "So get yourself gussied up so we can give 'em all something to really be jealous about."

And pinched my ass.

"Why you—" I turned to slap him—an instinctual response I had never had to use before—but he was already halfway out the door.

"Find me downstairs when you're ready."

My sandal hit the solid wood door with a thunk.

"Aaargh!" I screamed to no one in particular. Which was good, because no one else was in the room.

Because Phelps was on the loose with Jawbreakers and KYs to contend with.

I donned the dress and shoes and touched up my makeup with a little smoky gray shadow and extra blush—and consumed the remains of a package of cherry Nibs that I found hiding in a pocket in my suitcase—and was out the door in a record twelve minutes and thirty-two seconds.

DOWNSTAIRS I FOUND Phelps surrounded by all three KYs in the great room.

The room was a marvel of architectural and decoration styles. Elegant beams graced the high ceilings but had been painted white to diminish their presence. In fact, the entire room had been painted stark white, beautiful wooden floor to beautiful beamed cathedral ceiling.

Not that it lacked for color.

There was black and chrome silver and blood red.

Lots of red.

Along with innumerable textures and patterns. The once

elegant entertaining space resembled more a contemporary art gallery than a home. There was even an original—or excellent reproduction—Warhol on the wall above the zebra-print bar.

The KYs had Phelps cornered between the bar and a pair of red leather sofas. Three matching blond heads tilted at a vacant-but-attentive angle above matching push-up-enhanced cleavage. If breast augmentation weren't so taboo right now, I was sure they would have matching silicone implants. Maybe they could get a bulk discount.

Phelps said something and they all twittered in hair-raising girlish laughter.

And the most disappointing part was, he didn't look too unhappy about the situation.

Maybe he didn't quite understand the game plan.

"Phelps," I called across the cavern, hoping my bitter jealousy didn't show, "there you are, Sweet Tooth."

He turned to me with the kind of smile a girl wants to see at the other end of the aisle.

Like I was the sun in his dark, bleak world.

On the inside I melted like cotton candy.

I tried to remind myself that I had bought that smile, but the bliss just wouldn't go away and I beamed in return. My smile only grew when the KYs threw me identical scowls.

Rather than reply, he crossed the fluffy, sheepskin area rug, wrapped his arms around my waist, and drew me into a seductive embrace. His back to the room, he winked at me before leaning forward to whisper, "You look radiant."

Shivery goosebumps spread all over my body at the compliment. I couldn't answer.

"Show them you love me more than your lipstick," he teased. His teeth grazed my earlobe. "Kiss me."

36

"I-I can't," I stammered.

A fiery flush burned my cheeks and I wished I had skipped the extra blush. This was more boldness in one day than I had experienced in a whole lifetime.

He smiled against my temple. "At least grab my ass."

His arms tightened around me and my entire body pressed into his—separated by only the thin layer of gunmetal jersey and my flesh-toned thong. I felt every inch of his muscular form. My goosebumps got goosebumps.

I gathered every last ounce of courage and raised my hands to his hips. Resting just below his belt. Slowly, I started to slide them back—

"May I have everyone's attention please," Jawbreaker's booming voice thankfully stopped me before I lost all sense of public propriety. "If you would all adjourn to the dining room, dinner is ready."

The dozens of other people in the room—none of whom I had noticed in my fixation on Phelps and the KYs—started shuffling off in the direction of the palatial dining room.

Phelps held me captive.

"Grab my ass," he demanded.

"No," I countered, watching warily as the KYs slithered out of the room. "We have to go in to dinner."

"Grab my ass," he commanded.

"Phelps, really. No one's even here—"

"If you want this scam to work," he interrupted, "we have to act like a couple in love, right?"

I nodded—anything to get him to release me from the captivity of his arms and his attraction. His sweet compliments were weakening me, and he was starting to look far too Bubblicious for my health.

"I can tell you right now, I'm a very physical person and it's not going to look the part if we're not comfortable with each other's bodies." He sounded so logical. So clinical. So businesslike. "Suck it up and grab my ass."

So arrogant.

I was almost relieved by the return of the smart-ass.

Reaching around with both hands, I forcibly grabbed his cheeks—"How's that?"—and clenched.

Unfortunately, so did he.

My mind, which had not yet had the opportunity to appraise his derriere, came up with a very vivid image of the flesh in my palms. Holy Hot Tamales!

As if caught suddenly holding a flaming pineapple, I released him and stepped back. Two steps.

"Perfect," he drawled. "Now let's go in to dinner."

He held out one perfectly angled arm which I took out of habit. But my mind burned with the memory of his tight behind. And fantasizing about seeing it in the flesh— er, in person very soon.

I might have walked into the dining room with my shoulders drooped in resignation if he hadn't pinched my butt again.

THE HALLMARK of the first night of the Summer Sail Away was the beach bonfire. Twenty foot flames I was sure could be seen all the way from the Montauk lighthouse, generous amounts of champagne, and a club DJ spinning techno, jazz, and dance music.

Though I would have loved nothing more than to doff my

heels and wade into the moonlit surf, I had to use this opportunity to network. Only about one-third of the guests were
here tonight, and I had better odds at face time than I would
for the next two days.

Out of the corner of my eye I saw Phelps dancing with a
VP's wife. Typical middle-aged, upper-class housewife,
starved for the thrill of dancing with a gorgeous man young
enough to be her son.

For an instant, I saw a reflection of what my life might have
been if I hadn't found Gavin between his secretary's thighs.

I shuddered at the thought and again counted my blessings
that I got to the sour center of that sucker *before* the wedding.

Too many women don't find out until it's too late for even
prenups to help.

Turning from the sight of my future in an alternate
universe, I found my first target. Alberto Vermicelli, VP of
European Sales.

In the ten-year plan I had devised when I came on board at
Ferrero, earning his title was year nine. Currently in year six, I
should already have Jawbreaker's job—or at least be junior VP
of Something—but I hoped to make that goal soon.

Pulling off my heels to make my way across the sand, I let
them dangle from one hand as I approached Alberto.

"Alberto, how nice to see you." I kissed both his cheeks in
the Italian tradition and he took my hands in his.

"*Cara*, I am so happy you are here." He smiled, cosmeti-
cally whitened teeth bright against his swarthy complexion.

Alberto was the sort of man women crush on. He was tall
and athletically built, with thick black hair and dignified
creases in his handsome face. If I didn't know he was
devoutly loyal to his wife of nearly thirty years, I would think

he had affairs with every woman under thirty that crossed his path.

He was an old friend of my father's and the main reason I got my job. It takes good connections to get work in the fashion world. The KYs had Jawbreaker. I had Alberto.

And he brought me into the fold with the promise that he would retire in ten years and, if I worked hard enough to get myself into a promotable position, he would name me his successor.

One more step and I'd be there.

Hopefully, he could help with that one more step.

"It has been too many years you have not been invited." He swung my arms out wide and appraised me. "You are the most beautiful woman here."

"Except for your wife," I countered.

"Well, a man must protect his loyalties, yes?"

I smiled. Alberto was a kind man with a flair for fashion— as exemplified by his green and yellow silk shirt and elegantly tied white ascot. He also knew the ins-and-outs of the business like no other and could read people like a book.

"But you do not seek out your old friend for compliments, I think." He looked at me thoughtfully and nodded in approval. "You are looking for a little push in the direction of promotion."

"Yes," I answered. After thirty-three years, I was used to his uncanny assessments. "If the rumor about Jaw— Janice's promotion is true, I want to be in line for her job."

His gaze sharpened and scanned the guests littering the beach. "Then, *cara*, you should not waste time on an old man stuck behind a desk." Mischief sparkled in his light brown eyes. "Aim higher."

Following the direction of his gaze, I saw Jawbreaker—shudder—talking to none other than Ferrero himself.

I groaned. "Franco never remembers me. We've been introduced sixteen times, and if I go over there right now we'll have to be introduced again."

Alberto smiled like an indulgent father. "Then *make* him remember."

💜

"WHO IS THIS ENCHANTING CREATURE?"

If Alberto had come with me to schmooze Ferrero, I would have turned and said, "I told you so."

But how could a man who worked with supermodels on a daily basis be expected to remember scrawny, unadorned me?

As it was, I smiled blankly and said, "Mr. Ferrero, I'm Lydia Vanderwalk. Senior Account Executive for the Western US." And silently added, *we've met about a thousand times before.*

Ferrero stood out amongst the sea of navy and khaki sportcoats and black dresses in a white linen suit—to match his head of white hair—and bright orange silk shirt. He also stood barefoot on the sand.

"All that business makes my head hurt," Ferrero complained in a lilting—and I've always suspected fake since it sounds nothing like Alberto's—Italian accent. "If only I could just make my fabulous creations without having to worry about numbers and reports and sales."

I pasted on my best yes-I-understand-you-temperamental-artistic-types smile, curbing the desire to explain that without all those numbers and reports and sales he would be penniless, living in a cardboard box, and fashioning chic outerwear from garbage bags. Instead, he was a disgustingly wealthy million-aire with his gowns fought over by all the best starlets.

"But this weekend is for fun, not for business," he said with a dismissive wave of his perfectly manicured hands. "What do you do for fun, Lydia Vandowelk?"

"Van-der-walk," I enunciated. The chances of him actually remembering my name were slimmer than the chances of the strawberry-banana Starburst in my clutch making it through the night.

But Alberto had said "*make* him remember." That meant taking a risk.

Ferrero was the epitome of *artiste*. A man who thrived on creativity. And, if Marlene's gossip was right—and it usually was—flesh.

Deciding to hit both birds with one stone, I leaned forward to reveal a little deeper cleavage and draw attention to the pear-shaped pendant dangling therein and confessed, "I design jewelry."

"Jewelry," he exclaimed. "Such a fascinating field. What sort of pieces do you design?"

"Pieces like this." I did my best to drawl—imagining how Fiona would make a man remember her through body language and tone of voice.

She always said men needed to be hit over the head with the obvious, so I took one French-manicured finger and trailed it along the invisible wire of the necklace to the dangling pendant. Ferrero's pale blue eyes followed every inch of the way, alight with interest and—

"Who's the guy ogling your breasts?" Phelps asked conver-sationally as he came up on my left and slipped an arm around my waist.

I elbowed him in the ribs. My face burned with embarrassment.

Ferrero recovered admirably—surely he had yards of experience being caught ogling other men's women—and grinned at Phelps. "I was just admiring your young woman's work of art."

"That's one I never heard."

"I was showing Mr. *Ferrero*"—I pulled out of Phelps's grasp and lifted the pendant to his view—"my jewelry design."

Phelps examined the necklace closely—though I'm not sure he wasn't copping an ogle, too. "It's beautiful," he decreed. Then remembered that he should have already seen all my jewelry. "As always. But all the more beautiful because it has such a lovely canvas."

He took the hand that held the necklace and pressed a kiss to the back.

I was not appeased by the sweet gesture. Or the genuine admiration in his voice. Or the apologetic smile.

"Dance with me?" he asked as a slow song played out across the beach.

All right, I was appeased.

Not because he obviously realized his mistake and was trying to make up for it, but because Ferrero was taking this all in with rapt attention. Ha, let's see him forget me next time we meet.

"Go, go," Ferrero said. "Dance with your young man beneath the stars. Tomorrow, we must speak more about your designs."

"Yes!" I screamed. On the inside.

On the outside, I said, "Of course, Mr. Ferrero."

"Please," he argued as Phelps took my hand and led me away, "you must call me Franco."

I smiled like a kid presented with a 5-lb bag of Brach's Fun Mix. I hardly noticed as Phelps led me toward the surf, out of the circle of light thrown by the bonfire.

Ferre— Franco was definitely going to remember me.

"Sorry."

I looked at Phelps, a look of pure contrition on his handsome face. Hmmm, this night was getting better and better.

"I had no idea that was your boss," he apologized.

He looked really sorry. And I was a little amazed that this cocky, arrogant man—whom I had only known a few hours—had a remorseful bone in his body.

Rather than give in to the impulse to berate him, I let him pull me into a slow dance.

"You know, I should be mad." The wet sand felt cool beneath my feet. "I really should. But I'm not."

"You're not?" he asked, incredulous.

Maybe I had been a little high strung all evening. No wonder he expected me to rail him for embarrassing me.

His arms encircled my waist and I let him lead our sway to the soft jazz. This had to be the most incredibly romantic moment of my life—if only I weren't sharing it with a guy who was being paid to be here.

But I guess I could have a romantic moment of my own.

"I wanted to make an impression." I laid my head on his shoulder, closing my eyes and absorbing the moment with all my senses.

The smell of the sea—a little salty, a little fishy—and earthy cologne filled my nostrils. Small waves broke upon the sand with a rhythmic roar, somehow in tune with the rhythm of smooth jazz. Phelps held me close, but not tight. One broad hand flat across my lower back, the other smoothing circles along my spine.

I felt hypnotized.

When he turned his head to whisper, "Everyone's watching," I barely noticed.

One hand left my back to lift my chin. "Everyone's watching," he repeated. "Let's give 'em a show."

He smiled softly as his head dipped.

This kiss was nothing like the passionate one on the front porch.

His lips moved softly over mine. Tasting. Nibbling. Exploring. His hand, still cupping my chin, drew my mouth open. And I complied.

When his tongue slipped between my lips, I groaned. I was lost in the moment. My imaginary romantic moment had become a reality. And, if the bulge pressing against my abdomen were any indication, this was just as real for Phelps.

A piercing scream rent the air, followed by a soft explosion. We looked up to see a shower of glittering red and white embers rained down over the water.

Phelps tugged me closer to remind me that we were supposed to be showing everyone a different kind of fireworks.

FOUR

SLEEPING arrangements were easily dealt with; Phelps slept on the floor with the caveat that he had to be up before anyone might come to wake us.

I was a little concerned that he had much more depth than Fiona led me to believe. My dreams that night were of a Jacuzzi tub full of Hot Tamales, Phelps, and me. And let me tell you, the heat was not coming from the candy.

At one point I bolted up in bed, shocked by the ache between my legs and certain that he must have heard me moaning in my sleep. But when I peered over the edge, he lay soundly asleep on the floor, his expression angelic. I collapsed back into the bed and slept peacefully throughout the rest of the night.

BREAKFAST HARKENED the arrival of Gavin.

We were on the back deck, plates of eggs benedict and

exotic fruit perched on our knees, when I heard the melodious tenor of his voice.

I dropped my plate.

"Good morning, Lydia," he crooned, as I knelt to clean up my mess. Dubble Bubble Damn, why did his first sight have to be me on my hands and knees at his feet. Just where he wanted me, I'm sure.

"Gavin." I nodded my head in the barest tilt of polite acknowledgment.

Then my prince stepped in.

"Hey, you're the ex!" Phelps thrust out his hand, forcibly taking Gavin's in return and pumping it enthusiastically. "Can't thank you enough for being such an ass. Lyd's the best thing that ever happened to me."

I might have been mortified, but for the look of utter aghast on Gavin's pretty boy face.

"Um, you're welcome?"

Gavin. At a loss for words? Priceless.

"If you hadn't boinked your secretary, then where would we be?"

I clenched my jaw. Fiona must have told him more than just the particulars.

Gavin turned bright red—I had never thought to see Gavin Fairchild embarrassed—and could not come up with a single thing to say.

But I could.

"I don't know about you, Sweet Tooth, but I would be married to a louse who dropped his pants for anything dumb enough to put out." I stood, setting my plate on the bench behind me, and settled in at Phelps' side. "I'm much happier where I am."

Phelps grinned at me and I did the most startling thing; I kissed him. Right there in front of God, Gavin, and everybody.

Just a quick peck, but enough to send Gavin stalking back into the house with a vengeance.

"Bravo," Phelps whispered as he gave me a return peck on the ear.

Someone started clapping. I turned to find Alberto applauding my brilliant set-down, and several recently divorced female guests joined him.

Alberto stepped forward and patted me on the shoulder. "That was a very pretty thing. For you." He inclined his head to Ferrero, walking this way from the other end of the deck. "Just remember who your audience is."

With that, he disappeared, leaving me alone with Phelps to face the approaching king.

While I was proud of myself for putting Gavin in his place, I knew that kind of outburst was unprofessional and could not be repeated.

"We can't do that again," I whispered hurriedly before Ferrero arrived. "I need to maintain my professional image."

"Got it."

If he smiled that cocky grin one more time, so help me—

He grinned. But then made good his exit. "I'll just leave you to face the letch alone."

He winked and then he was gone.

"Good morning, beautiful Olivia," Ferrero greeted.

So much for my lasting impression.

"Actually Mr. Ferrero, it's Lydia," I reminded.

"Of course, but I asked you to call me Franco."

He smiled, his white teeth a perfect match to his white hair and white linen shirt. The shirt hit mid-thigh, and a far as

I could tell he had nothing on underneath. Great Mr. Goodbar.

"Since you have disobeyed, you must join me in the bubble tub." He frowned, searching for the English word. "The hot tub."

I hid my scowl, pretty sure I detected the teeniest bit of Jersey in his accent.

"I don't have my suit on," I objected.

"Nonsense. Who needs a suit?" At my look of horror, he added, "I only tease. Go. Fetch your suit." He waved me away. "And that man of yours. Bring him as well."

As he turned and walked off in the direction of the hot tub —its very existence a mystery to me since the ocean was only steps away—this time I openly scowled. His eyes had practically glowed at the mention of Phelps.

Maybe the rumor about his love of flesh was off by a gender.

♥

PHELPS IN SWIM trunks was a sight to behold.

Tall, six-one or six-two. Tan. Broad-shouldered, lean-hipped, and muscular—like he played a little football in the park on weekends. Only he probably didn't since any injuries might hinder his modeling career.

Then again, the man climbed the Andes for fun, so what did I know about his career conflicts.

But I did know a mighty fine ass when I saw one. And the ass emerging from our *en suite* bathroom, encased in gray nylon with white piping, definitely qualified.

Sweet Saltwater Taffy.

"Ready to hit the bubbles?" He cocked a brow and tucked two fluffy white towels beneath his arm.

"Yes," I said, tugging the belt of my French terry cover-up tighter around my waist. "But first we need to have a little talk about rules of conduct."

"Rules of conduct?"

I had been mentally reliving the interchange with Gavin for the past twenty minutes. And while I gloried at the flustered look on his pretty face, my behavior had been less than professional. The point of this weekend was advancing my career, not getting back at Gavin. That was just a bonus.

"Remember that the primary reason for this weekend—and your presence here—is my job." I grabbed my silver flip-flops and dropped them to the floor. "As much as I will always adore you for that brilliant shut down of my late-fiancé, we need to keep the rest of the weekend on a more mature level."

Phelps casually tugged his waistband into place. "You want me to act like a grown-up, then?"

"If you please."

He tossed a towel my direction, which I caught with a scowl. Nothing in his demeanor to this point suggested a capacity to act like an adult.

I dug my hands into my pockets, seriously wondering whether he could rise to the occasion. Oooh, my fingers curled around a paper-wrapped square. A mango tropical Starburst. Fumbling with the waxy paper, I unwrapped the treat and slipped it between my lips. But even mango sugar couldn't dispel my concerns.

"Relax, Chicken Little. I can do adult."

And he managed to say it with a straight face.

I stepped into my flip-flops and headed for the door. As I passed in front of Phelps, he pinched my backside.

Before I could turn to argue, he grabbed my shoulders and pushed me out into the hall.

"Just getting it out of my system."

♥

AS I LOWERED my bathing suit-clad body into the bubbling water of Jawbreaker's hot tub, I felt one step closer to heaven. Even in the humid August air, the enveloping heat felt blissful.

Unfortunately, Phelps and I were not the only guests Ferrero had invited into the bubble tub.

I sat wedged between Geoffrey Hildebrandt, retired men's accessories designer at Fendi, and Brant something-or-other, one of Jawbreaker's Southampton neighbors.

Geoff, whom I had met at several cocktail mixers, was gayer than the whole gang on that gay makeover show put together. He was a sweet man with an eye for leather goods and handsome young men.

Brant, on the other hand, was one of those old money, lacrosse-playing, sailing types. He was too tan, too smiley, and too blonde. He also happened to be too handsy. Before I could even settle into the bench seat, his hand slipped beneath my swimsuit-clad ass and wiggled. Rather than draw attention to his appalling-but-not-unexpected behavior, I smiled sweetly.

"Such a tight squeeze in here," I said as I gouged a set of crescents into the flesh of his palm. "Good thing I'm surrounded by such polite gentlemen."

My subtlety had no effect. Brant openly drooled over my

breasts, thrust into deceptively lush cleavage by the simple black one-piece with a silver buckle across the chest.

Removing his hand from my bottom, I forcibly placed it in his lap before grabbing an inch of tender flesh on his inner thigh and pinching with all my heart.

No one else even noticed his silent scream.

"Ah-hem, excuse me," he sputtered as he climbed out onto the teak deck. "Just remembered, um, left something, er, at home."

He turned and ran inside. I could see the darkening smudge of a delightfully placed bruise forming.

"Hurry back, Brant," I called after his retreating form.

Relaxing into the now ample space, I spread my arms along the edge and surveyed the rest of the tub. Phelps, directly across from me between a pair of exec's wives, winked.

And I was in such a state of bliss I couldn't even scowl.

"I hope there's room for us in there."

I cringed at the high-pitched squeal. My bliss shattered. Without looking, I knew Kelly stood behind me on the deck, sporting some teeny bikini as concealing as a trio of Necco Wafers, with Gavin in tow.

What was up with my run of luck this past week? All my fortune had fled to Palm Beach for the winter.

Maybe if I kept my eyes closed tightly enough, it would all go away.

"Always room for two more," Phelps boomed.

I briefly pondered the penalty for homicide of an infuriating hire-a-date. Surely I could get off with probation. And there are extenuating circumstances.

Mental Post-it: put criminal attorney on retainer.

Someone grabbed me by the shoulders, yanking me out of

my homicidal fantasy and pulling me forcibly through the water. As Phelps turned me and plunked me on his lap, he said, "Lyd and I can share."

Grrr.

Only Phelps heard me growl.

"Thought you wouldn't want to cause a scene," he whispered. "Besides, now you can schmooze the boss."

I turned, scowling, and found Ferrero sitting to my right. Score. Maybe Phelps was a little more business savvy than I—or Fiona—gave him credit for.

Kelly and Gavin made their way into the spots Brant and I had occupied. I was right, Kelly wore a barely-there, cherry red bikini I had seen in the last Victoria's Secret catalog. Gavin handed her down, following in his matching red swimming briefs. He eyed me warily, as if expecting me to do something outrageous and emotional and totally deserved.

I was above such petty behavior. Especially when he was getting everything he deserved with Kelly. If he thought he could cheat on her without becoming the next John Wayne Bobbitt, then he was dearly mistaken.

Letting all the other nonsense fade into the background, I tapped Ferrero on the arm. "Fe— Franco, you wished to discuss more about my designs today." I pinched my earlobes, tugging the pearl-dotted spirals into view. "These are my latest."

Franco leaned in to examine the silver pieces, and I could almost hear the steam shooting out of Kelly's ears from across the Jacuzzi.

Double score.

WHEN JAWBREAKER CAME to inform us of a sightseeing trip into the thriving metropolis of Southampton, nearly everyone in the tub clamored to go. Only Ferrero appeared uninterested. Even Phelps decided to go, swiftly whispering that I should "take a golden opportunity when it punches me in the face" before lifting me off his lap and following everyone else into the house.

Left alone with Ferrero and his rapt interest in my jewelry designs, I knew this was my chance to make the most important impression of all.

"Franco," I started.

"Dear Lyvia," he interrupted—I chose not to correct him since this was his closest guess by far—and placed his soft hand dramatically on my forearm, "I have been seeking for so long to find a woman of spirit, of imagination, of—" He paused dramatically. "—passion."

His pale blue eyes glowed and his grip on my arm tightened. A quick glance around told me the deck was deserted. We were alone.

And although I was pretty sure I wouldn't like where this conversation was heading, it had to be better than any conversation about Gavin.

"My creativity is, you see, a very fragile creature." He gazed wistfully at the sky above. "It requires much petting and great care. In short," he grabbed me by both shoulders and stared directly into my eyes, "it needs a muse."

"Muse?" I repeated.

That was not what I had expected him to say. And I wasn't particularly relieved to hear it.

He nodded emphatically. "Yes, a muse. An inspiration, like the great ladies of Greek mythology. Like Jacqueline Bouvier.

Like Princess Grace. And you—" He paused dramatically. "—shall be mine."

"But Mr. Ferrero," I argued, reverting to a polite distance, "I don't know anything about being a muse. I'm an account manager. I handle sales accounts, for Good&Plenty's sake. What do I know about being a muse?"

This whole thing was ridiculous.

"You already are, my dear." He smoothed his hand over my hair, along my ear, and then cupped my earring. "You have creativity," he said. He dropped his hand beneath the water and lifted mine to his mouth. "You have spirit." He cupped my cheek. "You have passion." He grinned. "You are already my muse."

Whoa there, Twizzler.

This exciting, spirited, passionate woman he described was not me. "I have *some* creativity, I'll grant you," I acceded, thinking of my jewelry designs. "But I'm not *spirited*."

I was so not spirited that when I found Gavin pressing flesh with another woman, all I thought was, *Guess I'll have to return the ring.*

"Nonsense." Ferrero waved a dismissive hand in my direction. "I have eyes to see the wildcat sharpen her claws."

Great Gobstoppers, did he mean on Gavin? Or Phelps? Or that toad Brant? I had to admit I had been behaving with a bit of spirit this weekend. But that wasn't the usual me.

The usual me set the ring on the counter and walked away.

"Fine, but I'm not passionate."

I was so not passionate that Gavin had to go to another woman—probably *several* other women, in fact—to satisfy his, um, needs.

"Ah, *chica*," he tsked, the Spanish endearment sounding

peculiar with his Jersey-tinted Italian accent, "no one could fail to see the passion between you and your young man. Fireworks were not the only thing lighting up the dark last night."

There was no way I could tell him how fake that was. He had to see reason, to realize that I was not muse material. I had a promotion to garner, and sitting around inspiring Ferrero or whatever being a muse entailed wasn't going to accomplish that.

"But—"

"Enough," he commanded, rising from the tub and tugging me out behind him, "you will be my muse for next Spring's couture line. Your jewelry will accentuate every piece."

"M-m-*my* jewelry?"

He didn't acknowledge my stammering, instead held out both hands expectantly. In a daze, I grabbed a pair of towels from a nearby bench and handed him one. I wrapped the other around my waist as I pictured my jewelry accessorizing the Spring line on the Ferrero runway. A dream I had never even dared to dream.

That was an opportunity I could not pass up.

Ferrero walked toward the house, toweling his snowy hair as he moved, and I blindly followed.

"And your young man," he decreed as he draped the towel around his neck rather than cover his wet, white—and obviously unlined—Speedo, "will be my muse for the menswear line."

I tripped over the negligible door jamb, righting myself just as Ferrero turned to say, "This will be my most inspired collection ever."

FIVE

I WAS SITTING on the front porch—fidgeting, worrying, hoping, *dreaming*—when the sightseeing caravan returned.

After changing into a colorful sundress, covered with bright yellow lemons against a white background and matching lemon yellow piping, my brain had calmed enough to realize the opportunities abounding. Not only would I be working in presumably close proximity to Ferrero, leading to many fabulous opportunities for great impressions wherein he might actually remember my name *and* think to promote me when Jawbreaker moves up, *but* my jewelry designs would be thrust center stage in the fashion world.

Accessorizing an entire collection on a prime runway during fashion week.

This was marketing no advertising dollars could buy.

An advantage the KYs could never hope to obtain and Jawbreaker could never hope to thwart. I would skyrocket up the ranks faster than they could blink.

Now all I had to do was convince Phelps to join in.

The shopping-weary sightseers climbed out of a trio of

elegant black limos Jawbreaker had hired for the weekend. They were a ragged bunch, a sea of wrinkled polo shirts and sweat-smudged foundation—on both men and women.

Kelly and Gavin emerged first, arm in arm and smiling falsely at each other. A perfectly matched pair of fakes.

They slinked past me. Kelly didn't so much as throw me a sideways glance, which suited me just fine, but Gavin slid his gaze over me as they walked by. I scowled at him.

Three dozen or so other sightseers drifted into the house, worn out from an exhausting two hours of shopping and riding around in air-conditioned limos. Oh the trials and tribulations.

The chauffeurs closed the doors after the last of the passengers disembarked.

I frowned.

Where was Phelps?

I watched blankly as the three black vehicles pulled away and headed down the driveway.

Had he bailed on me? Found some cute young thing in town and decided to ditch me? I was going to kill him. I was going to kill Fiona. I was going to kill *someone*.

A faint buzzing sound rang in my ears.

I shook my head but it didn't go away. In fact, it got louder. And I realized it wasn't in my head at all. Squinting down the long drive, I saw a streak of bright yellow heading my direction.

I blinked, watching in horror as Phelps flew up the drive and skidded to a stop right in front of me on a Vespa.

"What," I bit out, carefully swallowing the squeaky voice threatening to burst forth, "is that?"

"Hey, it matches your dress."

"What," I repeated calmly despite the overwhelming urge to launch myself at him, fists swinging, "is that?"

He looked at me like I was stupid—like I was the one roaring around Southampton on a child's toy. "This is a scooter." He revved the tiny rubber band engine. "See, *vvroom, vvroom.* Wanna ride?"

"No!"

"Come on," he goaded. "You know you want to."

"No, I don't." All I wanted to do was go up to my room— our room—and hide beneath the covers for the rest of the weekend.

Clearly he did not understand the meaning of the word decorum. His brain must have been absent the day they taught that in modeling school.

Or any school.

Had he even gone to school?

What kind of education had he had? Was he one of those wonder models discovered at fifteen and a high school drop out by sixteen?

For that matter, I wondered— "How old are you, anyway?"

"Twenty-seven."

Dear Mr. Goodbar, he was six years younger than me. I was robbing the proverbial cradle. Sort of.

At least I wasn't *really* dating him. That would be worse.

I groaned, wondering when I had begun resorting to rationalization to make everything seem okay.

Phelps climbed off the mini crotch rocket and took me by the shoulders, guiding me down the steps and into the driveway. "This opportunity won't come around every day, you know. I took the official Vespa training course in Italy. I'm a licensed scooter stunt driver." He climbed aboard and pulled me across his lap. "And she has to go back by five."

"You're making that up."

"Nope," he said. "I was filming a scooter chase scene and they needed me to do my own stunts."

"Let me go," I insisted.

Before I could launch an argument, he started the engine and roared off toward the street. "Remind me to show you the scar later."

I was a captive in his quest for adventure.

We sped through the narrow streets of Southampton. We spun doughnuts in the high school parking lot. We even raced long drives on the golf course, much to the dismay of the golfers and the groundskeeper.

And much to my surprise, I enjoyed every minute of it.

By the time we returned Daffy—so named because of her daffodil yellow paint job—to the rental place I was sad to see her go.

Mental Post-it: look into cost of buying and housing Vespa.

"Ray says his brother can give us a ride."

"What?" I was so busy with my mental debate I didn't hear anything but the end of Phelps's comment.

"I said Ray, the scooter shop owner, says the taxis are all at the train station, but his brother can give us a lift back out to the mansion."

"Oh, okay," I said, not having any other suggestions.

If I had known what that lift would consist of, I would have come up with some.

Ray-the-scooter-guy's bother drove a rickety old farm truck, the kind with two-by-fours nailed around the bed to hold in the piles of potatoes or apples or whatever they harvested in the far reaches of Long Island.

And the passenger seat was already occupied by a giant black and white Great Dane. I didn't think she would understand if I called shotgun.

So Phelps and I rode the five miles back to Jawbreaker's house on the tailgate of the farm truck. At least Rick, the brother, had a relatively clean blanket for me to sit on so my dress didn't suffer the effects of the dirty truck bed.

This was my punishment for even thinking about cheating on my baby.

♥

"YOU LOOK LIKE A MESS," Phelps observed.

Gee, like I expected to look like a Stepford Wife after a ride in a potato truck. I scowled as he lifted me down from the tailgate.

"You're no shining example yourself," I returned.

Though I had to admit, no man ever looked so good in a dirt-smudged grey t-shirt with wavy black hair wind-tousled to an Elvis-worthy peak. He was gorgeous, no matter the clothing.

Except for that space suit I had picked him up in. No one could make that work.

"We'd better clean up before dinner." And I still had to talk to him about Ferrero's proposal.

He grinned like a schoolboy. "I'll race ya!"

"No, thank you."

"Come on, it'll be fun."

"Um... no."

"You turned down the Daffy ride at first, too." His eyes sparkled as he poked me in the arm. "And look how much fun that turned out to be."

"This isn't the sa—"

"Chicken?"

"No, I'm just too—"

"Chicken," he declared.

Planting my hands on my hips in what I hoped was a determined nature, I said, "I am not a chicken, I'm just—"

"Afraid you'll lose." He looked at me sympathetically. "You're probably right. Better not to be humiliated like that."

He turned and headed up the steps.

As his foot hit the top step, I blew past him, calling back over my shoulder, "Just waiting to take advantage of your arrogance."

When we hit the staircase in the east wing, he caught hold of my hem and tugged me back. He made it two steps before I grabbed his sneaker and pulled him to the ground. I scrambled past him, just lunging out of his grasp, and bolted down the hall to our room.

I stood outside our door, fingers curled around the doorknob, as he raced down the hall in my wake.

"Guess I get the shower first," I teased.

He covered my hand with his own. "We could always share."

Sparks exploded where our skin touched.

"In your dreams, Elliot," I said, feeling carefree and maybe a little reckless.

I pushed open the door and preceded him into the room. Behind me, I swear he muttered, "Don't I know it."

It wasn't until I was under the stream of steaming hot

water that I realized he and his wild abandon had made me forget about all my worries and stress for an afternoon. I didn't want to dwell on what that meant.

THE COOL RUSH of the shower washed away the remains of the potato truck, leaving only the glaring unasked question. Would Phelps be willing to play the role of muse for Ferrero? And what would it cost me?

By the time I emerged from the bathroom, one fluffy white towel wrapped around my chest, the other vigorously rubbing the water from my dark blond locks, I was ready to ask him.

Nothing ventured, nothing gained, or some such rot.

"Phelps, I have a proposition for you," I began.

"Mmmm." He looked up from the book he was reading in the corner chair. "I like the sound of that."

I rolled my eyes. "Not that kind of proposition, you Nutty Bar." Sitting on the bed, I finished toweling my hair and wrapped the towel around my head. "A bus—"

He set the book down and stood. "How do women do that?"

"Do what?"

"That thing with the towel." He stepped in front of me and motioned to my turbaned head. "No man alive can do that."

"Phelps, can you please listen—"

"No straight man, anyway."

"Phelps!" I hadn't meant to shout, but he had a way of stretching my patience like Tangy Taffy, pulling until it spread so thin little holes appeared and grew until all that was left was a shredded lace of sticky candy.

"Can you please," I asked, calmly regaining my restraint, "listen to my proposition." When he looked ready to joke again about my choice of words, I added, "My *business* proposition."

Though he looked a little disappointed, he sat next to me on the bed.

"Are you familiar with the Ferrero menswear line?"

"I'm a professional model, babe, of course I know Ferrero Men. I think I have one of last season's shirts—the ones with all the heavy-duty zippers—from a shoot for Vanity Fair."

Ugh, I remembered those shirts. Not only were they ugly, but no man wearing one made it through airport security without a strip search. There had been a lot of store returns on that one.

"Right, well, Ferrero is apparently looking for a muse," I explained, wondering how on earth you ask someone to be a designer's inspiration. "He, um, asked me to be his muse for the couture collection, and—"

"His muse, huh," he interrupted. "The man has good taste."

I tried to fight my pleasure at the compliment. But it was no good. Any woman would be flattered to be asked to be a famous fashion designer's muse. And, try as I might to hide it, I was just as susceptible as the next woman.

"Then again," he said, tracing a finger over the fluffy edge of the towel wrapped around my chest, "you'd inspire anyone in this getup."

I might have blushed a little. "Yes, well, that's only half the bargain."

Phelps was beginning to look a little bored. Or maybe not

bored. Distracted. I needed to get to the heart of the proposition.

"He apparently needs a special menswear muse, too."

He shrugged, his gaze drifting down my bare legs, clearly not getting my meaning.

"You," I blurted. "He wants you to be his muse."

"Me?" Phelps asked, distractedly as he reached for the hem of my towel.

I smacked his hand away. "Yes, you."

For the first time in our twenty-four hours' acquaintance—and that was twenty-four solid hours with no potty breaks or anything—he had no witty comeback. Nothing, just silence as he stared at my thighs. He chewed on his generous lower lip, his dark brows lowered in thought.

Like maybe he wanted to decline.

Like maybe he was trying to find the right words to tell me to go piss off. No, no, no. I was not about to lose this opportunity.

"I'll pay you, of course," I rushed out, "for all the time spent as Ferrero's muse. I don't know how much time being a muse demands, but I'm sure we can work something out. We can sketch out a payment plan and—"

"Are you crazy?"

"You wouldn't be doing this for free," I continued. "I'll still pay you—"

"Why the hell would you have to pay me?"

I blinked at him, not really understanding his question. "I don't know if Ferrero plans to pay you—or me, for that matter—for this, but I'll p—"

He shook his head and laughed. "I would pay to do this."

"Really?" Now I was really confused.

"I don't know what you're getting out of this deal," Phelps said, "but this is a golden opportunity for my career. I mean, what model wouldn't want to be the muse of a couture designer?"

"You'll do it?" I squeaked.

"Of course I'll do it," he confirmed. "Modeling may not be my be all end all, but this will skyrocket my career." He braced one hand behind me on the bed and leaned in closer. "Why are *you* doing it?"

My first instinct was to make up a more legitimate and less, well, selfish reason. But he was so close, steadily meeting my gaze and probing my soul with those brilliant baby blues. He surrounded me. I could barely breathe.

I leaned back a little. "Because he wants to use my jewelry in the collection."

He looked unconvinced, as if he knew there was more to my decision. He was right.

"And because this will give me the advantage in the next promotion," I confessed, admitting to even myself for the first time how much beating out the KYs and triumphing over Jawbreaker meant to me.

"Well then," he said, extending his hand, "I guess we're partners in muse-dom."

SIX

AT 4:32 P.M. I set Jawbreaker's pug loose on the beach.

I didn't mean to. Really. It was an entirely accidental occurrence. Mostly.

When I came downstairs after the potato truck shower, the little monst— um, darling started nipping at my feet. My fabulous new pair of grass green flats with the cute flower cut-outs. The heels now bear several indentations that look remarkably like canine bites.

Where the little mon— um, darling had been until that point I had no idea. Probably sequestered in a bedroom or something. Or mingling quietly with the guests until Jawbreaker gave him the attack command.

I should have known there was a reason the French doors leading onto the deck were no longer wide open. I should have thought it at least a little odd.

But no, I just flung open the door, hoping to escape onto the deck and close the little mon—oh, all right, he was a monster—off in the house, securing a pane of hurricane glass between us.

Then I heard the scream.

"Miissterr Puuggssleey!!!" Jawbreaker wailed as the little monster—now the little escapee—squeezed through the closing door and raced across the teak decking as fast as his stunted little legs could carry him.

Quite fast, surprisingly enough.

"What have you done?" Jawbreaker cried as she reached my side, staring plaintively after the fast disappearing sight of Mr. Pugsley—no really, that's his real name—stirring up sand behind him as he made for the surf.

"I'm sorry, Janice. I had no idea he could run like that."

She glared at me like I had just eaten the last Junior Mint in a theater-sized box before the previews even started.

"You did th-that on p-purpose."

Oh no, those looked suspiciously like tears. I didn't know heartless corporate robots could cry. I guess when their Mr. Pugsley beat feet for the beach, all stereotypical bets are off.

Before I could stop myself—or realize what I was doing, for that matter—I put my arms around her shoulders.

"Don't worry," I soothed, "we'll get him back."

"Last time he didn't come home for three days." She sobbed and pressed her face into my offered shoulder.

I felt her tears wetting my second-of-the-day sundress.

Gingerly patting her back, I looked desperately around the room for any sign of reprieve. I found Phelps, heading our direction with that confident grin on his handsome face.

"Which way did he head?" Phelps asked.

"West," I answered, relieved to have the help. "Toward the city."

"L-last time," Jawbreaker lifted her head and sniffled, "the Monteforts said he came and made puppy love with their

Shitzhu." She wiped at her tears, smearing the pool of mascara out to her temples in a kohl-black sweep. "Their house is three properties down."

Phelps smoothed a reassuring hand over her platinum hair. "I'll get him back Janice." He turned and looked at the room full of stunned guests. "I bet Fairchild will even help me, won't you?"

Gavin grinned thinly. "I live to serve," he said as he followed Phelps out the French doors and headed onto the beach. Probably cursing every grain of sand that scuffed his leather loafers.

If not for my weeping boss at my side, I might have gloated. Yet a tiny little kernel of something deep inside my brain poked me with a feeling much like guilt.

Double Bubble Damn. Now I was going to have to be nice to Jawbreaker for the rest of the weekend.

♥

PHELPS and a very bedraggled Gavin returned with a grinning and well-satisfied Mr. Pugsley just in time for the scheduled lawn croquet tournament.

The front lawn had been set with a dozen different croquet courses, differentiated by variously colored wickets. Each guest was assigned a course color and a mallet color. Guests with matching colors were teammates. Twenty-four teams of two.

My card read: *Green Course, Pink Mallet.*

I never knew there was a pink mallet in croquet, but I was content because this color scheme coordinated nicely with my equally pink-and-green sundress—this one decorated with charming pink elephants on grass green, um, grass.

Spying a field of green wickets, I headed that direction as Phelps headed for *Yellow Course* to retrieve his *Blue Mallet*. Noticeably on the opposite side of the lawn.

A servant clad in white tie formals stood in attendance at the mallet stand, ready to quell any color conflicts, I assumed. I handed him my card as I watched Phelps receive his blue mallet. Why was I not surprised when Kelly bounded to his side, cheerfully waving her card that presumably also sported *Yellow Course, Blue Mallet*?

I briefly wondered how far a croquet ball could fly given enough motivated force. Then my brain jumped to a realization. If Kelly were paired with Phelps, then who—

"The gentleman already has the pink mallet, ma'am."

Following the servant's extended arm, I turned to see Gavin palming the pink mallet, slapping it against his khaki-clad thigh.

"Hello, Lydia."

Leave it to Gavin to try and single-handedly bring back the alligator shirt.

"Gavin," I answered in acknowledgment.

All guilt-induced sympathy for Jawbreaker and the plight of the lost-but-now-returned pug evaporated. Unlike Mr. Pugsley's purely accidental release—I mentally retracted any confession of knowledgeable intent—this was entirely deliberate. Malice aforethought.

"I hope my being here isn't making you uncomfortable." He even had the gumption to look contrite.

Gavin? Contrite? That was a first.

I flashed him a scathing smile. "Why should I be uncomfortable?"

Since I wasn't interested in having the highly overrated let's-put-this-behind-us-and-still-be-friends conversation, I focused every ounce of my attention on the idea that winning this tournament would be a terrific means of making up for this malicious match.

Beat Jawbreaker and the KYs at their own social game and redeem some measure of pride. If Gavin managed to benefit from my competitive determination, then I'd just have to take the bad with the good.

I eyed the mallet hungrily and tried to grab it from his hands.

"Don't be like this, Lydia." Gavin stepped back, holding the mallet securely behind his back. He placed his hand on my arm and gave me an all-too-familiar squeeze. "We can be civilized."

"What is civilized about a man boinking his already-married secretary two weeks before his own wedding?" I said. On the inside. On the outside, I said, "I don't want to talk about this. Just play the game."

A shrill whistle sounded and a voice over loudspeaker commanded that the games should begin.

As I stalked past him toward the first green wicket, I grabbed the mallet from his fist. And smacked the head into my palm for maximum effect.

My game had already begun.

♥

GAVIN and I played surprisingly well together. Not that I

would ever tell him, but he had skill with a mallet. We won our first three matches easily, ending up among the teams playing in the final on the white wicket course set up on the central lawn contained by the circular drive.

The other finalists included Jawbreaker and bottom feeder Brant, Kelly and Phelps, and myself and Gavin. Ferrero and his partner—some young metrosexual-looking hunk—also advanced, though from what I saw of their last game, they advanced because everyone kept granting Ferrero gimmes.

It paid to be the boss.

We all got to keep our balls. Even though another pink team made it to the final, ours had green stripes. They all had stripes that matched their initial courses.

My adrenaline was pumping. Years of practice at the Westchester Country Club assured that my game was head-on. And Gavin was much better on the other side of a croquet stake than he had ever been on the other side of an engagement ring.

We were going to win, I could feel it.

"Ladies and gentlemen," Jawbreaker called out, "before the championship match begins, you should know to the victors what spoils will go. Armando."

She motioned to an Italian-looking servant standing at the edge of the circle of guests. He made his way through the crowd and handed Jawbreaker a large white envelope with the Ferrero Couture logo embossed in gold.

"In this envelope are four first-class tickets to Milan, one-week for four at a five-star hotel and four week-long, all-access passes to fashion week for the Fall season." She waved the envelope above her head and announced, "To the winners and their guests."

The crowd cheered and on cue an army of servants appeared carrying silver trays laden with glasses of white wine.

"I don't know about you," Gavin leaned in close to whisper, "but I could use a week in Italy."

As much as I wanted to disagree with everything out of the man's mouth—for reasons of morality—I had to concede that Italy sounded wonderful. And if Ferrero really did use my jewelry in the Spring collection, it would be beneficial to have the experience of a fashion week extravaganza before I was expected to participate.

I smiled—an actual, unforced, genuine smile. "Then let's win this thing."

Gavin rested his hand at the base of my spine, guiding me toward the first wicket. I had to suppress a shiver at the memory of how his touch used to make me feel.

The teams drew straws for order of play. Jawbreaker drew the shortest straw and last start. Ferrero drew third to last. Kelly squealed as she and Phelps drew the longest straw. Looking at the straw in my hand I realized we would play second, directly after Phelps and Kelly.

Gavin realized this, too.

"Good," he said in their direction, "after you go, we can show everyone how the game is really played."

"Don't let your talk get bigger than your game, Fairchild," Phelps replied with that arrogant grin.

"A whisper would be bigger than your game, Elliot."

Oh no, the pissing contest began. I bit my lips to hide a smile as I took two steps away in an act of self-preservation.

That shrill whistle blew again, announcing the start of the match. Phelps grabbed the blue mallet from Kelly and dropped the yellow-striped blue ball at the starting stake. He whacked the ball, sailing it perfectly between the uprights of the first wicket and into position for the second. Gavin's triumphant smile dimmed.

Well, I was not about to give up after one shot. Besides, we were playing alternate turns. Scoring a wicket did not earn a consecutive hit. No one could get very far ahead at any one time.

And I planned on keeping right up.

"Give me the ball," I demanded.

Gavin smile, like he wanted to say something inappropriate.

I scowled, determinedly holding out my hand palm up for emphasis. He placed it in my hand without letting go. I snatched it out of his hand. "We're winning this trip to Italy," I said, "no matter what your stupid bet was."

For the first time in memory Gavin looked impressed. By me.

Had been part of our problem? Well, his problem really. Had I stopped impressing him? Men bored easily, didn't they?

Phelps interrupted my ponderings. "You going or not?"

I turned to him and smiled brightly. "Shut up, Sweet Tooth."

Setting my ball perfectly at the starting stake, I shimmied and aligned myself into perfect position before smoothly striking the wooden ball. Pink-and-green went rolling over the closely groomed lawn, through the wicket and into the blue-and-yellow ball. Knocking it several inches out of the path of the next wicket.

Gavin wrapped an arm around my waist and squeezed me close. "Looks like you might be eating those words, Elliot."

Part of me wanted to elbow him in the ribs. The rest of me saw the glare Kelly threw my way and leaned in closer to his side.

After my masterful stroke, if Gavin didn't hold up his end of the game, I would seriously reconsider my opinion on capital punishment.

The other teams played their turns, each pretty dismal after the first two shots. Ferrero managed to hit his black-striped pink ball into the driveway. And Jawbreaker's purple-and-red followed right behind.

Unfortunately, my need to kiss up to the boss was heavily outweighed by my need to win the trip. Or just win period. Other people clearly didn't have that problem.

After several rounds of play, we four were two wickets each from the finishing stake and the trash talk—if trash talk is even legal in croquet—had escalated to mountainous proportions. The other teams had actually given up, resigning themselves to shared last place and first dibs on the fresh round of wine.

"Why are you taking this competition so seriously?" Jawbreaker asked before downing an entire glass of Pinot Grigio in one gulp. "No matter who wins, all four of you will be going to Italy."

We turned to stare in unison.

"The glory," Gavin said.

"The bragging rights," Phelps added.

Kelly and I glared at each other.

"I don't like to lose," I said.

"I wouldn't know," Kelly replied. "I've never lost."

Oh, it was on.

It came down to the last shot, two balls side by side and

equally aligned for the perfect shot, Kelly stepped up to take her turn. She had two choices. Shoot the wicket and win the game. Or knock our ball out of play.

Guess which shot she chose. No really, guess.

As I retrieved our ball from a very thorny bush I could almost see the ego swelling her golden blonde head to monstrous proportion, glowing with the glory of my humiliation.

PHELPS HANDLED THE WIN GRACEFULLY.

If by gracefully you meant grabbed Kelly around the waist, spun her around like a cotton candy machine, and hollered at the top of his lungs, "Eat that, Fairchild!"

By the time we retired to our room at around three a.m. he had calmed down. Mostly.

"Did you see that last shot?" he called up from the floor. "Masterful I tell you, masterful."

I leaned over the side of the bed.

"I was there, remember?"

If I sounded bitter, it was only because I really wanted to win. Not because it seemed Kelly was everyone's golden child. Jawbreaker's favorite. Gavin's favorite. Now Phelps' favorite. No, that didn't bother me at all. Not. At. All.

"Knocked your ball out of play like a real pro." He waved his hands around, presumably reenacting the path of the redirected ball.

"Yeah, she should go on the international croquet circuit." My humor level was at an all-time low. And I had other things on my mind. "We need to talk."

He lifted himself up on one elbow. "Sounds serious."

"Not really." I sighed, thinking over everything that had happened in the last few days. "I just need to know if you are available for some upcoming business functions."

In the soft moonlight I saw him smile. Not that cocky, arrogant smile that sets my teeth on edge, but a genuine friendly smile.

"You asking me out on a date?"

"I guess," I replied. "What's the going per-date rate?"

He frowned and rose to a full sitting position. "What do you mean?"

"People will expect me to show up with you by my side. At least for now. I just want to know what each date will cost me. A date should run about two to three hours. There are a couple of cocktail parties that will probably be longer, but I figure we could come up with a set rate."

"Oh." Phelps laid back down and folded his arms behind his head. "I kinda forgot I was being paid."

That threw me for a loop. He sounded almost wistful. Almost *sad*.

Great Gobstoppers, Lyd. Get a grip.

The man was *only* here because he was being paid. Why else would a wild adventurer with Hollywood looks spend time with a dull Westchester girl at an even duller Southampton party?

"Can we just wing it?" he asked, rolling away from the bed to lie on his side. "I'm too tired to do math right now."

"Sure."

I collapsed back onto the mattress, feeling a little guilty for hogging the bed and for something else I couldn't quite name. At least I could do something about the bed. "Phelps—"

"Before I forget." He rolled off his makeshift bed and grabbed something from the pocket of his shirt that was hanging on the back of a chair. "Take this."

I leaned sideways and started to take it, before I realized what he offered me. "No, you earned the trip," I pushed the envelope back into his hand. "When the time comes take whoever you want. Consider it a bonus."

Snatching the envelope back, he shoved it back into the shirt pocket before dropping back onto his side.

Before I could even begin to apologize for whatever I had just done, he bit out, "Good night, Lydia."

Let me tell you, my dreams that night were not about tubfuls of hot tamales.

SEVEN

RATHER THAN SIT through the tedious Sunday morning brunch—and end up driving back in late afternoon traffic with the rest of the weekend suburbanites—Phelps and I headed back to Manhattan first thing in the morning. He seemed to have gotten over whatever I said to set him off the night before and I was over my momentary fit of jealousy. The three-hour drive passed quickly in pleasant conversation. When I pulled up in front of the Lower East Side tenement Phelps called home I felt like we had only just left Southampton.

He bounded from the car, grabbing his duffel from the back seat, and leaned back in the open window.

"You promise you'll call," he teased.

I smiled. "I think we have drinks scheduled Wednesday night at the Watering Hole."

"I'm there," he said, stepping back onto the sidewalk and shrugging the duffel onto his shoulder. "And Lydia—" He ducked down to peer in at me. "—I had a lot of fun this weekend."

"Me too," I replied. Yeah, me too.

With a sigh I waved and pulled out into the traffic on Avenue C. Who'd have thought I'd have so much fun with such an overbearing, arrogant underwear model?

Fiona. That's who.

I grabbed my cell phone, dangling from the charger cable connecting it to the dash, and punched her speed dial. She picked up on the fourth ring, sounding groggy and gravelly. "Herro?"

And masculine.

"Fiona?"

"Jacque," the man on her phone corrected. "Hold on."

There was the sound of rustling sheets and a muffled "phone call" before Fiona got on the line. "Who is it?"

"Who's Jacque?"

The other end of the phone sniffed and requested a cup of coffee. Strong coffee. "Hey Lyd. How was the Sailing Saga?"

"Summer Sail Away," I corrected automatically. "It was actually pretty fun."

"Good. Mmmm," she moaned as her cup of coffee presumably arrived. After a very loud gulp, she said, "Phelps is hot, no?"

That sounded an awful lot like a dangerously sticky question. I deftly evaded answering. "Wanna meet for lunch?"

"Lunch, my God, what time is it?" Fiona had never been much of a morning person. More like an after-midnight person. "It's only 11:30. Why are you calling me so early?"

"I just got into town." I merged my baby onto Broadway and continued south. "I'll be at your place in fifteen minutes. Get dressed. Bring Jacque if you like."

"No thanks," she grumbled. Fiona's love life was like a box of

Bertie Bott's Every Flavor Beans—one night she might get Soap, the next Earwax, and the next Grass. But she kept trying them, one by one, hoping to find that elusive Strawberries and Cream.

Clearly Jacque was something foul.

"Or don't. But be ready or I'm coming up and dragging you out."

"When'd you get so pushy," Fiona whined.

"I've always been pushy. I hide it well." Steering my way around City Hall Park, I made for the Brooklyn Bridge. "If you're not ready, I'm inviting Jacque to the Sweet Spot on Friday."

"God, I'll be ready already."

As she hung up her phone, she muttered something like "slave driver." But I knew she would be waiting on the sidewalk when I arrived. I'd bet my entire collection of Conversation Hearts.

♥

FIONA JERKED OPEN the door and dove into my car before I could pull to a full stop.

"Drive," she demanded. "Just drive before he tries to follow us."

"That bad?"

She looked at me and rolled her eyes in a you-have-no-idea gesture. "Carmella's. I need a pitcher of Bloody Maries."

I did so without question.

As we wound our way through construction-heavy streets, I allowed her to sit in disgruntled silence behind the protective shield of her mirrored aviators. Not until we were safely seated with a Bloody Mary in her hands and a Mimosa in mine, did conversation begin.

"The weekend," she grunted between gulps. "Details. Spill."

"Phelps is... something different."

"Shook your foundations?"

"Not exact—" I stopped as her eyebrow shot up from behind her sunglasses. "All right, yes. He rocked my world—that what you wanted to hear?"

Fiona, ignoring my concession, waved the waitress over to order another drink.

If she was going to act so smug about her matchmaking, she wasn't going to get any details from me.

I deftly changed the subject. " I have fantastic news. Ferrero is going to use my jewelry in the Spring collection."

"That's fantastic," she exclaimed as she whipped off her sunglasses. "What's the catch?"

"The catch?" I echoed.

"The catch." Her dark brown eyes bored into me with the intensity of all her Italian ancestors. "The hook. The price. The big *but* at the end of the sentence."

"Not really a catch," I explained. "More like a mutual exchange."

"Oh God, not of body fluids?"

"No! Of course not." Sweet Saltwater Taffy, where did Fiona come up with these things? Her mind resided permanently in the gutter. "He wants me to be his muse. His *muse*. That's all."

She scowled, as if weighing the pros and cons of such a situation before making her assessment.

"Just so long as his paws stay on the right side of the

sketchpad." Then she smiled. "This is a great opportunity. We could probably score you a few covers."

Our waitress arrived with Fi's third Bloody Mary—hair of the dog and all that—and our lunches. Fiona drooled hungrily over her stack of butter-slathered pancakes. She is one of those I-can-eat-anything-and-still-look-like-a-supermodel women— even violently hungover she looked runway-worthy in her black sleeveless turtleneck, denim micro-mini, and knee-high leopard print boots. Me, I had to balance my candy-rich diet with a carb-free fruit and cheese plate. After two days of heavy gourmet meals, I'll have to hit the gym for two sessions a day for a week.

I would still take a pass on her magazine offer.

"Keep me off the covers, thank you very much."

She cut off a giant forkful of pancake and shoveled it into her mouth. "Think of the publicity," she said around the mouthful of syrupy fluff. Waving her fork across the table in imitation of a headline, she added, "The new face of Ferrero: LIV Jewelry creator Lydia Ilene Vanderwalk."

I ignored her. My jewelry-making was never meant to be more than a hobby. Even now it was nothing more than some-thing to get me closer to a promotion.

There was no better way to distract her attention than with juicy news. "Guess who I was paired with for the croquet tournament?"

"Croquet tournament?" She washed down the pancakes with a generous gulp of Bloody Mary. "Did you travel back in time to party with F. Scott and Zelda?"

"Jawbreaker is a traditionalist." But Fiona has latched onto the wrong detail. "And she paired me with Gavin."

"Evil witch."

"That was my initial reaction, too. But,"—and I really had to think long and hard before admitting this—"it wasn't that bad."

Of all the scary things that had happened over the weekend, that had to be the most unsettling. Gavin and I working as a team. Something, in retrospect, we had never done as a couple. It was always him and me. Or him versus me. No matter my achievement, he had to top it with one of his own. If I got a 3% raise, he got a 5% raise. If I got a one-line quote in *InStyle*, he got a full interview in *Money*. Nothing I ever did was good enough to top his latest achievement. And the last thing I wanted in a relationship was constant competition. I got enough of that at work.

So it was startling that Gavin and I worked together as croquet partners. He wasn't trying to top my shots, he was trying to top Phelps.

And, much to my amazement and—to some degree—horror, it felt kind of nice.

Not that I was about to admit that to anyone. I was barely able to admit it to myself.

Besides, this time Fiona latched onto the *right* detail. "Then who played with Phelps?"

I managed not to roll my eyes as I said, "Kelly."

"Hell, I wouldn't know who to cheer against." She chewed and swallowed the last of her pancakes and moved on to the untouched grapes on my plate. "Gavin or her. Equally deserving of my booing."

"We were tied going into the final wicket, but Kelly knocked our ball into the bushes." That still grated, even though I would have done the same. "She and Phelps won a trip to Italy for fashion week."

"Together!" Fiona spit a half-chewed grape onto her plate. "Of all the devious, underhanded—"

"Not together," I soothed. "There were two pairs of tickets. They can each take someone."

Fiona grinned. That devious, self-satisfied grin that made me understand why she and Phelps got along so well. And confirmed my suspicion that her assurance that Phelps was pure eye candy had been downright manipulation.

She could be a calculating matchmaker when the mood struck.

"You and Phelps in the most romantic country on earth? Sounds like the perfect recipe for love."

I threw a grape at her, nailing her square between the eyes. "He's not taking me. Why would he?"

Fiona popped the grape into her smiling mouth. "We'll see about that. I'll just have a talk with our young man..."

I forked a bite of triple-crème brie and savored the smooth flavor. Personal experience dictated that ignoring Fiona was often the best course of action. Ignoring and distracting.

"So, Fiona. Tell me about Jacque."

She scowled as she stole another grape. "Fair enough."

And we spent the rest of lunch in the blissful absence of conversations about men. Hired or otherwise.

WHEN I GOT HOME I made the mistake of checking my voice-mail. One message from Bethany. Two from Dad. Sixteen from Mom.

They knew I was going away for the weekend, I told them

ten times, but when I called home the first thing I heard was, "Where have you been!"

"In Southampton." I rolled my suitcase into the bedroom and started mindlessly unpacking. "Did you need something?"

After setting two piles of folded clothes onto of the silver-gray silk duvet, I sorted into "Hang Up" and "To Cleaners" piles.

"The annual barbecue is next weekend," Mom said. "I need to know if you're going to come."

To Mom, the annual Vanderwalk barbecue constituted a crisis-worthy situation. I didn't roll my eyes, but it was a struggle.

"Of course I can come," I answered as I slipped one pile into the dry cleaners bag. "What day and time?"

"Saturday at six."

One by one I hung up my dresses and slacks on matching wooden hangers. "Need me to bring anything?"

"You could bring one of your friends..." she said with a deliberately pregnant pause. "Or a boy. A boy friend. A boyfriend. Unless..."

I sighed at my mom's version of subtle manipulation. Her *unless* signaled something as subtle as Fiona's taste in fashion. As I placed my shoes back in their labeled homes in the wall of plastic shoe drawers in my closet, I braced myself.

"...you want me to introduce you to Barbara Davenport's son. He's a doctor."

Like that would cure all my relationship ills. Maybe if he was a therapist. Or a candy manufacturer. Now that'd be something.

"No thanks," I declined politely.

"A radiologist," she persisted. "Top of his class at Harvard Medical School. He works at a private hospital in—"

"Really, Mom, I'm not interested."

Grabbing my toiletries bag I headed for the bathroom and unpacked the array of small bottles. As I looked at the collection of travel-sized products in my bottom drawer, a wanderlust longing hit me. It had been more than three years since I'd been out of the country. And that had been a one-nighter in Paris to visit Gavin on a business trip.

One night in the city of lights shouldn't even count.

Suddenly, I really wanted that trip to Milan. Maybe I would go anyway. On my own. Turn it into a real vacation and a chance to study fashion week from the audience's perspective.

"He lives in the city. Not far from you." Mom's sales pitch interrupted my Italian fantasy. "He knits sweaters. For cats. Isn't that darling?"

Mom was really scraping the barrel with this one.

"I'll just call Dustin and tell him you'll—"

"No!" If I didn't stop her now, she'd have the wedding planned before we even met. "I'll bring a guy, okay?"

The shocked silence from the other end of the phone was a little disconcerting. I mean it wasn't like I never had dates. Maybe since Gavin there's been a little lag, but—who was I kidding? Phelps was the first thing even resembling a date I'd had in two years.

"Oh," she finally managed. "Okay."

If Phelps could provide enough diversionary tactics to see my way through the matchmaking until either I found my one true or Mom gave up, he would be worth every penny.

Mental Post-it: Call Phelps Monday morning.

I SAT down at my perfectly clean desk Monday morning, ready to tackle my immense To Do list. I had already called to book Phelps for Saturday night. If only all my tasks would prove that easy.

Pulling the neat stack of Monday items from my top desk drawer, I started to dig my way through.

Ferrero popped in at 9:02.

"*Chica,*" he said in his increasingly fake Italian accent and I was certain he used the endearment because he still couldn't remember my name, "how is my beautiful muse?"

"Just muse-y," I replied with more cheek than necessary.

"Wonderful, wonderful." He looked around my office, a room he had never before visited, and nodded enthusiastically at the mahogany bookcases, tan canvas and leather armchairs, and Lempicka reproductions. "Pristine, elegant, sophisticated. Just like you."

"Thank you." Why was Ferrero eyeing my office like I ogled the candy aisle at D'Agnostino?

"This room is the perfect atmosphere." He scuffed his leather oxford along the lush carpet with reverence. "So soothing. Calming."

Ferrero lowered into the armchair on the left and looked around the room, as if gauging the view from the seat. He then stood, moved to the chair on the right, and did the same thing.

Artists, I thought, then shrugged and went back to the pile.

First task: Call Saks Fifth Avenue in San Diego to arrange preparations for trunk show.

Well, I couldn't very easily—or politely—make a business

call with Ferrero in the room, so I moved that note to the bottom of the pile.

Second task: Pull up numbers for second-quarter sales of men's accessories.

Ugh. My brain was not alert enough to compute a stream of numbers. That just might put me to sleep. Slipped that one to the bottom, too.

I looked up to find Ferrero dragging the side table next to the door toward the armchairs. He tugged it into place between the two and then sat in the chair on the right and reevaluated.

He smiled to himself and I went back to the pile.

Third task: Create PowerPoint presentation on implications of new advertising campaign for three o'clock meeting.

Okay, this I could do. And it had a hard deadline. I would need reinforcements, though. Of the sugar-filled variety.

I clicked open PowerPoint on the computer—ignoring the urge to check my email with willpower of steel—and pulled open my lower left drawer.

My gasp could be heard for a three-block radius.

"What is it, *cherie*?" Ferrero asked, slipping now into pseudo-French, and looking up from rearranging a shelf of photographs.

I could only shake my head in shock, but I did manage to close my mouth. He took this as a sign that all was well. "This room will be perfect, I have decided."

"W-what?" I stammered, dragging my gaze away from the drawer. "What h-have you decided?"

My whole body started to shake, like after a really hard yoga class when my muscles just gave up any pretense of working in their state of utter exhaustion. Like after I downed a whole 10-pack of Pixy Stix in ten minutes and my blood turned to sugar water.

I grabbed the arms of my chair to hide the quivers.

"This will be my creative center," he decreed. "The Spring Collection will be designed in this room. I shall have Antoine move my things in here this afternoon."

With a flourish and a swirl of his knee-length lilac kaftan, Ferrero exited my office.

I knew he had just announced he would be taking over my office, my personal space, for the duration of the upcoming season design, but my brain could not begin to process the loss. Instead, my wide-eyed gaze dropped back to the open drawer.

For several long minutes—until my assistant came in with a peppermint Frappuccino and shook me out of the trance—I just stared. Unseeing. At the empty drawer.

All my candy was gone.

EIGHT

TRYING to quell the surging panic, I grabbed my purse from beneath the desk and dug around for a treat. Any treat. A half-sucked Lifesaver. A dinner mint. A caramel wrapper with a tiny blob stuck to the corner.

Nothing. Not even a lone Nerd rolling around the dust and lint gathered in the bottom of my bag. How had I left home without a single piece of candy? How had I eaten every last piece in my drawer?!

Leaping from my chair, I pressed the intercom button and announced, "I have to go out for a minute. Please hold my calls."

My assistant Angela didn't respond from the other end of the phone line, but I didn't care. I dashed for the door. Just as I reached for the handle the door burst open.

Instantaneously, a dozen men dressed all in white began removing furniture from my office. Out went the armchairs and the side tables and the floor lamps before I could even voice a, "What on earth is going on here?"

Had I been fired? Had Jawbreaker found out that Phelps

was a fraudulent boyfriend? Had there been an unwritten rule in the croquet tournament that the loser lost her job?

"Mr. Ferrero's orders," one of the men said. "Wants everything out but that desk and chair."

Then, with all the offending furniture gone, they threw plastic sheets over the desk, the built-in bookcases, and the entire floor. One of the men carried in two paint cans and set them in the middle of my dropclothed desk.

He popped off the lids to reveal brilliant fuchsia and tangerine. Three other men made their way around the room laying strips of blue painter's tape in parallel, vertical stripes on the bare walls.

Oh no, I thought, my beautiful khaki and cream walls. Before I completed the thought, the painters started spreading garish deep pink and light orange stripes up and down my lovely walls.

I couldn't watch. As I turned to leave, I ran into Jawbreaker in my doorway.

"Lydia, I'm glad I caught you," she oozed.

Great Gobstoppers, can't she say *anything* without simpering. "What can I do for you, Janice?"

"I need to get the files for the trunk show tour."

"Oh, I haven't gotten the PowerPoint done yet." Or even started for that matter. I had more pressing concerns at the moment.

She smiled like a cat who came across an endless river of cream. "That's fine," she purred, "Kelly can do that."

No, Kelly can't do that. The West Coast Trunk Show was my project, my idea from the beginning, and no little KY tramp was going to take it away.

Giving up on getting out of the room anytime soon, I

walked back to my desk and plunked my purse on the plastic-covered desk. "Actually, I was going to start as soon as I get back. I'll have it to you before lunch."

She didn't look as taken aback as I'd hoped.

"You have too many other things on your plate right now, what with the Spring collection and all. Besides," she drawled, her voice positively reeking of unadulterated gloat, "that will fall under the purview of Kelly's new duties."

"New duties?" If not for the sheet plastic covering my chair I would have collapsed into the cushy softness.

"Ferrero's orders," Janice said.

I watched in horror as a gloating grin spread across her tanned, aging face. Where was candy when I needed it?

Wait, I thought I remembered seeing a stray Tootsie Roll in my file drawer last week. Dropping to my knees behind the desk, I flipped up the sheet plastic and jerked open the drawer. I shifted files desperately and, finally finding the dust-covered treat, stood as I tore off the wrapper.

Jawbreaker continued as I chewed my way to emotional calm.

"He ordered that all your duties be divvied up while you're working with him." Her eyes fell on the trunk show file beneath the transparent plastic. She carefully lifted the cover and slipped the file out without displacing anything on the desk. "Kelly will be taking over most of your duties."

I nearly choked on my Tootsie Roll. "I-I-I—"

"Maybe you two should get together later so you can show her the ropes."

"I have to go."

I needed more than a Tootsie Roll. Maybe one of those giant Tootsie Logs. Or a case of them.

This was my nightmare come true. KY Kelly was getting my job before I was even out. I had no delusions that she would treat this as a temporary situation. If she could find a way to snag my job permanently—whether by straightforward or ethically-fuzzy means—she would.

I dashed to the door, leaving a confused Jawbreaker at my desk amid the sheet plastic and rapidly forming pink and orange stripes. I made it to the doorway before remembering my purse. No way I could get my candy fix without my wallet. Unless I was ready to stoop to shoplifting. Though I actually considered that option for longer than was morally comfortable, I knew I had to go back to get my purse.

"Can't leave without my purse," I said through gritted teeth.

Jawbreaker looked confused. Perfect, I could retrieve my purse and get the heck outta Dodge before anything worse could come out of her mouth. I made it to the doorway again. Only to run into Kelly.

"Lydia," she exclaimed in that annoyingly high-pitched, enthusiastic voice, "I'm so glad I caught you."

Caught was sure the right word for it.

I pasted on my best glad-to-see-you-but-I'd-rather-eat-broken-glass smile. "What can I do for you, Kelly?"

"I just wanted to tell you what a fantastic opportunity I think this is for both of us, you working so closely with Ferrero," she stepped forward and hugged me, "and me getting the chance to work with you."

"Yeah," I managed to lift my right hand to pat her on the back in the kind of hug guys give each other at football games, "great."

"I was just saying you two should set up a meeting,"

Jawbreaker said. "Maybe you could have a standing appointment. At least until Kelly gets into the swing of things."

I extricated myself from Kelly's hug. I wanted to shout, *No, no, no!* There would be no getting into the swing of anything by anyone but me.

But the opportunity with Ferrero was more important than protecting my current job from devious KYs. I had to keep telling myself that. Reminding myself. Because if this worked out, I could drop the number-crunching job and focus on my designs. If I decided that's what I want to do.

What? No, I meant I could snag the promotion I'd been working so hard to get. I couldn't become a full-time designer. It was too… risky? Unstable? Terrifying. Definitely terrifying.

So, for now, I just smiled and nodded and pretended like helping Kelly learn how to do my job wasn't the last thing I wanted to do.

"Sounds great." I inclined my head to the door. "Gotta run now. We can talk when I get back."

This time I made it all the way out.

NINE

MY OFFICE LOOKED like a circus tent. All the walls were now covered in garishly bright stripes, the elegant cream-colored armchairs had been replaced by two semi-circular, red velvet sectionals, and Ferrero stood in the center like a ringleader directing the placement of two mannequins and a golden sculpture of a poodle standing on his front paws. A standard poodle.

I took one look and turned to run.

Unfortunately, Ferrero had keen eyesight.

"My muse," he called out.

Shoulders slumped in resignation, I walked into my office to face the disaster.

"Where have you been all morning?" he chided.

"Errands," I said dismissively, hoping he would drop the topic, "I am a very busy woman."

He waved both soft hands in front of his face. "No more," he clucked. "From now on you are only my muse. You shall eat, breathe, drink, love the Spring Collection. If I work, you work. If I rest, you rest. We are the same person."

Closing my eyes against his over-the-top display of artistic temperament, I wished this all away like the remnants of a bad dream.

Couldn't we go back, like, five days? Just before I walked through that door with Phelps and my life hurtled out of control. No, that wouldn't be far enough. I'd have to go back at least until before I told Jawbreaker about the NEB in the first place.

"*Cherie?*" His multi-accented voice invaded my delusional fantasy. "*Cherie*, we must to work."

Reluctantly opening my eyes, I found the workmen gone, the mannequins standing at either end of my desk, the golden poodle *on* my desk—where my monitor use to be—and Ferrero reclining on one of the red sofas with a sketchpad in hand.

He looked enthusiastic. Anticipatory. Predatory.

"All right," I replied hesitantly, "what do you want me to do?"

I crossed to my desk and rummaged around for a sketchpad of my own. And surreptitiously slid the bags of Jolly Ranchers, Cinnamon Bears, and Squirrel Nut Zippers into my lower left drawer. A feisty Zipper dropped to the floor and I knelt under the desk to fetch it.

I had just closed my fingers around the nutty treat when Ferrero said, "First, you must take off your clothes."

"Wha—aaack!" The crown of my skull connected with the solid wood of my desk drawer, sending lightning bolts of pain to every nerve ending I possessed.

"Are you okay?" Ferrero asked, in a suspiciously un-accented voice.

He rushed to my side and tried to help me up but I smacked away his hands.

"What did you just say to me?" I rose to my feet and put some extra distance between us as I rubbed my throbbing head. My left hand tightened into a fist around something solid. I looked down. The Squirrel Nut Zipper.

While Ferrero formulated a response, I unwrapped the prodigal candy and devoured it.

"I only meant," he began, Italian accent firmly in place, "that you should be in something more comfortable than what you have on."

He gestured to my ivory pencil skirt and matching cashmere turtleneck sweater. I scowled. "I am perfectly comfortable as is, thank you."

"Fine, yes, of course." Ferrero hurried back to the couch and sketchpad. "Only thinking of your comfort, *cherie*."

"Right," I replied.

With my own sketchpad in hand, I sat down on the opposite couch, facing him across the—I shuddered to think—black lacquer coffee table.

"Perhaps we should begin by looking at the sketches I have already completed," he offered.

When I showed no sign of leaping across the table to sit next to him, he handed me his sketchpad to study. As I flipped through the collection of elegant line drawings, he continued. "These are only rough drafts, of course, but you will see the direction this collection will take."

Every one of the rail-thin figures had shoulder-length light brown hair. And green-and-gold hazel eyes. And a heart-shaped face.

"When did you do these?" I asked.

"Yesterday," he looked nervously at his perfectly-mani-cured fingernails, "after the gala. You inspired me."

"Hmmm." I evaluated the sketches of all these models with my features wearing beautiful gowns and sophisticated sepa-rates and I actually blushed. I handed the sketches back across the table. "The collection is beautiful. What can I do?"

"You," he replied with a beaming grin, "can just sit there and look lovely." When that response earned him a scowl, he added, "And design some equally inspired jewelry."

"All right. If you sketch, I sketch." Pencil at the ready, I smiled. "We are the same person."

Ferrero smiled in return and we both dove into our sketching.

❤

THREE HOURS later I had initial jewelry sketches for several of Ferrero's designs. At four o'clock, Ferrero threw down his pencil and declared the workday over—although, if I had let him have his Italian way, we would have taken a four-hour lunch and worked until six.

"Enough of the work day. I need more inspiration." He looked at me with direct intent. "We must dine. You. Me. And your young man. Tonight."

"Franco"—I was getting used to calling him by his first name after three hours of insistence that I do so—"I don't think Phelps will be available on such short notice."

"Nonsense," he returned with a flick of his wrist. "How can he not have time for his young lady love and his favorite designer?"

"But Franco—"

"First I must rest. We will meet at Charpé"—pronounced Shar Pei, like the dog—"at eight o'clock."

He swept out of the room with a flourish, leaving scattered piles of sketches and fabric swatches everywhere.

Great, I hoped Phelps didn't have other plans.

I dialed him on my cell phone—not willing to examine the state of my social life when a hired escort rates number five on my favorites list—and waited for him to pick up.

"Yo Lyd." He sounded out of breath.

"Is this a bad time?" I asked between his grunts.

My imagination quickly supplied a vivid mental picture of exactly what my timing could have interrupted. Though why a man would answer his phone in the middle of—

"Naw, I'm on the stairmaster. Hold on," he said just before the whirring noise in the background shut off. "What's up?"

"Are you free for dinner tonight?"

"Absolutely," he replied quickly. "When and where?"

I gave him the directions to Charpé. "Be there at 7:30."

Half an hour earlier than planned, but I figured a guy like Phelps was chronically late.

As I ended the call, I caught sight of a cable cozy disappearing behind a gilded, antiqued armoire that had replaced two of my smaller bookcases. Crossing to the armoire, I flung the upper doors open and found my missing computer.

A whole day without checking email—at least not since leaving home at seven this morning—and I went into sudden withdrawal.

Quickly powering up my desktop, I logged into Outlook and checked my surprisingly few messages. The first was from Jawbreaker.

Lydia,

I have set up a temporary forwarding of the RegionSix@FerreroCouture.com account to Kelly so you won't be bothered with any business duties while working with Ferrero. If you have time tomorrow, can you meet with Kelly to go over her new duties? She is looking forward to working with you as her mentor.

Janice

That explained the sparsity— sparseness— sparsitude— um, small number of emails.

I could have been really upset. Invasion of privacy and delegation of my duties to a KY and all that. But I had actually —surprisingly—enjoyed spending all afternoon designing jewelry rather than crunching numbers and finessing store managers and tracking shipments and preparing presentations.

Putting that note aside in the mental you-win-some-you-lose-some file, I clicked open my personal email.

One email from Dad.

One email from Bethany.

One email from Phelps.

Three emails from Gavin.

Gavin? What could he need to email me about?

I clicked open the email from Dad.

Hey gumdrop,

Mom just wanted me to remind you about Saturday.

She also wanted me to find out about this guy you're bringing, but I know when you're ready to talk, you'll talk.

Loves and kisses,

Dad

P.S. Bring some peppermint bark from that hoity-toity grocery you like.

Bethany wanted the scoop on the weekend with the hire-a-date. I replied with a quick note that I would call her later.

Now the email from Phelps was unexpected.

Hey Lyd,

Just wanted to say I had fun this weekend. Who knew a bunch of upper crust stiffs could throw such a great bash?

Thanks.

EP

EP? Phelps Elliot? He must have just transposed the letters. In my experience, most men never learned the useful art of typing.

Finally gathering my courage, I clicked open the first email from Gavin. It was brief, with no greeting or signature. It just said we needed to talk. Whatever. I trashed it and did the same to his second and third message. The last thing we needed to do was talk.

I shut off the computer, closed the cabinet doors, and rolled the executive chair back behind the desk, the last vestiges of the beauty of what was once my office.

Slinging my purse over my shoulder, I headed home to get ready for dinner.

💙

CHARPÉ WAS the kind of restaurant that put a lot of stock in atmosphere. Zagat's calls the cuisine *Nouveau Chinois*, which I took to mean artsy Chinese food, and the décor reflected that premise.

The narrow ground floor lobby was painted bright red, bricks and all, and was about the size of my bedroom. Twin giant white canvases with gold-leafed Chinese characters hung on the two side walls. The only furnishings were the gilded maître d' counter and a long low bench with red cushions along the left wall.

The *maître d'*, a thin Chinese man with straight white teeth and a tendency to lean forward, approached me.

"Can help you, Miss?" he said in heavily accented English.

"I'm meeting a party—"

"Ah, yes." He smiled and nodded vigorously before I could say which party. "One already here."

I followed him down the steep, narrow staircase to the basement level. Ferrero must have been early.

But as we emerged into the dining area, a warm space with stained cork walls and cozy tables, I saw Phelps already seated at a table for four.

"Here, Miss." The maître d' pulled out the ladderback chair to Phelps's right.

"Tha—"

I started to thank him, but Phelps jumped up and took the chair before I could sit.

"I've got it," he said as he guided me into the chair.

The maître d' nodded and slipped silently away.

"You're late," Phelps admonished as he returned to his seat. He tried to scowl, but still smiled. "Thought you might stand me up."

"It's only 7:45."

"You said 7:30."

I couldn't stop the blush that burned my cheeks. "Yeah, well, I thought you—"

"You thought I would be late." He leaned close and whispered, "I'm never late for photo shoots or beautiful women."

"Phelps, you don't have to—"

"Good evening, my muses," Ferrero boomed, interrupting me before I could explain to Phelps that he didn't need to feign attraction when no one was around.

"Ferrero," Phelps stood and extended his hand, but kept his surprised eyes trained on me, "I had no idea this was a business meeting."

Oops. I guess I had forgotten to mention that Ferrero would be at dinner.

"Not business." Ferrero gave his hand to Phelps like a queen presenting her ring to be kissed. "Such an ugly, uninspiring word. No one shall utter it again in my presence."

Phelps and I exchanged a what's-up-with-the-crazy-artist-guy look, but he sat and I smiled prettily.

"Very well, Franco," I replied. "What shall we talk about?"

Ferrero ignored my question and waved the wine steward over. "We are ready to order," he said, not having looked at a menu. "A bottle of the Terra Rustica *Beaujolais*. A vegetarian springtime roll appetizer. Three *Sum Dim Da* platters. And a black bean ice cream tart."

The wine steward looked like he was trying not to explain that he wasn't a waiter, but decided Ferrero was too important a customer and simply smiled and walked away. I watched as he found our actual waiter and relayed the meal order.

Then, just as I turned back to the men seated on either side of me, a high-pitched, Jersey-accented, female voice shouted, "Frankie?" The voice grew louder as she drew closer. "Frankie Farris?"

A woman, hair teased to unnatural proportions, eyes caked with a rainbow of colors, and legs tightly wrapped in black spandex, walked up to our table and sat down.

"Frankie Farris as I live and breathe, it is you."

Ferrero, his face drained of all color, shook his head vehemently as his mouth gaped open-shut like a beached flounder.

The woman plopped her purse on the table and pulled out a thick billfold full of picture sleeves. After flipping open to a picture, she held it up to Ferrero and thrust it in my and Phelps's faces.

"This was us senior year. At the Boardwalk in Atlantic City." She looked at Ferrero with fluttering eyelashes. "We were one hot item, eh Frankie?"

Ferrero looked mortified.

Or embarrassed.

"I'm afraid you have mistaken me," he finally said, looking around the restaurant for salvation.

"Frankie, it's me." The woman pointed ten claw-like red fingernails at herself. "Marcy. Marcy Russignola. From Bay Shore High."

Like a trapped animal, Ferrero stared at her with eyes wide and unable to speak.

Now this may not have been incontrovertible as far as

evidence goes, but I felt pretty certain that my earlier doubts as to Ferrero's country of origin were well-founded. What a scandal. Franco Ferrero, designer to the stars, was really Frankie Farris from Bay Shore High.

This was the kind of scandal that could ruin a career.

No Hollywood ingénue wants to be dressed by a Jersey boy. They want to wear Italian. Or French. Or even British. But not Jersey.

Ferrero was speechless. I was speechless.

Thankfully, Phelps came to the rescue.

"Marcy, so nice to meet you." He stood and took her hand, planting a charming kiss on her frighteningly manicured fingers. "Please, join us for dinner."

Marcy flushed, a little embarrassed herself. "Oh, well, I came with someone," she stammered. She looked across the room at the table she had come from. "My husband. It's our anniversary. Thirty-five years."

"Congratulations." Phelps followed her gaze to the table and smiled at the older man sitting alone and waiting. "Don't let us keep you from your celebration. Enjoy your special night."

He kissed her on both cheeks and somehow she headed back to her table without the whole world of scandal erupting around us.

The wine steward arrived and took his time pouring three equal samples, then, after our hearty approval, three full glasses of the sweet red wine. By the time he left, our table had come to an unspoken understanding that Marcy Russignola was not to be discussed.

At one point, when I returned from the ladies' room, I saw Phelps smiling at Ferrero as the wine steward walked away. A few minutes later the steward delivered a bottle of champagne to Marcy and her husband. They raised a toast in our direction.

Marcy might not have to reconcile Frankie Farris with fashion great Franco Ferrero, but I knew I would never be able to forget. Even if we did continue to pretend that Marcy must have been mistaken and Ferrero's frequent slips in accent were auditory anomalies.

AFTER DINNER PHELPS insisted on seeing me home.

Even though the restaurant was on the same end of town as his apartment. Even though his apartment was either a very long subway ride or a very pricey cab ride from mine.

No protestations on my part would stop him, so when we stepped out into the night I moved forward to hail a cab.

"What are you doing?" he asked.

I raised one brow in sarcastic surprise, thinking the answer was obvious. "Getting a cab."

"Why?"

Again, obvious. Maybe I was missing something. "So I can get home?"

"I mean why a cab?" He pulled me back onto the sidewalk and out of cab-calling range. "There's a subway stop two blocks away."

"I don't take the subway."

He frowned like I had just recited the Presidents of the United States backward. Which I could totally do, by the way.

"It's dirty and dangerous and unreliable," I explained. And then, because he wasn't responding and because I felt the need to defend my opposition to mass transit, I added, "And there are drug dealers and gang-bangers and—"

"Have you ever been *on* a subway?"

"No, but—"

"Come on." Phelps grabbed me by the hand tugged me into a trot down the sidewalk.

He had the same look in his eye as when he pulled up in front of Jawbreaker's on Daffy. I was immediately suspicious.

"Where are we going?"

"On the A Train."

TEN

TWO HOURS and countless subway stops on what felt every line in the Metro Transit Authority later we arrived at my front door. I was exhausted and filthy and out of breath from running up the ten flights to my floor, but surprisingly enough I was having a good time.

Now I knew what older women saw in younger men.

"Admit it," Phelps teased as he poked me in the ribs, "you had fun on the subway."

I looked into those beautiful blue eyes and saw all the exuberance that was missing in my life. If only I were a few years younger.

"Yes," I admitted reluctantly, "it was actually pretty fun." My mother would have a heart attack if she ever found out. "You can't say anything about this on Saturday."

"About what? The subway?"

"Yes. It would kill my mother to learn I spent a night riding mass transit. For *fun*."

Phelps just smiled. Not that cocky, arrogant smile that grated my nerves—even though I was beginning to appreciate that smile, against my better judgment. No, this was a soft smile of indulgence. Of admiration.

"You, Lydia Vanderwalk," he said as he stepped closer and lifted a hand to my cheek, "are some piece of work."

His hand slipped behind my head and I felt the warm heat of his palm urge me closer. Hypnotized by his flame blue gaze, I leaned forward until my lips met his.

This was no hot and heavy, for public display kiss.

This was gentle and tender and I felt it all the way down to the tips of my toes.

My first response was, *Why?* Why was Phelps kissing me in this seriously romantic way?

But when he tilted his head and nibbled on my lower lip all questions—indeed all thought—ceased to matter. The soft fullness of his lips rubbed rhythmically against mine with a gentle pressure that begged me to open my mouth.

I was just about to accommodate when I heard a loud—as in this-is-not-the-first-second-or-third-attempt loud—*ahhem* from behind me.

Reluctantly pulling away, I turned to find Gavin standing in the hall. He looked furious.

I glance at Phelps, who looked gloatful—was that even a word?

At least now I knew why Phelps had kissed me.

It had all been for show.

"SO SORRY TO INTERRUPT," Gavin said as he thrust a grocery bag in my face, "but I've been trying to call you all day."

Stepping out of the awkward entanglement with Phelps I

took the bag. I hefted the several pounds of small, wrapped goodies and sighed. What was this? A peace offering? A bribe? A play in the chess match between him and Phelps?

"I know," I said.

Gavin scowled. "Did you listen to my messages?"

I nodded.

"Lyd, we need to talk. Can we—"

"Take a hint, man," Phelps said. "She's not interested."

"Listen, pretty boy, this is between Lydia and me." Gavin poked Phelps in the chest and I had a feeling this situation was going very wrong very fast.

I needed to step in. "Wait, let's—"

"Looks like I'm right in the middle of it." Phelps released me a stepped closer to Gavin, chest thrust out like a strutting pigeon. "You show up here with a bag of junk and—"

"Really, boys—"

"You need to get *out* of the middle." Gavin poked Phelps in the chest with two fingers. "And it's not junk to Lydia."

I clutched the bag to my chest.

This situation was escalating much too quickly. And nosy Mrs. Peepers—I didn't know her real name, but that fit the busybody well enough—was peering through the crack between door and jamb with avid interest.

"Can we please go inside and—"

Phelps threw his hands up in the air. "What is the big deal about a bunch of candy?"

I gasped.

Both men turned to look at me with disbelief.

The hallway fell silent.

I closed my eyes against seeing understanding wash over Gavin's face. He of all people would know that any man seriously interested in me would know about my candy addiction. That Phelps obviously didn't know... well, that was a problem.

The game was up.

Gavin smirked. "Have you been keeping your little problem a secret from Phelpsy here?"

But I wasn't going out without a fight.

The condescension in his tone pushed me too far. "What I have or haven't told Phelps is none of your business. You lost the right to meddle in my affairs a long time ago." I stepped between the two raging testosterone-fed egos and faced Gavin with all the confidence I could muster. "Please leave."

He looked like I'd slapped him.

Backing away slowly, he scowled as he said, "You always were quick to defend whatever side I *wasn't* on. It was a wonder we lasted as long as we did."

I stared blankly at Gavin's back as he stalked away, slamming the door to the emergency stairwell behind him.

What had that parting comment meant?

For years I had been the dutiful girlfriend, blindly taking Gavin's side in *everything* despite mounting evidence of his unfaithfulness. When he started staying late at the office five nights a week, I made excuses to family and friends that he was working really hard at his very demanding job. When he went away for long working weekends I attended all those social functions alone, putting on a happy face to hide the fact that our relationship was sinking fast.

"You should've let me punch him at the party."

Phelps placed his hands on my shoulders, giving me a reassuring massage. I turned into him, burying my face in his shoulder as tears of confusion and doubt stung my eyes. In his comforting embrace I let out all the frustration of two long years. Two years wondering what had gone wrong, what I had done do drive Gavin away.

Wondering how I hadn't been good enough.

Though I told myself it was better this way, there were still times on dark, lonely nights that I wondered if it might have been better if I'd never caught Gavin red-handed. If we'd just gone on as we were, gotten married, and lived the kind of marriage so typical of our peers.

Suddenly I felt very alone.

It had been two years since I'd been held like this. Like I mattered. Like I was cherished.

And it felt good.

Awkwardly wiping at my tears, I looked up into Phelps' brilliant blue eyes smiling down at me and smiled. I never wanted this feeling to end. "Want to come inside."

His smile faltered. "I don't think that's a good idea." He smoothed back the hair hanging across my eyes. "Not in your current state."

"Just for coffee?" He looked doubtful, so I added, "Promise."

He considered the offer for a minute before relenting. "One cup."

"I KNOW I've got a coffee pot around here somewhere." I rifled through all eighteen cabinets in my kitchen until I found the hunted appliance. "Ah-ha!"

"Not a coffee drinker, are you?"

Phelps looked around my apartment for the first time, and I wondered what it would look like to a relative stranger.

Bland probably. Most everything was cream, beige, taupe, or a combination of the three.

Sheer cream drapes. Taupe sofa. Cream and taupe throw pillows. Ooh, there was ivory in the wallpaper.

The only real color and warmth in the apartment came from the wood furniture. The rich walnut coffee and end tables, media cabinet, and bookshelves. Somehow the deep auburn-brown turned the beige room into a welcoming home.

Or so I hoped.

"I managed to get through college without catching the coffee bug." Plugging in the ancient coffeemaker—a graduation present from not-so-close Aunt Essie—I wiped off a layer of dust before taking the pot to the sink and filling it with water.

Phelps returned to the kitchen and leaned against the counter. "Candy's more your thing."

I had expected the questions. But that didn't mean I wanted to answer them. As I poured the water into the well I shrugged.

Water dribbled down the pot and all over the counter.

"Want to talk about it?" He pushed away from the counter and tore some paper towels off the roll hanging beneath the cupboard by the sink. Mopping up the dribbled water, he offered, "I'm a great listener."

"Can you grab the coffee from the freezer?" I asked, fully aware of my weak diversionary tactics.

Phelps was also a great interpreter, because he read my unwillingness to talk and let the subject of candy go. "If you don't drink coffee, why do you have three bags of it in your freezer?"

"I have friends. Family, too."

He started to read the label but I grabbed it away before he could finish. "Did that say Thin Mint Blend?" I scowled and started to retort, but he interrupted. "Never mind, forget I asked. You got music in this joint?"

I nodded to the armoire and went about making the coffee as Phelps flipped through my meager CD collection.

"The Bangles. Cindy Lauper. Boy George." The sound of CD cases clicking against each other as he flipped echoed through the apartment. "What decade are you from?"

"Every girl is an 80s girl," I answered.

Phelps plucked out a CD and popped it into the stereo. Soon the sounds of Etta James filled the room and my mood cheered exponentially.

"How old are you?" he asked.

"You can't ask a woman that question."

"But you asked me." He returned to the kitchen and searched through cupboards until he found a pair of coffee mugs. "It's only fair."

When he lifted one mug in question, I nodded. "I'll have tea." No need to mention it was peppermint tea. "And it's not the same. You're a guy."

"Thanks for noticing, but it's still your turn."

I punched the on button before turning to face him and his question. "I'm thirty-three." Crossing my arms over my chest I dared him to tease. "Almost thirty-four."

He wisely moved ahead without commenting—which I interpreted as "Jeez lady, you're old!"—and asked, "When's your birthday?"

"Next month. September 17."

Maybe he would leave the subject now. I already felt as old

as Croesus, and was getting older by the second. Almost to the point of regretting inviting him in.

Almost, but not quite. Feeling crummy and old was better than feeling crummy and alone any day.

"That's during the trip to Milan," he exclaimed. "Perfect. We can celebrate in Italy."

"First of all, I am not celebrating the birthday that will make me irrevocably *mid*-thirties." Though the excitement glowing in his beautiful blues could induce a woman to celebrate even her dreaded fortieth birthday, I turned away and worked on making my tea. There were some lines a woman has to draw in the world of birthdays. "And second, you're not taking me to Italy."

He came up behind me, so close I could feel the heat of his body. But he didn't touch me. He just whispered into my ear. "But I want to take you."

The coffee pot chose that instant to explode.

FORTY MINUTES later I tied my terry robe tightly over my pajamas as the washer in my utility closet spun a dozen coffee-stained towels and Phelps' clothes dry. My apartment was covered in Carpet Fresh soaked splotches and Phelps sported my fleecy gray robe. And nothing else.

I had to keep reminding myself not to think about that.

"Your clothes should be dry in half an hour."

"No problem." He looked me up and down, his attention caught by the neckline of my robe. And the jammies poking through. "Are those candy hearts?"

Clutching the robe tight to my neck, I made sure the terry

covered everything. "Of course not, they're just hearts. Simple, girly, romantic—"

"I can still see the pants, Lydia."

I looked down to see the candy hearts-covered fabric peeking beneath the hem of my robe. "All right, they're candy hearts. You have a problem with that?"

He laughed it off and collapsed onto my sofa as if he belonged there. "Not a one, firecracker."

Phelps had a way of fitting in wherever he was. It was his magical power—one of them, anyway. There was also his taste for adventure, his carefree attitude, his sculpted chest which I could see peeking out from behind my robe.

Which only reminded me that he was wearing nothing— and I meant nothing—underneath. My gaze unconsciously dropped to his basement, as Fiona put it. Darn thick fleecy robe! I couldn't see anything.

Man, was I so hard up that I was resorting to looking up a guy's skirts? Good thing he wasn't wearing a kilt or I'd be upskirting him with my phone.

He smiled like he knew what I'd been thinking. "Come here." He curled his index finger at me.

"I'm fine where I am." Leaning against the dining table a good fifteen feet away.

Instead of keeping the comfortable distance between us, he stood and crossed to me. When he was inches away—so close I could smell the faint remains of his aftershave and the lavender water on the robe he wore—he lifted his hands. I braced myself for another kiss.

Well, braced was not the right word. I arched my neck to present my mouth at a better angle, leaned forward, and closed my eyes.

Then I felt his hands on *my* robe. Pulling it open.

My door buzzer echoed through the apartment.

I laughed at his pained expression.

"Saved by the bell," I teased.

He released my robe and I made my way to the intercom.

"Hello?"

From the other end of the line I heard a serious of sniffles.

"Hello?" I repeated.

This time I heard a full out sob.

"Hello!"

"L-l-ydiaaa?" a vaguely familiar voice wailed.

"Yes," I answered hesitantly. "Who is this?"

"K-k-kaaathhhh—"

Now I recognized the voice. "Kathryn?"

All I got was a muffled "Uh-huh."

She sounded miserable. "Kathryn, honey, what's wrong?"

"Lydia," she wailed into the intercom, "my fiancé is having an affair."

ELEVEN

"WHERE ARE YOU?" I asked.

"D-d-downstaaairs."

What was KY Kathryn doing downstairs in my apartment building, coming to see *me* because her fiancé was cheating on her? Oh wait, that story sounded vaguely familiar.

"I'll be right there."

As I turned away from the intercom, the dryer buzzer sounded, signaling that the coffee casualties were clean and dry again.

Phelps made a face. "That's probably my cue to head out."

"Sorry." I gestured at the door. "I need to go down and get her."

"Only builds the anticipation," he said as he pressed a soft kiss to the corner of my mouth. "I'll see myself out."

I lifted up on my toes and gave a kiss of my own. "You're the best."

While he headed for the laundry room, I grabbed my keys and opened the door.

"Oh, and Lydia," he called without turning back, "I *am* taking you to Italy."

The door closed behind me with a whooshing click and I sighed. There was something about Phelps Elliot that made a girl quiver. On the inside *and* the outside.

Now if only I knew whether that was a good thing or not.

On the ride down in the elevator, tissue box in hand, I mentally ran through all the possible reasons that KY Kathryn had come to me, of all people.

Not only were we not close, but we had never even had a complete conversation. She had her perfect life and her perfect friends and didn't need me, a thrown-over fiancé with no ring on my finger and no Barnard on my transcript.

The only answer I came up with was that I had once played the role of jilted fiancé.

The elevator doors slid open and I entered the tear-fest. Kathryn looked worse than I had ever seen a KY look. Her hair hung in ratty strings around a face free of makeup except for black smudges beneath tear-reddened eyes. Unlike the polished Kathryn I usually saw at work, this defeated Kathryn wore a holey Barnard t-shirt with half the letters rubbed off and a pair of well-worn sweatpants. This was a picture not of an elegant, vengeful KY, but of a downtrodden and heart-broken woman.

Kathryn looked up at me with all the haunting desperation of the world in her eyes. And broke into a fresh round of wails.

"Come on, Kathryn." I patted her awkwardly on the shoulder in an attempt at friendly sympathy. "Let's go upstairs and you can tell me all about it."

Handing her the box of Kleenex, I guided her to the elevator. She only sobbed harder.

"Tell me what happened," I encouraged as we entered my apartment, hoping the ride had given her time to get control enough to actually talk to me.

She plopped inelegantly into my chofa and wiped at the tears and mascara smudged beneath her eyes. "Victor is cheating on me."

"Did you catch him?" I grabbed the basket under the end table and pulled out the pristine package of Belgian chocolate seashells. Serious situations call for serious sugar.

Kathryn plucked a dozen tissues and blew her nose like a foghorn. "He said he was working late and I called the office and they said he wasn't there."

"Maybe he had a business dinner," I proposed as I held out the box and she took a marbled seahorse from the selection. "Maybe he—"

"No," she said around a mouthful of chocolate. "I called his driver. He was at that new dinner club in Midtown."

"It could still have been a—"

"I saw him. With his secretary." She dabbed at her eyes as they watered again. "Huddling."

"Huddling?"

"*Close* huddling."

Well that did sound pretty incriminating. And it sounded like Kathryn had some doubts in the first place. "Why did you call to check up on him? Are you two having problems?"

Tucking her feet up under her on the chofa, she reached for another seahorse before continuing. "He's been spending more and more nights working late. And he's more distant. Especially when we're intimate," she continued despite my sudden fidgeting at the encroaching too-much-information zone, "he seems preoccupied and he's spending less time on fore—"

"What did he say when you asked him about it?" I rushed out before she could divulge all the secrets of her sex life.

She didn't answer, instead focusing on tearing her tissue to shreds.

"You didn't ask him?

She shrugged. "I know what I saw."

"It would be better if you talked to him, Kathryn." I retrieved the cordless from the kitchen and handed it to her. "For your peace of mind."

She stared at the phone then looked up at me with sad eyes. "Did you talk to Gavin when it happened?"

I shouldn't have been surprised by either her question or her apparent knowledge of the details of our break-up. As I looked at her, a sorry heap surrounded by crumpled Kleenex, I saw a reflection of myself two years ago. Me in ratty Columbia sweats planted on Bethany's couch and surrounded by empty candy wrappers. Drained of every last drop of energy and confidence. If Bethany hadn't kicked me out of the apartment every morning at seven I would have lost my job.

It had been months before I went out for anything even resembling a social occasion. Months of days filled with work and self-pity and weekly trips to the candy aisle.

And as much as I despised the KYs and all they stood for, I would never wish that miserable agony on any woman.

So I answered honestly.

"No, we never talked." I pushed the phone into her hand. "And look how that wound up."

After several silent moments of consideration and tissue shredding, Kathryn took the phone and dialed the number.

"Victor?" she asked, her voice breaking with emotion.

She looked to me for encouragement and I managed a genuine smile.

Her jaw set in determination and she boldly asked, "Are you having an affair?"

♥

ONE HOUR and countless apologies and assurances later, Victor escorted Kathryn from my apartment. Turned out he had been working tons of overtime to surprise her with an Aegean cruise for their honeymoon.

By the time they left I was so sick of baby talk and endearments that I might have given up Jelly Bellies for life just to silence them.

I closed the door on their clinging embrace and faced my suddenly empty apartment. It had always felt like home. A comforting and welcoming space with the right mixture of cozy and spacious.

Right now it felt desolate.

Something was missing, something more than a table or a painting. Something emotional.

"Maybe I need candy," I said out loud, maybe to hear the sound of a voice and maybe convince myself that was all I really needed.

But for once in my life candy was not the solution. That in and of itself should have floored me, if not for the greater problem at hand.

For the first time in two years, I began to question whether I had done the right thing in dissolving the relationship with Gavin without so much as a this-is-over talk. Admittedly, I had caught him in a significantly more compromising position—

meaning his secretary kneeling at his feet and his pants around his ankles—but that didn't mean I didn't need closure.

He'd said we needed to talk. He was right.

Before I could think myself out of it, I picked up the phone and dialed Gavin's number.

When the machine picked up I nearly wimped out. Then I thought of all the heartache I had gone through, and all the heartache I had just saved Kathryn from, and I firmed up my resolve.

At the beep I left my brief message. "You're right. It's time we talked."

With that long-due conversation irretrievably in the works, that left me with a looming realization. Somehow I had just made friends with a KY and I didn't know what to think about that. And the scariest part was realizing that they—or at least Kathryn—had all the same feminine insecurities as other women. As me.

The fresh pint of Heath Bar ice cream in my freezer called to me, promising to help digest this new information.

I had just dug a spoon from the drawer when the door buzzer rang.

This night was never going to end.

TWELVE

"HEELLOOO, LYDIA!" a pair of male voices shouted through the intercom.

Something in the background yipped.

"I'm ba-a-ack," one of the voices sing-songed.

I pressed a palm to my forehead, certain I was feverish in explanation of this hallucination. Hadn't I just sent Phelps home a few short hours ago? A quick glance at the kitchen clock confirmed my suspicion that it was after two.

Clearly I was not meant to sleep tonight.

"Wake up, my muse," Ferrero's thickly-accented voice cried. "No sleep for the creative."

When a sharp pinch to my thigh and counting to ten did not wake me from this nightmare, I relented. I pressed the buzzer.

No way I was fetching those two. Whatever the reason for their visit. Of course I wasn't going to turn my boss away from my doorstep in the middle of the night, either.

I managed three quick and painfully cold bites of ice cream before they knocked on my door. Peace of mind was not immediately attained. Giving the sugar a chance to work, I waited as long as I could to answer.

Even willing the sugar into action didn't work.

They started banging harder.

"We know you're in there, Lyd."

"Please, *cherie*, let us in. We have a problem."

Bang, bang, bang.

I glared at the ice cream carton, knowing it was willfully denying me comfort in my hour of need. Shoving it into its new home at the *back* of the freezer, I steeled myself for whatever was to come.

Whoever said *bad things come in threes* grossly underestimated the persistence of problems.

Bang, bang, bang.

"Don't make us sleep in your hall," Phelps goaded. "What would the neighbors think?"

Probably that I have a pair of stalkers.

Fortified by a deep breath, I swung open the door. "What's this big prob—" I caught sight of something furry in Phelps' arms. Pointing a shaking finger at the furball, I demanded, "What is that!"

"A puppy," he answered with a smile.

"No," I backed cautiously into the apartment, away from the tiny brown fluff, "puppies are soft and round and behind glass at the pet store. That," I accused, waving my hand in an encompassing gesture, "is a rat."

"Please, *cherie*," Ferrero soothed as he approached me, "give her a chance."

"H-her?" That thing was female?

Oh no, a tiny brown head popped up and a tiny pink tongue dropped into view. Big round puppy-dog brown eyes blinked against the light of my apartment. She was... she was... the most adorable thing I had ever seen.

But that didn't explain why she was here.

Unless...

"No, no, no. I don't want a dog. I hate dogs, ever since Sissy Kowalchuk's bulldog trapped me up a tree when I was nine." I tried to back further away as Phelps approached, but ran into the couch. "And dogs hate me back. They bark and drool and snarl and pee on me. It's a mutual dislike. They—"

Phelps held the little furball out and she had the nerve to lean forward and lick my nose, undermining my entire argument.

"See," he waved the dog before my eyes, "she likes you already. And she's housetrained."

Ferrero approached, reverently petting the furry little head. "Take her. You were made for each other." He winked and elbowed me in the side. "I can tell these things."

I met his eyes and knew he referred to more than just the dog. If his intuition saw a blissful ever after for Phelps and me, then the dog and I were doomed.

"No, I—"

"She has nowhere else to go."

Phelps smiled sadly, clearly knowing he played the trump card. How could I turn away a sad little ragamuffin with no home and no one to love her?

"Why can't you—"

"My place doesn't allow pets," Phelps argued.

"And I," Ferrero interjected, "travel all the time."

I was beat, and they both knew it. Phelps held her out and I reluctantly took her in my arms. She immediately settled in, snuggling her cold nose into the crook of my arm.

Tempted as I was too coo and baby talk—despite my repulsion at the same only minutes earlier—I was not about to show my maternalistic weakness in front of them.

So I focused on business.

"Is this the problem you were moaning about?" I looked them both in the eyes, indicating my disapproval of their underhanded techniques. "Or was there something else we need to discuss at, oh, two o'clock in the morning?"

Neither had the decency to look ashamed.

"We," Ferrero spread his hands dramatically, "have a crisis."

With Ferrero, there was always a crisis.

Last month it was the color of the hangers Barney's was using to display his ready-to-wear collection.

The month before it was the number of stitches per inch on the lining of one of his men's coats.

Naturally, I was not overly concerned.

"You are going to the suburbs this weekend," he accused.

"Yes, my parents—"

"And you are taking your young man with you."

I was starting to wonder whether Ferrero could remember his *own* name. "Yes, *Phelps* is going with me."

"This is a disaster." Ferrero collapsed onto the couch.

Phelps looked to me, brows raised in question. I shrugged and shook my head, not understanding myself why my parents' annual barbecue was a disaster when it hadn't even happened yet.

"And," he continued, his accent growing stronger with each successive word, "he does not even own a trench coat."

Rather than give in to the temptation to fling a pillow at his eccentric head, I sat in the chofa, facing him, and calmly asked, "*Why* is this a disaster?"

Phelps, choosing to squish in next to me on the chofa rather than have a whole cushion to himself on the couch, also took the calm approach. "I have a parka. Can that work?"

"No. You are going away this weekend. Next week we prepare for Milan and the following weekend we go." Ferrero pleaded with his eyes. "I have an inspiration that requires two days of sketching and a trench coat. If I do not manifest this inspiration soon I will lose it. And the world will never see this wonderful design."

"What the—"

I elbowed Phelps in the ribs before he could blurt out what we were both thinking. Ferrero was off his rocker. But I was not about to lose my job by pointing out that my boss was a nut case.

"What can we do to help?" I knew that solving Ferrero's crises usually required only a little effort and a lot of imagination.

Like last month when we got Barney's to tie feathered hair clips to all the hangers. Made Ferrero happy, and every customer got a little extra accessory.

"This weekend," he lamented, shaking his head, "would have been the perfect time. But since you're going away..."

He trailed off and I knew what the answer to the first part of the crisis.

"Why don't you come along? I'm sure my parents would love to have you."

His face lit up.

One down, one to go.

"And I can take Phelps shopping tomorrow for a trench

coat." Especially now that I had no official duties left to take care of at work. "Then this weekend you can have him in a trench coat"—why did that sound like a dirty fantasy? —"without the distractions of the city."

"Does that work for you?" I asked.

He shrugged. "Sure."

"Perfecto." Ferrero clapped his hands before jumping up from the couch and pulling out his wallet. "Now you can show me your humble abode. I must see where my muse sleeps."

Phelps and I shared an eye roll as we headed down the hall.

PHELPS AND FERRERO finally left at three thirty. I crashed the instant they left, not regaining consciousness until the phone— which I was seriously considering powering down permanently—rang at seven thirty.

How Phelps had not only the nerve but also the energy to call me that early to go shopping was beyond me.

Still, I managed to drag myself into the shower and get some orange juice and toast down by the time he called from the lobby. Grabbing my purse and keys, I was almost to the door when I heard a plaintiff whine.

Dyllie. Right. I was now a dog owner.

Darting into my bedroom, I peered into the makeshift den I had made for her from a cardboard box and an old blanket. I was not relying on Phelps' assurance that she was housebroken.

She hadn't piddled in the box, which I took as a good sign, but that meant she needed to go out. I had no leash, no collar, and no idea where the nearest green spot was. We would just have to wing it.

Plucking her meager five pounds from the box, I tucked her into my purse with the promise that we would get a dog carrier before the day was out.

💜

"MORNING SUNSHINE," Phelps greeted as I stepped out the front door.

He looked fresh off a full night's sleep, blue eyes bright and glowing above the fitted black t-shirt that spread sculpturally across his chest. His hair was as tamed as those thick curls ever could be and he looked delicious enough to eat.

I glowered. "Let's go."

He stopped me before I could hail a cab. "The *Artiste* sent us his car."

Following the direction of his inclined head, I saw a beautiful black sedan stopped in front of my building. My morning improved dramatically.

"You ready?" I asked.

He waggled his brows. "For what?"

I grinned and climbed into the back seat, settling into soft gray leather. "For Bradford's."

"Never been."

He shrugged and shut the door behind us. As the driver pulled into traffic, I stared at him with unabashed shock.

"You've *never* been to Bradford's?" I watched him shake his head as if it were no big deal. No big deal. This was Bradford's. Mecca to shopaholics and socialites alike. This was Saks for the serious label hound. How could a man who sported designer on a daily basis never have been to Bradford's? "Where do you buy your clothes?"

"I don't." Again he shrugged, like he couldn't fathom what I thought the big deal was. "I get to keep the samples from shoots and shows."

That explained the couture wardrobe.

"What do you do with all the money you make? Clearly you don't spend it on housing or clothing."

"I'm saving."

"For—"

My purse wiggled off my lap, sending Dyllie and all my belongings flying across the floor.

"Is that a dog in your purse or are you just happy to see me?"

"Come here, Dyllie bean," I cooed, scooping her off the floor with one hand while trying to corral the contents back into my purse with the other. "Don't let the mean man make fun of you."

Before I could argue, he was half kneeling on the floor, gathering my scattered things and setting them back in my purse.

"We need to make a stop first," I announced.

The whole day would go smoother if we got Dyllie's needs out of the way first. I had done my research last night and found the best pet store in the city.

"To Puppy Love," I instructed the driver. "We need a leash."

Phelps handed me my purse with that cocky grin on his face. "Does this mean you're keeping her?"

Dyllie circled around on my lap until she found just the perfect position and plopped down and promptly fell asleep.

For someone who had such a bad history with canines, I fell for this one quickly. I credited my turnaround to the fact that she didn't really look or act like a dog. She looked like a mini teddy bear and acted like a house cat.

By the time we got to Puppy Love, Dyllie was awake and whining like she needed to do a number one.

"Hold on, girl. We need to get a leash first."

Out of the corner of my eye I saw Phelps smile as I nuzzled her nose. Grabbing my purse, I tucked her safely back inside and silently prayed to the gods of new dog-owners that her bladder held out.

Inside, I wandered the aisles of pet-related goodies with an awe usually reserved for a new candy store. Who gets paid to think up things like the "Pooper Picker Upper" and "Wilderdog Rain Booties"?

"Think this is what Ferrero meant?"

I turned to find Phelps holding a tiny doggie trench coat on a tiny doggie hanger. It was camel colored with plaid lining and a matching plaid belt. Sickeningly adorable.

Dyllie would never be subjected to such humiliation. "No, thank you."

"Admit it, this is cute." He flipped up the bottom hem to reveal a bright red ruffle.

Clutching at my purse, and the whining furball inside, I shook my head vehemently. "Put it back. We have serious shopping to do."

"You shop," he agreed, "I'm getting this."

He jogged off to the front of the store, tiny doggie trench coat clutched in his hand, and left Dyllie and me to find our necessities. When we made our way to the front of the store, Phelps stood chatting with the cute clerk, a perky twenty-something smile and matching perky twenty-something breasts.

Stalking to the counter, I slammed the black microfiber leash and collar and matching doggie tote down on the melamine surface.

"Good morning, ma'am," Perky greeted. "How are you today?"

"Fine." As if I needed to feel any older. Especially around twenty-something hunks with eyes for perky redheaded clerks.

My personal history with redheads was not good.

Mental Post-it: Next time a redhead says, "Hi," run the other way.

Dyllie poked her wet pink nose out the top of my purse as Perky slid the items across the scanner.

"Oooh," she cooed, "what a cute puppy. What's her name?"

While I tried to decide whether I could ignore her question without looking like a capital witch, Phelps supplied, "Dyllie. She's a Yorkie."

Was that what she was? Better than furry brown rat, I supposed.

"Hi precious." Perky reached beneath the counter and pulled out a doggie treat and held it out.

Dyllie, against my strongly broadcast mental wishes, leaned out and gingerly took the offered treat.

"What kind of diet do you have her on?" Perky asked as she placed my purchases in a large plastic bag covered in puppies and kittens.

"Diet?" I didn't know what kind of stick-figure dog world Perky came from, but Dyllie was not overweight. She was a puppy for Good&Plenty's sake.

"Yes," she explained. "Diet is crucial in a puppy her age. She needs food rich in fat, protein, and nutrients to help her little body grow big and strong."

That kind of diet. I knew that.

"You're a new pet owner, aren't you?"

I nodded, suddenly feeling woefully inadequate as Dyllie's mother. What did I know about rearing a healthy and well-adjusted dog?

Perky apparently understood my self-doubts. "Not to worry," she said, handing the plastic bag to Phelps and indicating I should follow her. "We'll get you all set up."

Though I was tempted to throw Phelps a please-save-me-from-perky-twenty-something-pet-shop-clerks look, I dutifully followed. I should have known to be afraid when she pushed a shopping cart in my direction and asked, "So how big is her bedroom?"

TWO HOURS, five-hundred dollars, one full shopping cart, and a pit stop in Central Park's Sheep Meadow later, Phelps, Dyllie, and I climbed back into the limo and headed for Bradford's. I never knew a little puppy could need so much stuff.

Leash, food, and, in the city, doggie tote, I knew. I would have eventually figured out food and water bowls, too. But there were treats and treatments. Shampoos, toothpaste, and vitamins. Beds and mats.

Dyllie's new possessions filled the trunk.

Tucked safely in her doggie tote beneath my arm, she napped peacefully as we walked past the store windows and through the elegant metal doors into the world of high-class shopping at Bradford's Men.

"Outerwear is on the sixth floor," I explained as I led the way to the elevator.

Everything in Bradford's Men screamed wealthy business-man. From the button-down oxford shirts on display to the warm wood paneling covering the walls. And this season, all the displays were very brightly colored. Though I couldn't imagine a powerful, heterosexual man wearing hot pink and lavender, I knew they did. Maybe because they were powerful and knew no one would question their masculinity.

Or maybe they were secretly not so heterosexual.

"Sixth floor," the elevator announced.

We stepped off into a sea of black leather and heathered tweed. A flash of camel canvas caught my eye.

"There are the trenches." I pointed to the racks of trench coats in a rainbow of neutral colors along the far wall. Appar-ently powerbrokers restrict the bright colors to shirts and ties.

"Lead on, captain."

Phelps followed as I wove through the pea coats and bomber jackets and waterproof parkas.

"I still can't believe you've never been to Bradford's," I reflected as we came to a stop in front of a rack. "How can a New Yorker *not* come here? It's like church. Only without the preaching."

And occasionally without the guilt.

"Don't know," Phelps shrugged as he grabbed a hip-length coat and held it up. "Never needed to, I guess."

I shook my head at the coat and at him. "Bradford's is not about need."

Setting the coat back on the rack, he shrugged again. "I

have more clothes than I could ever ne—" He paused when he noticed my mouth preparing to repeat my last comment. "More than I could ever want. I have better things to spend my money on."

"Like trips to the Andes?"

"Nah, that was work." He shoved his hands in his pockets, as if he'd been admonished not to touch anything.

"You don't spend your money on clothes or trips and you obviously don't spend it on rent." I scanned the racks from just the right coat. "What do you spend it on? Drugs, whiskey, and women?"

"Children."

I stopped my search and stared at him. *He had children?* Not that I believed it wasn't possible, but he just did not strike me as the fatherly type. More like the troublemaking older brother type.

"Ch-children?" I repeated, incredulous.

He turned away, presumably to look at a rack of black leather pea coats, but I had a feeling it was to avoid my questioning gaze.

"I started a charity." His voice was flat, like he didn't care. Or was afraid to show that he cared. "A foundation to get underprivileged kids involved in their community. In making their community a better, more prosperous place."

Great Gobstoppers. He was a philanthropist.

Now that was a surprise.

"That is a noble thing," I squeaked, unable to hide my shock at his revelation.

He shrugged again, keeping his back to me. I took that as flashing neon sign to drop the topic. Reluctantly, I returned to my coat quest.

Then I saw it. The perfect, damp English night, Sam Spade trench. Knee-length camel with polished horn buttons and cashmere lining. I held it up to Phelps' back and nodded.

"This is the one."

He turned.

"Let's get it on."

The seductive look he gave me could have fried ice.

THIRTEEN

"I MEAN *TRY* IT ON," I quickly retreated. "You try it on."

Jeez, some people just have a one-track mind. Usually men. And usually the same track.

"You're welcome to join me." He flashed that cocky grin as he slipped past me, grabbing the coat and heading for the three-way mirror.

"Just try the coat on, Elliot."

I barely managed to twist out of the way as he reached to pinch my backside. I was getting faster.

"You know," he said as he shrugged the coat onto his broad shoulders, "I've always had a trench coat fantasy. It never involved having to pay for one."

He tightened the belt around his lean waist, tugging it into a knot and turning for inspection.

"As a matter of fact, it never involved *me* wearing the coat." His smile turned seductive. "But I'm always open to adaptation."

Stepping closer, I brushed at the shoulders of the coat,

smoothing out the wrinkles across the yoke and down the arms. Phelps was only inches away.

Before I could stop myself, I stood on my tip-toes and pressed my lips to the corner of his mouth. "You're a good guy, Phelps Elliot," I whispered before pulling back and proclaiming, "The coat looks good."

"I'm not that good," he returned. His hands gripped my shoulders and crushed me to him in a heart-stopping kiss.

I was instantly on fire and devouring. His mouth opened, urging mine open to let him in. As his hot, hard lips pressed furiously into mine, I clutched at him, slipping my hands beneath the brushed canvas trench to sculpt his muscles with my palms.

One masculine hand pressed into my lower back, sending my body into full contact with his. I felt something cold at my back and distantly registered that he had backed me up against a mirror.

Unfortunately it was a freestanding mirror that started to topple the instant I leaned back.

With quicker reaction time than mine, Phelps wrapped one arm around my waist to hold me up while catching the tumbling mirror with the other.

"That was fast," I breathed.

"Too fast," he answered, dipping his head to resume our interrupted kiss.

But sanity returned. We were in the middle of Bradford's outerwear on important shopping business—to some extent—and he was not only my hire-a-date, but was also several years my junior. One lapse in judgment with dismissible. Two was a pattern. Three would be a habit.

I held him off with a hand to his chest. "We'd better pay for this and get out of here. I have work to do."

Not really. Ferrero was busy this week with preparations for Milan. Kelly had my job and with it all my responsibilities. Still, I felt I should make a showing, to remind everyone that I still worked there.

The last thing I needed at this point was someone cleaning out my desk.

"You can't hide forever, Lyd." His voice purred as he caressed a finger down my cheek. "There's a heat between us and someday we will find out how hot it can be."

My mouth went dry.

I backed away slowly, my eyes locked on his, unable to look away.

"Lydia," he began and reached out, "don't—"

I hastily stepped back.

Right into the mirror.

The elegant gilded frame fell to the floor with an echoing crash.

"—step back."

And I tumbled down right on top of it.

Before Phelps could stoop to help me up I rolled to the side and jumped to my feet. Thankfully my stomach had cushioned Dyllie's doggie tote in the fall, but my stomach learned that even a tiny little puppy can pack a punch with enough velocity.

"Here, let me—"

"Don't." I shrugged off his offer of help, not because I didn't want or need the help. Because I was afraid of his touch.

I was afraid to find out he was right.

That we would be scorching together.

"Let's just get the coat and go." I tried for a steady, unaffected voice, but knew that my fears quavered through.

In the tote, Dyllie whimpered and I reached in to soothe her fears. Too bad no one could soothe mine.

♥

MY DESK WAS COMPLETELY obscured by the piles of shopping bags from Puppy Love. Ferrero was in the construction studio, overseeing the final details of the Fall collection, so I had my office to myself for the first time all week.

In less than ten minutes I had checked my email, voicemail, and snail mail, thus exhausting all my current duties. I had two choices: Stay at the office trying to look busy and bored to tears, or go home and set up Dyllie's new possessions. Perky had told me the most important thing you could do for a new dog was make them feel at home, give them their own space.

I had already decided to give her a corner of my bedroom.

Decision made—there was only so much solitaire a girl could play—I lifted Dyllie into her tote and began gathering the bags.

When the phone rang my gut knew who it was before I answered.

"Hello," I reached into my drawer and found a bag of Bon Bons.

"It's Gavin."

"I know."

I started to unwrap a shiny pineapple, but his words stopped me.

"Can we meet somewhere?"

My heart thudded. Or maybe that was my stomach. Dread. Sheer dread.

But I'd left the message. I knew we need to have this conversation.

I told myself it would be better to talk in person. "The café around the corner?"

"I'll be there in five."

The phone clicked dead in my ear. He must have been nearby, far from his Wall Street office.

"Come on, Dyllie-girl," I slung the tote over my shoulder and slipped my hand through all the shopping bag handles. "Let's go have The Talk."

Gavin was waiting in the café when I got there. With a cup of coffee in front of him and a frothy drink at the place opposite him at the small metal table.

"Hi," he greeted and stood as I approached. He even took the bags from my aching wrist and set them in the corner of the terrace barrier. Always the gentleman. Well, almost always. "You look good."

I almost said, "I look haggard," but thought better of it. Let him think I looked good.

Because he damn well looked good enough to eat on a stick.

His dark blonde hair—full of the kind of highlights women paid hundreds for—brushed neatly back, as always, but for one runaway lock curled across his forehead. Soft brown eyes smiling in anticipation or expectation, with little crinkles at the corners that befit a man of thirty-five.

Would Phelps ever get those crinkles?

When I didn't say anything, Gavin tried to start the conversation. "So, you wanted to—"

"Why did you cheat on me?"

"—talk," he finished lamely. "Why did I *what*?"

"Cheat. Sleep around. Two-time. Cuckold." I didn't know if cuckolding applied to women, but it sounded good.

He looked shocked. Genuinely shocked. Maybe he never knew I found out. But could he be that stupid? Why else would he think I broke off our engagement and never returned any calls or emails? I mean, I knew adulterers never expected to get caught, but they should realize when they were.

"Lydia, what are you talking about? I never—"

"Don't deny it, Gavin, I don't have the energy." I swirled a sugar cube into my tea with a spoon, too emotionally tired to look him in the eyes. "I just want to know why."

"Look at me," he commanded.

I resolutely stirred the coffee until the sugar melted into the steaming drink.

"*Look* at me." He slammed his fist on the table when I still refused. "Damn it, look at me."

Blinking away the thin sheen of tears, I lifted my head and met his burning gaze. His eyes were open and honest and intent on me. In complete opposition to his lies.

"I never cheated on you." He enunciated each word with specific clarity. "I was unwaveringly faithful."

"Ha!" The shocked laugh burst out before I could stop it. "Then we must have a different definition of faithful. Let me clue you in: mine does not dismiss a hook-up with a secretary as a business meeting."

He closed his eyes and shook his head, as if he could not comprehend what I was talking about. Man, he was good.

Must have had a lot of experience.

"I don't know what you're—"

"Let me refresh your memory, just so you know exactly which time I caught you." I gripped the edge of the table, seeking an anchor before my hands started shaking. "It was the night before our anniversary and you were working late. I decided to surprise you with Chinese take-out, but when I showed up I found Rhonda on her knees at your feet and your pants around your ankles. There was nothing to misinterpret."

You would think that after two years, I would have these emotions under control. But when you loved someone that much... I shook my head. *This* was a result of lack of closure.

Which made it all the more imperative he tell me why. I had to understand what drove him to cheat. Was it me? Had I done something wrong? Not done enough?

Or was it him?

That was what I'd been telling myself for two years, but what if I was wrong? What if I was delusional, and it was really a deficiency in my makeup that drove him to the arms— or rather the bed—of another woman?

"I don't know—" His eyes widened suddenly. "Hell, I remember."

Well that was good news. At least there hadn't been so many that he couldn't recall them all.

"Lydia, what you saw wasn't... Jesus, it wasn't a hook-up."

I snorted. He must have thought I was born without the capacity for direct observation.

"Listen, I want you to listen to me very carefully." He spoke softly, as if speaking to a distraught child. "And keep in mind the picture of what you saw."

"As if I could forget," I snapped. As if I didn't see that mental picture every single day.

"Rhonda and I were working on a presentation for the

Kleinfitch meeting. We had to finalize everything and make copies for all fifty attendees."

Not that it made a difference, but I did remember how stressed he had been about that meeting. It was the meeting that could make his career. And had.

"She got back fifteen minutes before the meeting with the copies and coffee. I took one sip and spilled the scalding coffee in my lap. Not only was it burning my thighs, but my pants were stained with coffee. When you must have walked in, Rhonda was dabbing at the coffee on my thighs and I was getting my pants off so I could rinse them in the sink. That's *all* that happened."

"That," I bit out when he finished his tale, "is the most ridiculous story I've ever heard."

Gavin looked taken aback that I didn't believe him. He had truly thought I would accept that fabrication as an explanation of what happened. And why did he insist on lying? It's not as if he had anything to prove with *me*. I just wanted the truth. For my own mental health.

For several long, uncomfortable moments he just looked at me. Watched me. Assessed me.

"You never knew me at all," he finally said. "You couldn't have, or you never could have believed I would do such a thing." He ran his hands roughly through his hair, sending the neat locks in every direction.

I hadn't wanted to, that was for sure. It broke my heart into a million little pieces, leaving a box of Nerds rattling around in my chest.

Was it any wonder I hadn't dated anyone since we broke up.

When his eyes met mine, they shone with wetness.

"The truth is," he sounded resigned, deflated, "*you* never really loved *me*. Because love is trust. Clearly you didn't trust me."

My mouth dropped open.

His lies were impressively elaborate. Who but a pathological liar could turn his own adultery into an accusation that I'd never loved him? I had loved him more than I thought possible, and I got a great big dose of heartbreak for it.

This was not how I expected this conversation to turn out. I wanted answers, not blame. Gavin was not the injured party in this failed relationship.

"Tell yourself whatever you want," I said airily, shrugging Dyllie onto my shoulder with an indignant huff. "We both know what really happened."

"No, we don't—" He frowned. "Is your bag whining?"

I looked down to find Dyllie struggling to peek out of the tote, probably curious to see who I was talking to.

"It's nothing." Reaching into the tote, I tried to settle her back into her nap, but she was apparently up and ready for action. Faster than I could think, let alone react, she pulled herself up over the edge of the bag and let out a friendly *yip*.

"When did you get a dog?" Gavin sounded like it was beyond the realm of comprehension that I would have a pet. Guess he hadn't noticed all the puppy-covered shopping bags.

"Last night," I answered sweetly. "Phelps gave her to me."

He scowled.

The perfect opportunity for my exit.

"Goodbye, Gavin."

I tried to sound decisive. Final. But he stood and collected the shopping bags from the corner.

"I'll walk you home." He waved off my protest. "I can't let

you struggle to carry all these home. Especially this one,"—he hoisted the bag containing the food—"it weighs a ton."

As I left the café, Gavin on my heels with my shopping bags, I wondered how the conversation that had gone so wrong had ended with him helping me home.

♥

"HE EVEN HAD the nerve to question my love for him." Swirling the ice in my Lemon Drop, I pondered how I had ever believed Gavin Fairchild was the picture perfect prince of my dreams.

He was a cad and a liar and I was well rid of him.

Bethany tapped a preoccupied finger on the bar. "I still can't believe Phelps gave you a puppy."

"A puppy is serious business," Fiona added. "Giving a girl a puppy is practically a billboard announcing he wants to be around at least as long as the dog."

From her sleek black tote, Dyllie whined at the sound of conversation she innately knew was about her. As much as I was growing to love her, and wondered what had prompted Phelps to think I needed or wanted a dog, my mind was preoccupied with the late afternoon conversation with Gavin.

"*I* still can't believe," I announced in a loud and authoritative and conversation-redirecting voice, "Gavin denies having an affair. Or that he walked me home."

"Maybe he thinks you're lonely," Bethany mused. "It has been over two years since you... you know."

"Yes I do know, thank you. But Gavin doesn't." Really, at the moment a nonexistent sex life was the least of my problems. "And I am not lonely. I am very satisfied."

Next to me, Fiona sputtered pink drink all over the bar. "So you *have* been using your Christmas gift." As she dabbed at the mess with a cocktail napkin she threw me a conspiratorial smile. "The reviewers at thehotteststuffaround.com gave it a top rating for ease of use and explosive org—"

"That was not what I meant!" Sometimes I felt like life was one big joke at my expense. "I am not lonely and I don't need a man to—"

"A man?" Bethany's brow furrowed in puzzlement. "I thought we were talking about a dog."

"Both," Fiona added.

That was enough! "Neither."

Slamming a handful of cash on the bar, I shoved my stool back and tried to stand so I could stalk away. I was not in the mood for Bethany's single-minded focus on the dog and Fiona's single-minded focus on sex. There were more important things going on, like, say, a weekend with my parents, a trip to Milan, and a lying late-fiancé.

Unfortunately, as the Fates looked down on me with malicious hoots of laughter, the stool caught on the sticky floor and I went flying. Landing on my back on a bar floor with a stool between my legs was not the indignant exit I was going for.

Bethany and Fiona leaped into action, Bethany lifting the stool out of the way and Fiona pulling me upright.

In some ways this was all too familiar. Only unlike the first time I had to be pulled upright from a sticky bar surface—first the counter, now the floor—my problem was no longer no man in my life. Now I had two, and I kind of missed having a short list of zero.

"What was that about?" Fi asked as she dusted some questionable material off my gray cashmere cardigan.

"Nothing," I mumbled. Humiliation was bad enough without having to explain your motivation after the fact.

"Has Gavin really upset you that much?"

Leave it to Bethany to see past the muck and get right to the point.

"I just—" I frowned, trying to figure out to put into words why the conversation with Gavin had gotten me into such a knot. "I just wanted him to admit it, that's all. Just a simple, 'Yeah, I was a letch.' so I can forget about it and move on."

So much for that much-needed closure.

Fiona assessed me with her soul-exposing brown eyes. "You wanted him to say it wasn't your fault."

"Pretty much."

"You know it wasn't, sugar." Bethany laid a reassuring hand on my arm.

"I know, I know," I agreed.

We went through this merry-go-round right after it happened, trying to snap me out of my self-pity and restore my confidence. But something about this conversation brought back all the fears and insecurities and—great—the tears.

"Dubble Bubble damn." With a sniff, I reached for a cocktail napkin to mop up the salty streaks.

Fiona beat me to it. She gently patted at my cheeks until they were dry. Then, looking me square in the eyes, she said, "But there's something else you're afraid of. You—" She squinted, as if trying to see deeper into my psyche. "—are afraid it wasn't a lie."

"What?" Bethany and I said at the same time—although mine was more like a high-pitched squeal.

Roused by the excited pitch, Dyllie roused from her nap and poked her head out to look around. I was too taken aback to shoo her back down, even though animals were not allowed in Sweet Stuff. Or any New York bar, for that matter.

No, I was entirely focused on Fiona's outrageous proclamation.

"Are you crazy?" I demanded. "I *saw* them, Fi. With my own eyes. *In flagrante delicto.*"

"I don't doubt that." Her voice was calm and soothing, and my hackles dropped enough to listen to what she said. "But somewhere, deep inside, you are afraid that maybe you were wrong. Maybe what you thought you saw wasn't precisely what happened, and now Gavin has dredged up those old self-doubts. You are afraid you made a huge mistake."

By the time she was done tears poured rivers down my cheeks, wetting the soft cashmere of my sweater into spots of steel gray.

Was she right? Was I afraid that Gavin hadn't really cheated on me and that I broke off the engagement based on nothing but my own insecurities and misguided assumptions?

"Did I ruin it all for nothing?" My words came out choked with tears and heavy on the sniffles. I dropped my head in my hands as I relived with absolute clarity every second of that night at Gavin's office.

He had stood there with an expression on his face that I interpreted as ecstasy, but could it have been pain. Rhonda was on her knees, fully clothed, and from the doorway I couldn't make out what she was doing. From the movement, I had imagined the worst. But could she have been hastily wiping scalding coffee off his skin? It was... possible.

A cry escaped me as I realized what a horrible mistake I had made.

Instantly, Bethany and Fiona were there, soothing me.

"No, not for nothing," Bethany said.

"There had to be a reason. Even if it wasn't cheating."

"Sugar, your subconscious knew something was wrong."

Fiona wrapped an arm around my shoulder and hugged me close, even as my sobs shook us all. "The affair was only an easy excuse to do something you knew you needed to do anyway."

Several cocktail napkins and wrenching sobs later, what they said finally penetrated.

And it made sense.

For weeks before that night, I had worried that Gavin was having an affair. That he was being distant. That something about our relationship was not right.

Then I had caught him with Rhonda and I felt relieved. Because that became the reason that our relationship was failing. It wasn't my fault—because he was having an affair. It wasn't cold feet—because he was having an affair. It wasn't a fear of commitment—because he was having an affair. That became my excuse for everything.

Most people even bought it.

But the fact that I've spent the last two years without even speaking to him, without seeking the closure we both needed, should have been the big clue that all was not right with how things ended.

"Order me another," I asked before downing the remains of my Lemon Drop. Sliding off the stool, I grabbed my purse for a much-needed trip to the powder room. "I think I'm gonna need it."

Because whether it was cause for celebration or despair, I was facing the cold, hard truth that I had never been in love with Gavin Fairchild.

THE DRIVE to Westchester Saturday morning took ninety minutes. About three times as long as usual, and not just because of the road construction and three traffic accidents on the New York State Thruway.

About halfway there Ferrero decided that he needed to see Phelps in his trench coat. Immediately.

The trench coat was, of course, in the trunk. Ferrero instructed his driver to pull the limo over at the next possible stop. Which turned out to be a Shell station with an inviting patch of grass. As Phelps dug through the suitcases in the trunk to find his trusty duffel bag, I snapped Dyllie's leash on and pranced her over to do her business.

You know how sometimes you turn your back for a second and all hell breaks loose?

This was hell and all its suburbs.

FOURTEEN

WHEN DYLLIE FINISHED INSPECTING every blade of grass for the perfect spot to squat, we turned to head back to the limo.

In what couldn't have been more than sixty seconds, the limo had disappeared, leaving Phelps, Ferrero, and the driver standing next to the pile of luggage. One of the bags—mine, of course—had fallen open in a brisk wind, sending my weekend wardrobe flying across the heavily trafficked Cross Westchester Expressway. And a dozen police cars had the parking lot surrounded.

"What the hell happened?" I shouted, running as fast as my kitten heels could carry me, and tugging on Dyllie to keep up.

A stern voice on the megaphone stopped my return. "Don't move and raise your hands above your head."

I froze and tried to lift my hands, but Dyllie's leash kept my right hand from rising above shoulder height.

"Both hands above your head."

Stifling a growl of frustration, I shouted back, "I can't, my dog is attached to my—"

"Lydia Vanderwalk?" The voice asked.

"Y-yes," I ventured.

"Hey, it's me," the voice continued, as if that were an enlightening statement of identity, "Rick Pearson."

In the space of two words, I was back in high school, crushing on the Bingley Academy quarterback. Rick of the surfer boy good looks, West Coast laid-back attitude, and truly generous nature. Always in the nebulous zone between popular and not, I had flourished under the platonic friend-ship Rick offered when his family moved in next door.

I remembered Mom telling me he'd become a cop.

"Sir, take off the trench coat and lay it on the ground."

Seeing a swarm of cops with service revolvers aimed at her hire-a-date had a way of popping a girl out of the past.

"Rick, what the hell is going on?" I asked as he sidled up next to me.

"We got a—" He dropped the megaphone, probably real-izing that if he could hear me I could hear him. "We got a report of a carjacking."

"That was us, you moron," Phelps shouted, trench coat in hand. "We were carjacked."

A ruby blush colored Rick's cheeks.

Turning his attention to the gathered police, he announced over the megaphone, "These aren't the perps. Spread out into a vehicular canvas of the area. Kirby, post an APB on a black Lincoln limousine."

In a flurry of activity, the cops rushed back into their patrol cars and roared out of the parking lot, sirens blaring.

"Sweet Saltwater Taffy, Rick," I gasped as we met in front of the sad pile of luggage. "What was that about?"

"A mistake," he admitted. He always had more integrity

than any ten men. "I apologize. We've had a rash of carjackings lately, I guess we rode into the wave before we figured if it was rideable or not."

I took that as surfer-speak for leaping before they looked.

"Um, Lydia..."

"So you really became a cop." I smiled and gave him a hug. "You always said that's what you wanted to do."

"Yeah." He baby blue eyes sparkled with the excitement of someone who loves their work. "Became sheriff even."

"Um, Lydia..."

"Sheriff? Really? Aren't you a little young?"

I felt old. Very old.

"Nah. I worked hard to get this job."

"I would imagi—"

"Lydia!"

"What?" My irritation at being interrupted made my question snappish. But Phelps should see that I was happily catching up with an old friend—

"Don't you think we should retrieve your underwear before it succeeds in hitchhiking to Canada?"

Just then a blur of pink rolled past my feet. Rick and I both bent to grab it, but his reaction was quicker. As he handed me the thong, color again staining his sculpted cheeks, I tamped down my own embarrassment.

I stuffed the wad of lace in my pocket and took off to save the rest of my belongings from a trip to the border.

RICK DROPPED PHELPS, Ferrero, and me at my parents' house before heading to the police station with the driver to take his statement. Ferrero was inconsolable, bemoaning the loss of his precious limo and wondering how we would ever get back to the city from the godforsaken country. No attempts to explain that Westchester is suburban and not rural could convince him that we had any number of options for transport home, not the least of which was my dad's SUV.

But from the moment the squad car pulled up in front of my house, there was not a moment for self-pity.

"Lydia, my God," Mom squealed as she ran down the porch steps, "what happened? Are you hurt? Have you—"

"No, Mom, we're fine."

"—been to the hospital? Have you—"

"Really, no one's hurt."

"—done something illegal? And what—"

"Of course not."

"—is that?" She finally stopped to point an accusatory finger at me.

"What?" I turned in a circle, trying to discern what had her so concerned. Finding nothing, I asked, "What is what?"

"That *thing* under your arm."

Lifting my arm I saw Dyllie poking her furry head out of my purse. Though the carjacker saw fit to leave us our luggage —my guess was that Ferrero negotiated for that—he did not leave the doggie tote.

"Oh, this is Dyllie. She's a— um, I'm not sure what she is, actually."

"A dog?" Mom squealed.

"Yes, I'm just not sure what kind."

"Yorkie," Phelps offered.

"Oh right," I said. "A Yorkie."

She looked odd, both horrified and furious, like she could

go either way. When she rushed me with arms outstretched, I instinctively tucked Dyllie behind my back. Mom had the tendency to be a little emotional, and I didn't want a defenseless puppy to bear the brunt.

Next thing I knew, Mom threw her arms around me and engulfed me in an enthusiastic hug.

"How wonderful, darling," she exclaimed. "I thought you would never get over your fear of dogs. I can't believe you actually bought a pup—"

"Actually," I interrupted, "it was Phelps who bought me the dog."

Mom jumped back, as if she just remembered my purported boyfriend was present. She quickly brushed down the floral apron covering her skirt in a homemaker's instinctive primp for company.

"Mom," I said by way of introduction, "meet Franco Ferrero, my boss. Franco, my mother, Jeanette Vanderwalk."

While they exchanged pleasantries I looked at Phelps, uncertain if I could carry on the charade in front of my mother. Could I pull it off in front of the people who knew me best? In two steps he was by my side, his arm around my waist. No turning back now.

"And this—" I took a deep breath and leaned into Phelps's side. "—is my date, Ph—"

"Elliot," he interrupted, thrusting out a hand in offering. "Elliot Phelps."

I blinked what felt like a thousand times, watching as Mom took Phelps's hand in both of hers, welcoming him into her household.

Why had he introduced himself that way? Did he not want my parents to know his real name? It made no sense.

"Welcome home, gumdrop." Dad emerged on the porch, barbecue tongs in hand and sporting an apron that read, *Kiss the Cook*. "Let's get these city folk settled so we can start the party."

Just like that, Dad set everyone to action. Ferrero picked up his worn leather briefcase. Phelps hoisted his duffle bag onto his shoulder and grabbed the two suitcases. I tucked Dyllie down into my purse. Mom herded us up the steps and into the house.

I had told Phelps that we would probably be in separate rooms. My parents were old-fashioned in a lot of ways. So, when Mom showed Phelps and me to my old bedroom—now devoid of all traces of my youth except the bed and nightstand —and told us to come downstairs when we were ready, it only added to the shock.

"I can't believe she put us in the same room."

Phelps set the luggage and his duffle at the end of the bed before flopping his lean length onto the quilt-covered mattress. "After the day I've had," he exhaled as folded his arms behind his head and closed his eyes, "I'm just glad to have a bed at all."

"What?" I asked. Spying a few inches of space, I sat down next to his hip. "You mean more than being stuck in a limo with Ferrero in an artistic tizzy, pulling over to get a trench coat out of the trunk, and getting carjacked in the process?"

He unfolded one tan arm and rubbed his eyes. I'd never seen him look quite so worn out.

"I had the gig from hell this morning."

I leaned down on one elbow and took over his temple massage. Come to think of it, he had been uncharacteristically quiet during the drive up. I had chalked it up to Ferrero's obsessive attitude, but maybe it was more.

"Tell me about it," I ventured as I rubbed gentle circles across his forehead.

He smiled a wicked grin. "I spent six hours surrounded by fawning swimsuit models."

His eyes flashed open and before I could react he reached around my neck and pulled me flush across his body. Settling me across his chest, he clasped his hands over my lower back and held me close.

I closed my eyes and absorbed the feeling of every single inch of his fitness model body. I found myself sinking into him. Startled, my eyes jerked open, only to find him fully relaxed against the pillow, his own eyes dreamily drifted shut.

"Poor baby," I whispered, laying my head down on his chest. Mesmerized by the rhythmic rise and fall of his breathing, my mind drifted.

I felt... content.

How long had it been since I felt this way? So content. There was something about this wild man that, paradoxically enough, soothed my mind. He might not be the kind of guy I would settle down with, but he sure made me feel like a princess. And most of the time I didn't even remember that he was seven years younger.

Most of the time.

He was fun and exciting and always came up with ways to shake up my life. Like when he—

"Hey," I admonished, shaking him out of our contented slumber. "Why did you introduce yourself to my mom as Elliot Phelps?"

"Because that's my name," he answered sleepily.

"Your what?"

"My name." His eyes drifted open and he looked at me with the blurry admiration of a puppy dog—not that Dyllie would ever stoop to blurry admiration.

"No," I argued, "your name is Phelps Elliot. Fiona told me. You told me. I saw it in a magazine."

I rolled off his chest and off the bed to better project my indignation. He sat up, stretching the tight t-shirt across his beautiful chest.

"I'm sure you did." Stifling a yawn, he jumped out of bed and pulled me into a hug. "But my real name is Elliot Phelps. Elliot Richard Phelps, actually. Famous Faces thought Phelps Elliot sounded a little more fashionable. A little less—"

"Geeky?" I supplied.

"I was going to say less stiff," he said. "But yeah."

"Why didn't you tell me the truth before?"

"Never came up." He shrugged, as if it didn't matter.

"Then why tell my mom the truth? Why not just keep up the façade?"

"It wasn't a façade, Lyd. It was just... easier." He looked away for an instant before meeting my eager gaze. "I didn't want half-truths between us anymore."

Holy Hot Tamales. There was some kind of intensity in his eyes, in his entire body as he confessed this. He might as well have said *I want there to be more between us.*

My first instinct was to run. To back away and never, ever mention this again. But his arms tightened around me before I could flee.

Forced to look at him, to answer, I faced the deep down realization that maybe I wanted there to be more, too.

My eyes dropped to his mouth, so full and masculine and

begging to be kissed. To kiss. He licked his lips and I lost the ability to breathe. At that moment I *had* to kiss him.

Framing his beautiful, chiseled cheeks with my hands, I looked up into his searching, questioning eyes. Phelps, the man who whisked me around Southampton on a yellow scooter, would never reveal that much uncertainty. But Elliot, the man who came home to meet my parents with an open heart, showed a vulnerability that tugged at me.

In answer to his silent question, I lifted onto my toes and pressed my mouth to his.

Right there in my childhood bedroom.

It was like magic. He tasted better than any penny candy or gourmet sweet ever could.

His arms tightened around my waist, pulling me into him as his tongue nudged my mouth open. I willingly let him in.

We were as close as we could get, but I needed to be even closer. Finding the hem of his t-shirt, I tugged it up to reveal his washboard abs. The instant my fingers touched his heated flesh, I knew what real passion felt like.

I felt the red-eyed monster take over, urging me to uncover more skin, feel more, reveal more. Lust was carrying me away.

Until my mother burst in.

"Oh, my, dear, I didn't— I mean, I'm sorry to— well, color me embarrassed."

I tried to jump away, but Phelps—no, *Elliot* held me close.

"What is it, Mom?" I asked as I finally broke free of his embrace just as another figure stepped into the doorway.

"There's a young woman here who claims to know your Mr. Phelps."

After seeing to it that my clothes were back in order—it seemed that he had done some uncovering of his own—I looked up. My jaw dropped at the sight of the extremely pregnant woman in the doorway.

"Rhonda?" Phelps and I exclaimed at the same time.

Then Phelps ran up to embrace the woman I had last seen on her knees in front of my fiancé.

FIFTEEN

"WHAT ARE YOU DOING HERE?" Phelps asked.

I watched in horror as he tried—unsuccessfully—to lift the obscenely pregnant Rhonda into a twirl. Though he couldn't get her off the ground, he threw his arms around her and returned the hug she gave him.

"You got fat," he teased.

She swatted at his shoulder. "Pay no attention to him," Rhonda advised me. "He's been incorrigible since we were children."

I must have looked as confused as I felt, because Phel— Elliot explained. "We're cousins."

Cousins? Well that explained the big bear hug. But that didn't mean she was welcome in my bedroom.

"Rick called me as soon as he dropped you off," Rhonda explained. "Said he thought he recognized Elliot from the family reunion a couple years back. And when I found out he was with you, Lydia, I rushed right over."

All this happy coincidence was making me ill. "If you'll excuse me," I said rather curtly, "I need to change for dinner."

I shut the door on three bewildered faces.

Whatever actually happened that night in Gavin's office, I was not ready to forgive all the involved parties. Rhonda may have found herself a new man—a husband even, if the nine-month bulge and impressive solitaire were any indication—but that didn't mean she was entirely innocent.

What kind of secretary kneels before her half-naked boss, no matter the situation?

My shoulders slumped. I knew I'd been rude. Mixed feelings about kissing Ph—Elliot, getting caught by my mom, and facing the woman responsible for breaking up my last relationship overwhelmed me. Definitely mitigating circumstances.

A soft knock roused me from my recriminations. I figured it was most likely my mother.

When I called out, "Come in," the last person I expected to see was Rhonda.

"Lydia," she said gently as she closed the door behind her, "I'm sorry if my presence has upset you."

"It hasn't. It's just—" I fidgeted with the hem of my blouse. "—it was a surprise."

She smiled softly. "We used to be friendly."

I sighed. "Yeah, before."

"I never knew what happened." She stayed next to the door, as if afraid to venture too far into the room. "Between you and Gavin."

She glowed with the inner light of expectant motherhood. A woman ready to nurture, and willing to use that nurturing instinct on me.

"Actually, Rhonda," I confessed as I lowered onto the bed. "What came between us was,"—my brained screamed out the word *you*, but my heart knew the real answer—"me."

"I don't understand."

As I started to explain what I saw that night, what I thought I saw, Rhonda walked over to the bed and sat by my side. Tears came as I recounted how betrayed I felt at the thought of Gavin cheating on me. And with a woman I had considered a friend.

"Sweetheart," she soothed, rubbing a reassuring hand along my back, "you know that never happened."

"It looked that way," I sobbed, "I was so sure of what I saw."

Rhonda patted her protruding belly. "This little angel will be our third. I've been happily married, and fully satisfied thank you very much, for five years. I would never cheat on my Rick." She leaned in for emphasis. "And if he cheated on me, I'd chop off his wiener and throw it in the blender on puree."

She spread her arms and I turned into her hug.

The tears didn't stop. My heart hurt.

"Did I make a horrible mistake?" I asked.

"If you were that quick to judge, even in the most compromising of circumstances, there must have been something wrong already."

What she said made sense. I'd always believed that if a woman has doubts about the man she's with, then he's not the right man. I never wanted to acknowledge that I had doubts about Gavin. I wanted to believe our relationship was perfect, that we were made for each other, that, beyond a shadow of a doubt, we would be happy forever.

Yeah right.

Gradually the tears dried up and I realized that what Gavin and I had was never a relationship. It was a façade. At least on my part.

He was the picture perfect boyfriend—two years older, highly successful, dangerously attractive, and willing to settle down. When I looked at him that was all I ever saw. A good catch. A cardboard cutout of the perfect man I could unfold and stand next to on social occasions.

Gavin was right; I never really loved him.

I never really *knew* him.

"How did my life get so messed up?"

"Sweetheart, everyone's life is messed up," Rhonda countered. She stood and pulled me to my feet. "Most just don't realize it. Now let's go eat, I'm starved."

"LYDIA, YOU REMEMBER DUSTIN DAVENPORT," Mom called out the moment I walked in the kitchen. She indicated the well-dressed man to her left. "He's a doctor."

I rolled my eyes—on the inside—and smiled. He wore a navy suit with a pale gray shirt and matching tie, but his frizzy black hair detracted from his classy look. Maybe if he got it professionally straightened and used a weekly deep conditioning treatment and—

I stopped myself.

Judging on appearances again, Dum Dum?

What good was coming to a life-altering realization if you didn't let it alter your life? I was judging Dustin on the same superficial criteria with which I'd judged Gavin and everybody else.

This was not a path I wanted to continue traveling.

Forcing myself to relax into an open stance, I stepped

forward with hand extended. "Hello, Dustin."

After five minutes of conversation that concentrated on his medical practice and his relationship with his mother, I knew this was not a guy I could be interested in. But at least I *knew*, which was a lot better than assuming.

Besides, I already had a compatible guy at my side for this party. Who, at that very moment, was buddying up with my dad at the grill on the back porch.

At that moment, there was nowhere I'd rather be than by his side. I gracefully made my exit and sidled up next to Ph— Elliot. His name was Elliot, and I was determined to remember that.

"Hey, Hot Tamale," he teased as I slipped an arm around his waist. "I was just thinking about you."

"Really?"

"We need more barbecue sauce."

He winked and I twisted out of his reach before he could pinch me on the backside.

"Don't get used to this kind of service," I admonished. "One time only."

When I returned with the jar, I paused in the doorway to watch Elliot—yes! got it on the first try—and my dad deep in discussion about the best placement of chicken parts on the grill. This was not a conversation I would have witnessed between Dad and Gavin.

Elliot turned to me, that cocky grin spreading across those full lips. We shared a simple moment of connection as Dad concentrated on the chicken and Mom and Rhonda were in the kitchen chatting with the ever-growing number of arriving guests. One shared moment of knowing that, of all the people filling the house, he was thinking of me and I was thinking of him.

Feeling all warm on the inside, I marched across the deck and handed the bottle over.

"That's the last time you'll see me fetch, mister."

He reached out the take it, but I pulled away before he could. His brow furrowed in a petulant pout.

"I expect payment for services rendered." My boldness surprised me, but then again a lot of things were surprising me lately. Even with my dad standing not two feet away, I tilted my head back and offered up my mouth.

"Oh, you'll be paid." His voice was a predatory growl.

With lightning fast reflexes, he snatched the barbecue sauce out of my grip, spun me around, and pulled me flush up against his chest.

"Here you go, Mr. V." He clutched my wrists in one hand and tossed the sauce to my dad. "Excuse us for a moment, your daughter and I have a payment to discuss."

Dragging me—well, not really, I went willingly—around the corner of the wrap-around porch, Elliot—gee, that name was really growing on me—led me to the isolated porch swing and lowered his graceful frame onto the seat. When I tried to take the spot next to him, he held me back, swung his legs up on the bench, and pulled me down on his lap.

Arms wrapped tightly around my waist, he set the swing into a gentle sway.

"Hmmm," I sighed, "this is nice."

Though the simple words didn't capture the depth of my contentment—with both the current situation and, for once, myself—they were all we needed.

"Nice," he said, reaching around to turn my face up, "is not what I was going for."

It wasn't what I wanted either. With a wicked grin, I twist my torso and lifted my mouth. He didn't close the distance, though. Instead, he held back the fraction of an inch from my lips.

He smiled. He did wicked way better than I ever could.

"Did you want something?" he teased.

"You know what I want."

Slipping my hand behind his head, I tugged his mouth towards mine. For a second he resisted. Then he relented and his hot lips brushed mine briefly before pressing harder and—

"Muses!" The lyrical call came from within the house.

With an instinctive reaction, I twisted back around and ducked down. My head thumped back against his warm, solid chest behind me. "Maybe he won't find us."

I felt Elliot's chuckle rumble through his chest and mine.

"He's not like the kind to give up easily." Elliot nipped at my exposed neck with quick kisses. "Maybe we should hide while we still can."

"Have you seen my muses?" I heard Ferrero ask, followed by a negative response from Rhonda.

"No chance," I answered, eyes closed and absorbing the sensation of his lips against my pulse. "The only way out is right past the open kitchen door."

Ferrero forgotten, I sank deeper into Elliot's welcoming warmth. If I closed my ears to the sounds of chirping crickets and televised football announcers, I could almost imagine we were hanging in a hammock over the turquoise blue waters of Tahiti. Cool breeze coming off the lagoon. Wind rustling the palm fronds above. Water lapping at pure white sands. Solar eclipse.

Eclipse?

Blinking out of my reverie, I found Ferrero standing over us, a beaming smile on his tanned face as he blocked out the fading light of the setting sun.

"Here you are," he exclaimed. He grabbed my hands and pulled me up from the swing in one swift motion. "We have much work to do."

Just as quickly, I was unceremoniously nudged aside so Ferrero could tug Elliot up and toward the house. Looking back over his shoulder as Ferrero dragged him inside, Elliot silently pleaded with me to save him.

"Sorry, Sweet Tooth." I didn't even try to hide my grin at his distress. "A muse's work is never done."

How right I was. Except for meals, I scarcely saw Elliot the entire weekend.

AFTER A RELAXING WEEKEND in the country, I found myself full up on inspiration and initiative and short on things to do. With Dyllie sufficiently passed out after countless hours of squirrel chasing and ball fetching I headed for the workroom and worked on turning my industrious mood into inspired pieces.

Two hours later the phone rang and Bethany's face lit up my screen.

"Hi Beth," I said as I brushed some eraser crumbs out of my way.

"Hey sugar, what's shakin'?"

"Working on a new design."

The line was silent for a few seconds.

"On Monday morning? Shouldn't you be at work."

Should was the operative word. I *should* be making sure KY Kelly was not getting too comfortable with my job. I *should* be *doing* my job. But Ferrero, Jawbreaker, and Kelly had seen to it that I stayed far away from my duties. Ferrero's exact words on dropping me off at my apartment yesterday afternoon were, "Channel your creativity. Meditate. Do nothing."

Do nothing? That wasn't in my DNA.

He had this absurd notion that I needed to "clear my creative *chakra*" before we went to Milan. Five long days of nothing but packing, meditating, and channeling. That was going to get old fast.

"Lydia?" Bethany prodded, reminding me that she had asked a question.

"Work doesn't need me right now. Kelly's doing my job and Ferrero's focused on finishing up the Fall collection but won't let me do anything 'non-muse-like'. I'm bored."

I doodled absently as I spoke, unconsciously letting my mind wander through my pencil.

"You've never had so much free time to work on the jewelry before. How's that going?"

"Actually, it's going really well. In fact," shifting the phone to my other ear, I elaborated on the tangle of vines that appeared in my doodle, adding strategically placed red M&Ms, "I'm having a lot of fun. I have about a dozen sketches for the Spring Ferrero collection and the makings of some spectacular designs of my own. I feel like I have time to actually flesh out a design. To work it out until it's right instead of just good enough."

"Sounds like you're having fun." She paused, her hesitation reclaiming my full attention. "You've never gotten this excited about the day job."

"It's not just a day—"

"Listen, sugar. I know I keep saying I want you to go into design full time because I want your pieces in my shop, but that's only part of the reason. I want this for you because you're talented and you're wasted as a number-cruncher. The only time I hear you really, truly happy is when you're talking about your jewelry."

We'd had this conversation several times. Even though she said it was for purely selfish reasons, I had always known that there was deeper meaning in her urging. Bethany didn't have a selfish bone in her polite, Southern-raised body.

"I—"

"You need to quit your job."

I dropped my pencil and held the phone away, staring at the receiver. She never was one to beat around the bush much, but Sweet Saltwater Taffy this was more frankness than I was prepared to hear.

If for no other reason than I had been thinking the very same thing.

When I woke up this morning I bounded out of bed, took a leisurely shower, and made myself an indulgent breakfast of sparkling orange juice and a chocolate croissant. I sat at the breakfast counter in my candy-hearts jammies and let myself enjoy the unhurried peace.

For the first time in a long, long time, there was no weight of worry in the pit of my stomach. No dread over what might happen at work, if today would be the day Jawbreaker gave her position to Kelly. Or the day she found a way to have me fired for not really *enjoying* my work.

And the number-crunching? Calculating sales data, projecting sales, evaluating advertising expenditures. Maybe this was what I should expect with an econ major from Columbia, but that hadn't been my dream.

As an idealistic college student, I had dreamed of getting my degree in economics and pairing it with my jewelry design and starting my own business. But when graduation came around, the panic of not having a steady job with benefits struck and I bit the corporate bullet and took the job at Ferrero.

Steady. Benefits. Opportunity for advancement. And the prestige and cool factor of working at a couture fashion house.

I enjoyed the company and my coworkers—for the most part—and I let the idea of my own jewelry business melt away, like cotton candy in the rain.

Several years and a master plan later, the dream was but a distant memory.

But memories tend to flood back in when you have some free time. It started as a tickle at the back of my mind after filing the sketches for Ferrero into a portfolio and turning to my own designs. As I sketched out a necklace made from ceramic peppermint beads, the first teasing thought of what a good central piece that would be to a collection wiggled its way into my head.

Inspiration bombarded me and I now had plans for two dozen candy-themed pieces.

I could almost picture them on the "Must-Haves" pages of Lucky Magazine.

When the tinny sounds of my name repeated over and over

reached my ears, dragging my wandering brain out of the land of daydreams, I held the phone back up to my ear.

"Lydia?" Bethany called. "Earth to Lydia."

"Yeah, I'm here." I chewed my lip.

"Just promise me you'll think about it," she said.

"I—" I closed my eyes and took a deep breath. "Okay, I'll think about it."

"That's my girl."

Beep-beep.

"I've got to go, Bethany," I told her. "I've got another call."

"Okay, talk soon."

"Will do." *Click.* "Hello?"

"Lydia?" the hair-raisingly sweet voice asked. "It's Kelly. Can we meet?"

SIXTEEN

"UM," I stalled, wishing I had *any* plausible excuse for saying no, "sure."

"Great, I'll be there in ten." Kelly hung up before I could protest. Or disagree. Or agree, even.

Lurching off the stool, I dashed into the bedroom to change into something moderately more presentable than candy hearts pajamas. I was just slipping my pantyhose-clad feet into a pair of pumps when the doorbell buzzed.

Two and a half minutes later, I opened the door, tasteful makeup hastily applied and hair twisted up into a messy bun to hide the fact that I couldn't find my brush.

"You look fabulous," Kelly exclaimed as she burst into my apartment like an overfilled balloon. "You'd never catch me looking so glam on a home day."

Ha, I snorted—unintentionally out loud—and earned a scowl from Kelly.

"No, really," she asserted. "It's sweats and slippers for me. Every day, if I could."

One glance at her head-to-toe designerwear and I knew this KY had never seen the pilly side of a sweatshirt. Since the day they started at Ferrero, all three KYs had dressed impeccably. The only exception was the night Kathryn showed up in emotional distress, but that was a definite once-an-eon occurrence.

"Yeah, I'm sure you snuggle up in your designer workout suit on chilly nights." My tone came out a lot snippier than I intended. Rather than apologize, I got to the point. "What's so urgent?"

She looked taken aback by my abrupt change of subject.

"I think you have the wrong idea about me, Lydia."

What idea was that? That she was a career- and social-climbing siren set on stealing my job and my fiancé?

Whoa! Fiancé? That came out of nowhere.

First of all, Gavin was no longer my fiancé. And second of all, what did I care if she stole him—not that someone can steal something that doesn't belong to you.

Deep breath, Lydia.

"Sorry. I'm a little wound up at the moment."

Leading the way into the living area, I headed for the buffet cabinet and plucked the lid off the antique soup tureen that had belonged to great-great-great-great-grandma Vanderwalk. A sea of gummy bears smiled up at me.

"Gummy bear?" I offered, ladling out a handful into my palm.

"No... thank you." Kelly looked a little frightened.

As I glanced down at my fistful, I was a little frightened, too. To prove I wasn't some insane candy freak, I poured half of the gummies back into the tureen. And slammed the lid down before I could retrieve them.

For a second, I thought I heard the tiny, high-pitched screams of a hundred little voices.

Was hallucination one of the signs of addiction?

I closed my eyes and tried to remember the addiction checklist from that recovery book Mom gave me last Christmas. One was denial, and then concealment. Oooh, yeah, personification was number seven.

Turning off my inner voices, I lifted the lid once more and dropped the rest of the bears back inside.

When I turned back around, Kelly was eying me like you eye the crazy person walking down the street talking to himself. A little wary and a lot concerned.

I crossed to the chofa and sat as if nothing bizarre had happened. Kelly snapped out of her deer-in-headlights stare and lowered herself onto the couch, perching on the edge of the cushion and clearly ready to get back to business.

"I know we've never gotten on real well." She set her briefcase on the floor and leaned forward, forcing a conversational intimacy I had no interest in sharing. "I just want to tell you that I—"

"Can we get to what you came for?" I cut in.

What was my problem?

She looked taken aback, but quickly recovered her composure. "Yes. Of course. I had a few questions about the numbers from the Bay Area campaign."

As I looked over the papers she handed to me, I realized that she had caught a couple of errors. Not significant, career-breaking errors, but errors nonetheless.

My heart sank. I knew that everyone made mistakes, especially in such a high pressure, fast-paced world. But it bit that I had screwed up and Kelly had been the one to catch it.

Sitting up straighter in my seat, I knew I had to do the right thing.

"You're right. I miscalculated the overhead," I said, handing the papers back to her. Hard as it was for me to form the words, I made myself add, "You have a real head for this business. Nice job."

And I even did it without cringing.

Her eyes brightened and for a second she looked like she might cry. "That," she gasped, dabbing at the corners of her eyes with her fingertips, "was the kindest thing you have ever said to me."

Now it was my turn to be taken aback. Kelly was not the sort of girl who made it through life without being praised at every turn. She was beautiful, stylish, obviously intelligent, and must have been regularly swamped with compliments. She didn't need mine on top of all that.

"Well, I'm sure—"

"No." She stopped me, refocusing her attention and pinning me with an earnest look. "Let me say this. I have not had the easiest life, and I know I don't relate very well with other women. But I've always wanted to be a fashion executive. From the moment I came on board at Ferrero, you were my role model. I wanted to do everything as smoothly and gracefully as you. And what you just said—well, that's the greatest thing that you could ever say."

Before I could react, she was out of her seat and next to me on the chofa. Her arms wound around me in what felt alarmingly like a hug. This was getting a little bit too friendly for me.

I stood, grabbed her briefcase off the floor, and urged her to her feet.

"You'd better get back to work," I blurted. "Those spreadsheets aren't going to fix themselves."

Kelly smiled, but it didn't reach her eyes. "Of course."

She started gathering her paperwork, neatly stuffing spreadsheets and summaries into colorful folders, and tucking those folders into her fuchsia work tote. I hadn't meant to be harsh, but after a year of conflict, I was not quite prepared to bond with KY Kelly. Things couldn't change that fast.

I got her out into the hall, briefcase in hand, and was about to shut the door when she turned back to face me.

"Before I go," she said, "you should know there isn't anything going on with me and Gavin. We're friends, that's all."

I scowled and nudged her toward the hall. "Great. Thanks."

"I mean, I know you're with Phelps now, but the only woman Gavin ever talks about," she added as she stepped into the hall, "is you."

I stood there frozen in shock as she walked away.

"HAVE YOU PACKED?" Fiona asked, reclining on my couch as I recounted the events of the past few days.

There was a lot to catch up on.

"For Milan? Not yet. We don't leave until Friday." I heard her *mm-hmm* around the piece of chocolate on her tongue.

When Fi showed up at my door with a 16-piece box of gourmet chocolates I knew she'd had a tough day. Nothing but the roughest of days could induce her to bring out the big guns. And, although chocolate was not my personal favorite—

if it's not gummied, sugared, sour, or caramelized, it's not really for me—we shared this indulgence once every black and blue moon.

Choosing a dark chocolate chili pepper truffle from the box, I leaned back into the chofa and bit into the sweet and spicy ball.

"Do you know what you're taking?" she asked.

"Haven't even thought about it."

"Think about it now," she suggested. "Let's have a look at your wardrobe."

Fi was on her feet and heading through my bedroom door before I could answer. Slowly rising, I replaced the lid on the truffles box so Dyllie wouldn't get interested, and followed to my room.

In the span of twenty seconds, she had half my closet draped across the bed. The half from the back. The half I was too chicken to wear.

"I am *not* taking any of that!"

"You've been hiding behind your suits and cardigans for too long, sister. You have the perfect body to pull all these off. All you need is a little confidence."

I looked down at my scrawny self. Flat chest. Chicken legs. Protruding collarbone. My body wasn't perfect for anything. Hence the carefully concealing layers of wool and cashmere.

"These clothes," she added, holding up white eyelet sundress, "were designed for models with your figure."

"You mean *your* figure," I countered. Fiona had the perfect body: tall, lean but shapely, full-breasted. I'd always envied her that.

And she had the fashion sense to show it all off. Right now she wore a red v-neck sweater that accentuated and displayed her pushed-up chest and a skintight black pencil skirt that molded her hips into seductive curves.

Without hesitation she pulled off her sweater, peeled off the skirt and tugged the sundress over her head.

Though we wore the same size, the dress stretched way-too-tight across her hips and chest. Her pushed-up breasts were pushed even more into view, nearly cut in half by the low neckline of the dress.

"So one dress doesn't fit," I conceded. I held up my gunmetal gray cocktail number, knowing it would look better on her. "Try this one."

After struggling out of the tight cotton sundress, Fiona slipped into the slinky number. Like the sundress, this dress stretched tighter across the hips than it should, and her ample breasts pushed out on the panels of the halter top, leaving a gaping view of her bra and abdomen.

"All right, so two dresses—"

"No," she interrupted, passionate in her argument. "*All* dresses. There isn't a single designer dress in my closet that hasn't been professionally altered to fit my figure. I probably spend as much on tailoring as I do on clothes. Maybe more. So trust me when I tell you, *these clothes were designed for you.*"

Shocked, I stared at her like she had sprouted Sour Straws for hair. A candy-haired medusa.

"Really?" I finally ventured when I could speak.

She rolled her eyes dramatically before slinking out of the cocktail dress and pulling her clothes back on. "Not that I would trade figures for anything—my C-cups have many fans —but yours is the body type gracing all the runways and magazine spreads. So shove your body image issues into the garbage disposal and let's pack you a wowser wardrobe for Milan."

My courage bolstered, I headed for the closet and dug into the way back. "And this," I said, finding the hanger and lifting it off the bar, "is the first thing in."

Holding the strapless minidress up to my chest, I faced Fiona. Every golden bead and sequin sparkled in the bright light of my room.

Her beaming grin said everything.

I hung the dress on the valet hook next to my closet and reached for the silver-gray shoebox on the top shelf. Strappy stiletto sandals in matching metallic gold.

"You wear that outfit around any guy with eyes and you won't be wearing it very long." Fiona grinned when I threw a wad of tissue at her. Which only made her goad me more. "Better wax up that zipper."

I was just about to forget the six-hundred-dollar price tag and fling a shoe at her when the buzzer sounded.

And a good thing, too. That was six-hundred *per shoe.*

SEVENTEEN

"THIS IS A CRISIS."

Ferrero threw up his arms and marched into my apartment without preamble.

"Won't you come in," I offered to his back.

He whirled around on me as I closed the door. "It has come to my attention," he boomed, "that *you* are a sales executive."

He looked tired.

"That is true."

Fashion week was always stressful for him, and I had heard there were problems with suppliers and an embargo on a tiny Eastern European country that exported handmade glass beads. Top it off with the whatever had thrown him into a tizzy and no wonder he appeared on my doorstep looking haggard and pointing out a well-known fact.

"That is unacceptable," he continued, pacing nervously on my living room rug. "A muse cannot be concerned with... *business*."

He said it like it was a bad word.

"Well, at the moment, I'm not really—"

"Unacceptable." Stopping in the center of the rug, Ferrero faced me with a determined set to his jaw. "I should fire you."

I gasped. Was he really firing me? Fiona had said there had to be a catch. Well, hello there, catch. Welcome to the party.

"No," I replied. "You can't fire me. I quit."

I gasped again. Had I really said that? Out loud?

This was all Bethany's fault. She had pushed me into saying I would think about focusing full time on my jewelry. Otherwise I never would have said something so rash. But if Franco was firing me, what did I have to lose?

He was struck frozen for the space of two seconds before his lips spread into a beaming, cosmetically-whitened smile. "No, I said I *should* fire you. But I am not."

I glared at him, more than a little skeptical.

A yip from the direction of my bedroom drew my attention to Fiona standing in the doorway with Dyllie in her arms. From the scowl on her face I knew she had heard everything. She looked ready to gut him from neck to nuts. Fiona might have a bit of a flakey streak, but she was loyal to the point of violence.

Straightening her spine, she pasted on her own brilliant smile and strode into the room like she owned the place.

"I don't think we've met." She extended a hand to Ferrero. "I'm Fiona, a friend of Lydia's."

Oh yeah, that should clear things up, since Ferrero still didn't know my name. Still, he took her hand, lifting it to press a gentlemanly kiss on her knuckles.

"Miss Vanderwalk is an inspiration. And you," he said, lowering but not releasing her hand, "are a vision."

Fiona smiled politely, but lacking genuine warmth. She was well-versed with the social platitudes of the world of fashion. It was often her job to smooth the feathers of designer and model alike at a show-gone-bad.

"Thank you, Ferrero," she replied, and when he began to correct her she added, "Franco. You are very kind to say so. Now what were you saying about *not* firing Lydia?"

"Oh yes." He turned back to me. "I am not firing you. Instead," he continued, "I am offering you a choice."

"What kind of choice?" I asked before Fiona could ask for me.

"I offer you a promotion to junior Vice President of Marketing," he said, and all the air left my body. "Or a creative position as lead accessories designer, to start your own line within Ferrero Couture."

All the blood left my body, too.

How could I choose between two such amazing opportunities? I had been angling for Jawbreaker's job since day one. It was on my ten year plan, and now it was within my reach right on schedule.

But starting my own line under the Ferrero name? That was... incredible. Few designers ever got that kind of opportunity. It was a risk, though. It meant committing to my creative pursuits full-time, leaving the safe, stable business side behind.

I just stood there, staring at Ferrero, blinking and unable to process his offer.

Fiona, ever one to read situations with startling clarity, stepped forward. "Sorry to interrupt, but I actually have to go. Lydia," she said, placing Dyllie in my arms and screwing her face into an apologetic-but-leaving-you-anyway look, "I think you have your packing under control."

She said her goodbye to Ferrero—presumably not giving him a similar look—and make quick for the door, turning to mouth, *Call me!* as she left.

Dyllie squirmed in my arms and I set her on the floor.

"Franco," I began, "I—"

"Stop." He quieted me with a wave of his hand. "Do not answer in haste. Think about this offer. You may give me your answer when we return from Milan."

Thank goodness, because I wasn't sure I would be able to decide right now. Who was I kidding? I wouldn't be able to decide after Milan, either. But at least that gave me time to think about it, to talk things out.

"All right," I agreed. "After Milan."

"Good." Ferrero nodded in approval. Glancing briefly over his shoulder, he smiled broadly and came forward to shake my hand. "And, since it appears your little angel needs to be relieved, I will take my leave."

I peered around him to find Dyllie doing the potty dance, whimpering and tapping her little toenails on the wooden floor of the hall like rapid-fire Pop Rocks. Based on previous calculations, I figured I had about ninety seconds to get her outside before she decided that the chofa seat was as good a spot as any.

"I'll see you out," I threw at Ferrero as I ran to the front door and grabbed the leash. Dyllie dashed with me, pausing only to wait for the click of the lobster clasp snapping onto her collar.

For a little dog, she sure had a heck-of-a-lotta power in those tiny legs. If the floors of the main hallway hadn't been tile, she probably could have pulled me all the way to the elevator.

As it was, Ferrero and I made our way accompanied by the sliding clicks of doggie toenails and desperate whimpering. The elevator arrived promptly and within moments we were crossing the lobby and stepping onto the sidewalk, searching out the nearest patch of dirt.

Ferrero signaled his driver who immediately emerged from the limo and opened the rear door. Before lowering into the seat, Ferrero called my name. "Lydia," he said when he had my attention, using my correct first name for the first time, "you are an inspiration to the entire company."

His white head ducked into the car before I could respond.

I stood there, on the sidewalk of 76th Street, long after the limo pulled away and Dyllie began tugging on her leash to go back inside. I wasn't a fool, I knew what Ferrero had just done. By taking away the disadvantages of either option, he had just forced me to make an actual decision.

For good or bad, I had to choose which path I wanted to take. And, as I let Dyllie lead me back through the lobby, I knew that was not going to be an easy decision to make.

Did I really want to focus more on my jewelry hobby?

Or did I want to keep my paycheck-secure business position?

Dyllie looked up sympathetically when I sighed.

"Well," I asked her, "what would you do?"

Just like a dog. She stuck out her tongue and looked away.

WHEN THE BUZZING sounded at six a.m. on Friday morning I picked up the phone and groggily told whoever was calling, "I'm packed, really. Just about to get up."

Silence was my first clue. The continued buzzing—coming from the area around the front door—was the second.

"Good&Plenty," I muttered as I stumbled out of bed and hurried to the front door. Pressing the intercom button, I asked, "Hello?"

"Helloooo!!!" Two cheerful voices screeched through the speaker, jolting me out of whatever sleep haze remained.

I jabbed at the door release button, letting Fiona and Bethany in against my better judgment. They sounded much too cheerful for so early in the morning. If I didn't know they both had to work today, I'd think they hadn't gone to bed at all last night.

They showed up at my door, laden with shopping bags and Fiona's luggage-sized makeup case.

"*Buongiorno!*" Bethany squealed, dropping her shopping bags and flinging her arms around my neck. "Are you ready?"

"For what?" I asked around her tight embrace.

"Italy, silly," Fiona answered. She set her case down on the kitchen counter before adding herself to the hug.

"Yeth. All packed." It was a little difficult to speak through Fiona's fuchsia feather boa.

"Not quite." Bethany eased away, grabbing the shopping bags and holding them into view. "We brought some last-minute extras."

Each girl took me by an arm and led me to the couch, pushing me down until I sat. They moved in front of me, Fiona holding the shopping bags as Bethany prepared to display everything inside.

Under Where was not my usual lingerie shop. I was a simple undergarments girl. Give me a pair of cotton bikinis and a full-coverage bra any day.

The first thing Bethany pulled from the bag looked more like doll clothes than underwear for a grown woman. Tiny and turquoise with gold accents; no way was that designed to fit an adult.

"*Femme Fatale,*" Bethany announced, tossing the scrap into my lap.

"The very best," Fiona added, eyeing the bit of lace with undisguised envy.

I inspected the g-string thong, shocked to find a tag identifying it as an adult small. The thing barely fit across my hips, let along cover— "Oh no," I announced, "I'm not wearing this. Ever."

Fiona frowned, clearly disappointed.

Bethany, however, looked determined. Digging into the bag again, she pulled out a matching bra. She flung the coordinating scrap at me, admonishing, "Just try it on."

Looking from one friend to the other, I read their unrelenting determination. Reluctantly, I headed for the privacy of my bedroom, chased by the promise that I would like it once I tried it on.

Stepping out of the candy-hearts flannels, I turned the thong around every which way until I found the right orientation. As I pulled the undies up into place, I was shocked to realize I didn't feel a thing. No uncomfortable wedgie sensation I'd read about in magazines. I could hardly feel the satin and lace that barely covered parts I'd always left under a solid layer of cotton.

Intrigued, I quickly slipped my arms through the bra straps and reached back to maneuver the hooks into place. Again, it was like I wasn't wearing anything. The straps lay softly against my shoulders without cutting and the lacy cups provided support without the chaste appearance of full-coverage.

Only one test left to pass.

Eyes closed, I crossed to the full-length mirror hanging on the back of my closet door, managing to avoid the dresser and the bed without incident. When I felt sure I stood directly in front of my reflection, I opened my eyes and ... *marveled*.

I looked like an underwear model. Without the ample chest, of course. The color and texture against my bare flesh—an awful lot of bare flesh, to be sure—made my fair skin look as smooth as cream. Rather than merely covered, supported, and protected, my body looked—dared I say it?—sexy.

Lifting my gaze to smile at myself in the mirror, I noticed that the colors made my eyes glow. I always knew my hazel eyes changed depending on what I wore, but this was extreme. The three tiny patches of lace turned my plain eyes brilliant turquoise. And the gold accents brought out the golden flecks in the centers.

Nothing could deflate my grin.

"Come on, Lyd," Fiona called from the living room, "what's the verdict?"

I was not about to walk out into the living room virtually naked—even if these were my two best girlfriends out there. Quickly changing back into the jammies, I carefully folded the lingerie and placed it on the bed to be packed.

My grin still intact as I emerged, Fiona and Bethany smiled knowingly at each other.

Bethany stood and handed me the rest of the shopping bags. "Now you know Victoria's *real* secret."

Knowing that you and only you know what goodies lie beneath the business suit or the ball gown. Knowing every guy would be panting at your feet if he only knew. *That* was the secret.

Bethany was right; now I knew.

"Have I told you guys how much I love you?"

Neither answered, but I found myself at the center of another group hug.

"Okay," Fiona said, her voice sounding suspiciously sniffy, "are you ready for The Extras, Part Two?"

Eyeing the makeup case warily, I had a pretty good idea what they had in mind. An image of Fi's lime green glitter eyeshadow popped to mind, but I shoved it aside. Though they might each be outrageous in their own way, there weren't two people I trusted more.

"Do your worst."

Something reminiscent of absolute power glinted in Fiona's eyes. Hoping I hadn't just handed myself over to be Picasso's next project, I let them lead me to a stool at the breakfast bar.

"Just remember, I have to get on a plane with my bosses and my enemies in a few hours."

"Don't worry, you'll put them all to shame," Bethany assured. "He'll be at your feet."

I frowned. Gavin and Elliot would both be on that plane. "Which one?"

Bethany smiled. "Which one do you want?"

Saved from giving Bethany an answer by Fiona's order to close my eyes, I knew I would soon have to answer that question for myself.

"MISS VANDERWALK," a male voice announced over the inter-com, "this is Howard with your limo to the airport."

A shiver of excitement tickled up and down my spine. The same shiver I got every time I traveled, but this time it was much, much stronger. Like an iceberg parked itself on my back. There were so many things this trip signified. The start of a new phase of my career. Maybe the start of a new relation-ship—or the renewal of an old one? And in some ways, the start of a whole new me.

"Wow," I breathed to no one but myself.

Bethany had graciously volunteered to dog-sit for the dura-tion of the trip. Both girls had left me with identical orders to enjoy myself in Italy.

And I didn't think they meant with my sketchpad.

Handle of my rolling suitcase in hand, I turned and surveyed my apartment one last time. Everything was neat, clean, and put away. Sterile came to mind. Mom always made sure we cleaned before going on a trip so the house would be nothing but welcoming when we returned. Somehow, that had become a mainstay in my life—that everything be sterile so I would never have to face a mess.

Well that had worked out just swell. It seemed like every-where I turned in my life I faced a mess on top of a mess. Since everything else in my life was changing, this might as well change too.

Marching into the kitchen, I grabbed a glass from the cupboard, filled it with pineapple Fanta, took a single sip and dumped the rest right down the drain. As I set the dirty glass in the sink I smiled.

My life was changing; starting on the inside.

I said goodbye to my apartment—mess and all—from the front door. With a whoosh of the door and a click of the lock I bid farewell to neat and plain Lydia. The woman with a mess in her sink and an nightclub-worthy wardrobe in her suitcase was taking over. About damn time.

But as I waited for the elevator, I looked longingly at the black metal door with gold-toned numbers and matching peephole. All I could picture was that dirty glass and all the ants and roaches it might attract during the next few days.

By the time the elevator finally arrived I had added rats and feral cats to the image. Maybe a girl can't change all her stripes in one day.

My heart pounded and I knew I couldn't do this. Mental Post-It: send Danielle an email about the glass.

Decision made, my pulse calmed down to near normal as I crossed the lobby and emerged into the city night. While the driver struggled to load my suitcase in the trunk, I absorbed the magic of New York at night.

Other parts of town might be crazy with seas of people going clubbing, eating out, or just trying to get somewhere—anywhere—else, but my neighborhood saw only a few couples and families out for an evening stroll. A taxi cab dropped off an elegant looking woman clad in fur and heels across the street. My imagination pictured her knocking on her sweetheart's door, unwrapping her fur to reveal nothing but lingerie and stockings underneath when he answered.

A commotion from the limo drew my attention. The sound of raised voices and the shattering of fine crystal.

Trying to ignore whatever was going on I turned to the driver. "Do you have many more to pick up?"

"No, ma'am," he answered in a heavy Brooklyn accent, "you're the last."

He took my hand and lowered me into the back seat of the limo. Into the fashion world version of *Animal House*.

EIGHTEEN

"*BUONA SERA*," Ferrero greeted. "Welcome to the Italian Express. Strap yourself in for a bumpy ride."

The limo could have seated at least twelve, but only five others occupied the soft leather benches. Ferrero sat at the head of the limo, his back to the driver and the privacy window. Kelly sat to his very near right and Jawbreaker to his very near left. I had half-expected Jawbreaker's husband to be there. She always made him sound like such a perfect doting husband. He worked a lot, I knew, but I figured this could have been a vacation for him.

The other two occupants, Gavin and Elliot, knelt on the carpet in front of the bar, carefully picking up shards of glass.

"Good evening," I responded, choosing to ignore tension and awkward glances all around me and whatever had resulted in a broken champagne flute. "How is everyone tonight?"

Though I was just making polite conversation, the question prompted Kelly to leave Ferrero's side, climb gingerly over the two men on the floor, and plop herself on the seat next to me.

"Oh my god, Lydia," she squealed. "Isn't this just the most exciting thing ever?"

She threw her arms around me in a stranglehold, squeezing until I finally patted her on the back in reciprocation.

"I mean, not only is this my first trip out of the country, my first time on a plane, but Milan? *Milan?* This is like my holy pilgrimage!" She could hardly keep her wiggling behind in the seat.

It was hard to believe she'd never flown before. Never been out of the country. Everything about Kelly screamed jetsetter sophistication. Dressed entirely in winter white, in her light-weight wool slacks and chunky knit cowl neck she looked like she belonged on a private Greek island.

Unlike the outfit Fiona had selected for me to wear.

Which Kelly suddenly noticed.

"You look amazing! Like you're ready to step onto the runway." Her grin faltered for a second before adding, "The fashion runway. Not the airport kind."

All eyes in the limo—even the driver's, since the partition was down—turned on me. A long, low whistle let me know that Elliot approved of my new look.

I had to fight the urge to tug at the ruffles of the pacific blue satin tank, wishing they covered just a little more than they revealed. Though I had to admit, the way the ruffles accented things that weren't there and the way the bright blue made my eyes glow more than made up for the amount of flesh showing.

It had taken a lot of convincing to get Fiona to let me wear pants instead of a miniskirt. In the end, the statistics about the friction of bare skin on emergency ramps won out. To save my legs from third-degree burns she had consented to a pair of tight black skinny cords. They had just enough stretch to let me move freely and shaped my butt into a perfect curve.

And then there was the face.

Fi and Beth had taken almost two hours applying my makeup. Both were experienced with professional makeup application—Fiona from working with makeup artists at the model agency and Bethany from working with makeup artists from the lines of cosmetics she sold in her shop. So, two hours later I really did look like a model.

Of course the worst of it was they expected me to remember how to recreate the look.

I probably could, as long as I mastered the eyeliner. How Fiona lined the inside of my eyelids was still a mystery. But when I looked in the mirror and saw Brigitte Bardot looking back I had to admit that my past makeup skills had been lacking.

Bethany had even managed to spray and tease my limp, straight hair into a mass of voluminous, sexy waves.

A pair of cat-eyes and pouting lips later, I knew that the old Lydia—the one who used an all-in-one kit full of neutrals to the exclusion of all other makeup—was long gone, a lone brown M&M sitting out in the rain, melting away into oblivion.

Hoping the cosmetic blush disguised the real color heating my cheeks at the attention, I managed a sincere, "Thank you."

While Elliot couldn't take his eyes off my screen siren face, Gavin's gaze dropped to my feet. He had always had a thing—almost a fetish, really—for sexy heels. Boink me pumps, he called them. And the four-inch snakeskin stilettos I wore were as sexy as they got.

Of course, I had a pair of comfortable flats in my carry-on

for the plane—it would defeat all the effort to get permission to wear the pants if I broke my ankle on my way to the emergency exit—but for the trip to the airport I wanted to feel the full effect of my new look.

The fire in Gavin's green eyes was unmistakable when he finally met mine. But the fire banked quickly as Elliot crawled across the carpet to my feet and settled into the seat on my right.

Gavin quickly disposed of the last of the broken glass and filled two of the remaining flutes with champagne. Taking the seat next to Kelly, he handed a glass to her and I waited for him to make a toast.

Instead, he handed the second glass to me and smiled.

Though I half-expected Kelly to giggle and squeal, "Bubbles," she merely raised her glass, indicating I should raise mine as well.

"To Italy," she toasted.

"To Italy," I echoed, my gaze dancing briefly over Elliot and Gavin before resting on Kelly. "And to new beginnings."

As Kelly chattered on about Milan and all the things she wanted to do, I felt Gavin and Elliot's eyes on me the entire way to JFK. I knew they each wondered which new beginning I was toasting. If I knew myself, I might have told them.

THE PLANE TOUCHED down at 7:46 the next morning; almost twenty minutes early, but not a second too soon. Through some cruel trick of fate—or the fact that Kelly requested the seating assignments—she and I were seated next to each other in the last row of the first class cabin.

Somehow, even the soft leather seats and fresh baked cookies couldn't overcome the fact that I had to listen to her gushing for the entire seven hours and twenty-one minutes of the flight.

Jawbreaker, of course, took the seat next to Ferrero in the row in front of me, leaving Gavin and Elliot neighbors in the seats across the aisle in my row.

Needless to say, there was not a lot of conversation from the other side of the gray patterned carpet.

As the plane taxied through the runways of Milan's Malpensa Airport—an unfortunate name for an airport, roughly translating as "badly thought"—and Kelly *oohed* and *ahhed* at the Gothic spires and Romanesque bell towers, I gathered my belongings back into my carry-on.

I had resisted the urge to pull out my sketchpad and work during the flight. Feedback from Kelly was not on my birthday wish list.

Electing not to change out of the oh-so-comfortable-and-yet-still-fashionable driving mocs, I checked on the carefully tucked away heels before zipping the bag shut. I would just have to rely on my dove gray pashmina to exude my jetset-terness.

We emerged into the insanity that was Italy in the morning.

"We go this way," Jawbreaker called when I headed for the sign with a suitcase on it, beckoning with the promise of baggage claim.

I frowned. "Shouldn't we—"

"We have a car waiting," Ferrero interrupted. Spying a young Italian man wearing a black suit and muted gold tie and casually holding a sign that read *Ferrero Couture*, Ferrero made a beeline and immediately pushed his nearly empty briefcase into the man's arms. "I am exhausted. I need a *siesta* before the shows begin at ten. The hotel will arrange for the luggage."

The driver, clearly used to the eccentric temperament of Americans—fake Italian accent or no—simply shrugged the briefcase onto his shoulder and led the way to the car.

Following closely behind, I had a feeling Fiona would have enjoyed the view. The car service did not skimp on their drivers. Fi would already be enumerating the boundless opportunities provided by a hunky chauffeur and an empty limo.

But, rather than push me backward into the car for a steamy interlude, the driver politely held the door as we all climbed in and then closed it softly behind us.

"Here is a rough schedule." Jawbreaker handed out a stack of papers printed on Ferrero letterhead. Tasteful gold embossed ivory stock.

What should my letterhead look like if I started my own line? More fun, definitely. Maybe a bright lilac paper with blue lettering that matched my top. Ooh, and maybe something sparkly—

"Did you hear me, Lydia?"

"Wh—" I returned from my brief daydream to find all eyes on me. Jawbreaker's, weary and above purple-smudged sags, looked tired. "Um, sorry. Could you repeat that?"

"The first show is a ten o'clock, but we should be able to relax and unpack a little beforehand since the hotel is only a couple blocks from the catwalk venue."

"Oh, yes," I said mostly because I felt like I needed to contribute something, "that's convenient."

As she looked down at the sheaf of papers in her hands I almost thought Jawbreaker rolled her eyes.

"Do you even know where we're staying?" she asked.

If she didn't sound so tired and run down, I might have taken offense.

Before I could shake my head, she answered her own question. "*Hotel della Regina,* in *Via di Modo.*"

"Oh," I answered quietly, "thank you."

Why did I feel like I had done something very, very wrong?

"THIS IS *GORGEOUS!*" Kelly exclaimed, not subtle as we stepped into the elegant Renaissance lobby of the *Hotel della Regina.*

"That's an understatement," Gavin concurred.

Elliot let out another low whistle as he came up at my side and slipped his arm around my waist. Exhausted from the long journey, I laid my head against his shoulder and sagged into his embrace. A growl resonated against the polished marble, emanating from the vicinity of where Gavin stood.

I was too tired to get in the middle of the testosterone contest. Instead, I pulled away from Elliot and walked away from them both.

Drawn to a beautiful oil painting of the hotel's façade, I was leaning in for a closer look at the brush strokes around the windows when Jawbreaker tapped on my shoulder.

"I understand there's some conflict about the sleeping arrangements." When I only looked confused she explained. "Gavin and Kelly have requested separate rooms. Something about only being friends and Kelly's use of counter space. Do you and Phelps need separate rooms as well?"

Across the lobby I could see Gavin and Elliot glaring at

each other from about ten feet apart. If looks could wound there'd be blood all over the pristine white floors.

I weighed my options.

To request separate rooms would be a clear indication that I didn't want to be with Elliot. Not necessarily meaning that I chose Gavin, but a definite message that I had *not* chosen Elliot. A choice I was not ready to make.

I couldn't make either decision without knowing more about both of them. Sharing a room—for a week instead of just a weekend—would be enlightening. And if Gavin had a problem with my exploring my options then he could go hang.

"No," I declared, "we're fine the way we are."

Jawbreaker nodded and turned to the front desk. I went back to studying the painting until I was again interrupted.

"And Lydia?"

I turned around at her uncharacteristically soft-spoken question.

"I ... I apologize for snapping at you earlier." She massaged her temples wearily. "There's just so much going on and ... there's no excuse. I'm sorry."

Something about the despondent look on her tired face—shockingly bare of makeup, I noticed—made me ask, "Is something wrong?"

"No, n-nothing."

She protested, but the moisture in her eyes was unmistakable. When I laid a reassuring hand on her shoulder a single tear dropped from each eye.

"Carmello left me. He—" She wiped brusquely at the tears, smearing them into oblivion. "—he went back to his ex-wife."

"Janice," I soothed, her true name coming out without thought, "I'm so sorry. Is there anything I can—"

"No. It's fine. I just—" Patting my hand, she smiled gamely. "He could have chosen better timing, is all. I'll be fine."

I watched in awe as she shook off the momentary display, strode purposefully across the lobby, and checked in. There weren't many women who could suffer a husband's leaving right before a gargantuan career event and rise to the occasion. I felt something tickling at my stomach that felt disturbingly like respect. For Janice. Jawbreaker! I meant Jawbreaker.

Sweet Saltwater Taffy, I hoped this was just the effects of jetlag. I wouldn't know what to do with myself if I suddenly found respect for everyone I worked with.

Jetlag. That was all.

THE GUEST ROOMS were even more lavish than the lobby. Rich golds and lush velvets everywhere. Even the four-poster king-size bed had gold velvet drapes and gold quilted jacquard bedding. The gilding on the light fixtures alone must have cost more than my entire apartment.

Our baggage managed to beat us and my suitcase stood empty in the antique armoire, the contents neatly folded into drawers and hung on smooth wooden hangers.

Never underestimate the value of five diamond service.

"Ready to see the sights, sugarcakes?"

Elliot came up behind me, wrapping his arms around my waist and hugging me to his chest. His energy was boundless. Maybe I wasn't the only one needing to cut back on the sugar intake.

"No." I turned within the circle of his arms and slipped

mine around his neck. "I need to rest before the shows begin. We have almost an hour and I need a quick cat nap."

"Oka-ay," he drawled, "but don't think you're getting out of a moped-driven city tour."

I smiled at the exuberance in his sky blue eyes. "Just be sure and get a yellow one."

He grinned in return. "Daffy II."

Then, with a quick kiss to my forehead, he bounded out the door. Off to take Milan by storm, no doubt.

I stepped out of the driving mocs and padded over to the bed, lovingly caressing the sensuous duvet and testing the downy softness of the mattress. Sleep beckoned.

Before I could lift one knee, a hesitant knock sounded at the door. Not Elliot, I knew. I didn't think he knew how to be hesitant. He took life by the horns in every situation.

Still, I shouldn't have been surprised when I swung open the paneled door to find Gavin standing in the hall.

"Hey," he offered in greeting.

"Hey back."

His eyes hovered over my shoulder, scanning the room behind me.

"He's gone," I answered the unvoiced question. "Sightseeing."

"Oh, well..." Gavin scuffed a perfectly polished oxford on the carpet and jammed his hands in his pockets. He looked like a recalcitrant schoolboy in his button down and khakis. Golden hair a little mussed and guilt heavy in his bright green eyes. "I want to apologize for acting like a jerk. Earlier. In the lobby. In the limo."

"Accepted." Though I had expected a little more than this

unnecessary apology when he showed up at my door. "Is that all?"

"No, of course not." Taking a deep, sighing breath, he shrugged and relaxed into a more casual, but undeniably confident stance. "If you don't have plans for tonight would you like to join me for dinner and maybe visit a museum? The *Pinacoteca di Brera* is only a few blocks away."

My eyes shot up and I held his gaze intensely.

He remembered. My favorite painting in all of history, *The Kiss* by Francesco Hayez, hung in that museum. How could he, two years later, still remember my favorite painting? And he had obviously gone to the effort of finding out where it lived.

A tiny, self-effacing smile lifted the corners of his mouth. As if ashamed to be caught being so thoughtful.

"That," I managed through the emotion swamping me, "would be wonderful."

" Why don't we go to the museum straight from the last show and then to dinner after?"

I nodded. "Are you going to the show?"

"No, I have a couple of calls to make to New York. Time change and all that. Besides," he raked a hand through his hair and stepped back into the hallway, "you know I'm not much for the whole fashion thing."

This was an opportunity I couldn't resist.

"But Gavin," I cooed, "you *were* on the cover of GQ."

He shook his head. "A horrendous lapse in judgment. The firm's publicity rep owes me big time." He grinned, confidence and mischief sparkling in his eyes. "Need tickets to the Super Bowl?"

It felt like forever since I'd laughed with Gavin. Forever

since he pulled back the reserved façade to let his inner class clown show. I was surprised to realize I missed this.

"I'll let you know," I joked back.

We shared a smile. One that bridged a gap that had long kept us isolated. Different than the completely spontaneous and outrageous ones I shared with Elliot. One that felt like home.

He lifted his wrist and checked his watch. "I'd better let you rest," he said as he backed down the hall towards his room two doors down. "I'll meet you in front of the *Fiero Pavilion* at 5:30."

"See you then."

I'd lost track of which new beginning this was, but it sure felt like a Whopper.

💜

"I NEVER IMAGINED how beautiful it would be in real life."

Though it had to be the millionth time I commented on the exquisite beauty of the Hayez painting, I couldn't help saying it again. And as we strolled along the narrow streets of a Medieval city, Gavin let me gush.

I wondered what Elliot would have thought of *The Kiss*. Would he have been awed by the emotion in the lovers' embrace? Or would he have turned to me and swept me into an embrace of our own? Maybe I would bring him to the museum before we leave.

I also wondered how to tell him I'd spent the evening with Gavin. Even though we were *not* committed, he had an endearing streak of jealousy. Especially where Gavin was concerned.

"If I could afford it," Gavin said, interrupting my thoughts, "I would buy it for you. Just so you could see it every day."

"Oh no," I exclaimed, horrified by the thought. "It should never leave this museum. The public needs it more than I do."

Gavin laughed at my adamant response.

"You were joking, weren't you?" I asked. Sometimes with Gavin I couldn't tell. He had a kind of humor that made you wonder if he was laughing with you, at you, or if he really laughed at all.

"If you want me to be." He batted his eyelashes in feigned submission.

When I stuck out my lower lip in a pout, he laughed and put his arm around my shoulder, deftly guiding us across *Via Broletto* and onto the sidewalk on the opposite side.

Gavin was the sort of man who always knew where he was going. In a new city. In a car. In life.

Navigation was not my strongest suit.

"I don't know how you know where you're going." I shook my head in wonder. "Do you ever get lost?"

"Not when I look at a map beforehand," he answered, distractedly reading the sign above a door on *Via Dante*, a street blocked off as a pedestrian area and strewn with sidewalk cafes and full of tourists and locals alike. "This is it."

Gavin pulled open the unassuming, carved wooden door and ushered me inside. Down a flight of ancient tile steps we met a *maître d'* with a pair of menus in his hands and a welcoming smile on his lips.

"*Buona sera, signore Fairchild. Come stai?*" the *maître d'* asked musically.

"*Molto buono, grazie Carlo.*"

Gavin's fluent response surprised me. "I never knew you

spoke Italian."

"There were a lot of things you never knew."

Carlo motioned for us to follow him. "I have saved you the very best table, *il migliore*. All is ready."

"Thank you Carlo."

After setting the menus on the small corner table, Carlo pulled out my seat. Gavin stepped around and took the chair and slid it in beneath me as I sat. With a quick nod and a smile of commiseration, Carlo disappeared.

"What is ready?" I asked as Gavin sat.

"A special order," he replied cryptically. Picking up the open bottle of local *Valpolicella* to his right, Gavin carefully poured two equal glasses. Lifting his glass, he indicated I should raise mine as well. "To Italy."

I smiled, holding my glass higher. "To Italy."

"And to you," he added, interrupting my first sip, "Lydia Ilene Vanderwalk. You are an amazing and beautiful woman."

Not knowing how to respond—a woman with more social savvy would have said "Thank you" with grace and aplomb— I merely nodded and lifted the glass to my lips.

The meal was slow, in a leisurely and sensual way. Several minutes passed between each lavish course and the conversation never waned. I told Gavin about my promotion offer from Ferrero and my thoughts about maybe, possibly, someday starting my own jewelry line. He gave me advice, as both friend and businessman, for both options.

We never spoke about that night two years ago when I walked out of his life or that afternoon two weeks ago when we finally talked about it.

Getting to know Gavin all over again was more like realizing that I had never known him at all.

"I didn't know you spent a summer in college volunteering at Sustainable Development International." I looked at him in a whole new light. "That must have been very rewarding."

He shrugged as if it meant nothing, but I could see in his eyes that he regarded that time very fondly.

"It was okay."

Yeah, if okay meant life-altering. "Where were you sent?"

"West Africa. Ghana mostly. Digging canals and planting soil-retaining vegetation in areas that suffer from soil erosion-induced droughts."

Rather than continue the conversation, Gavin looked around and caught Carlo's attention. A cryptic signal passed between the two and Carlo quickly disappeared into the kitchen.

Moments later he reappeared, a grinning chef and two waiters following in a mini-parade.

"For you, *signorina*." Carlo bowed and stepped out of the way.

The chef stepped forward and set a large, covered platter on our table. One waiter lifted the lid as the other handed each of us a dessert fork and wished us, "*Buon appetito!*"

On the platter sat an enormous, spherical scoop of *Semifreddo al Limone*—a rich ice cream parfait that was my absolute all-time favorite dessert—in a bed of strawberry sauce. Written in the strawberry sauce, in carefully piped chocolate, were the words, "Guaranteed to melt in your hand."

My mind sped back to a clear blue morning several years ago—lying in Gavin's king-size bed, decadently wasting away the first half of a lazy Sunday. One where he miraculously didn't have to work and I had no plans but being with him.

He had rolled over and reached under the bed to pull out a

brown paper bag with *Sugar and Spice* imprinted in vibrant red. From the bag, he produced a sable artist's brush and a small paint can.

"What's that?" I had asked.

He had grinned wickedly in return. "Chocolate body paint."

With a swift twist of the lid, he popped the can open and dipped a finger into the liquid inside. He held the chocolate-coated finger out, waiting until I had closed my lips around him to add, "Guaranteed to melt in your hand."

Needless to say, we had been lucky to make it to work on time the next morning. And I bet his sheets still bore traces.

"Lydia?"

Gavin's voice jarred me back into the present. Into a new moment. A memory in the making.

He held a forkful of *Semifreddo* hovering in front of my mouth. Our eyes met and, as I leaned forward in slow motion, taking the frozen treat into my tongue, the tension built and crackled between us.

"You know," I breathed after swallowing the bite, "I'm not really hungry."

Not taking his eyes off mine, Gavin called out, "Check please."

Carlo appeared with the bill before I could even lick the little drop from the corner of my mouth. Clearly he had expected things to go this well.

We were out the door in a taxi to the hotel moments later.

Our mouths met before Carlo closed the door behind us. The taxi only took three minutes to get to the hotel, but already I was overheated and trying to get on Gavin's lap.

He threw a few *euro* at the driver—far more than a three-minute ride warranted—and climbed out the cab, pulling me out behind him. Hand-in-hand, like anxious school children, we dashed across the lobby to the elevator which, thankfully, was waiting on the ground floor.

"God, I've missed you," Gavin exclaimed as the doors slid shut and he pushed me against the back wall.

His mouth captured mine, his tongue sweeping across my lips before forging in to taste all of me. I couldn't get enough. I had to touch him everywhere. My hands grabbed at his shoulders. His back. His tight behind. Finally, needing more, I tugged his button-down out of his waistband and smoothed my hands over the rippling planes of his chest.

"I've missed this," I breathed when his mouth released mine to devour my jaw and neck and collarbone and ... oh my.

A faint ding registered in the back of my mind, but I was too swept up to even notice. It wasn't until I felt Gavin move away suddenly that I opened my eyes to find out why he left.

"I guess I know why you missed our moped tour," Elliot said, his voice cold as he held Gavin by the shirt collar.

Dropping his catch, Elliot turned abruptly and stalked down the hallway to our room.

"Elliot, wait!" I called after his swiftly retreating form. "Elliot!"

The door to our room slammed with a resounding thud.

Dubble Bubble Damn!

I looked from the empty hallway to Gavin, still panting from our heavy petting and obviously confused by what had just happened. Did I stay and satisfy some long-unaddressed urges with Gavin, or go to Elliot and do a lot of explaining?

That was the trouble with new beginnings; you had to make choices to get them started.

NINETEEN

DECIDING SIMPLER WAS BETTER, I dipped my key card in the reader and slipped into the room in order to offer my apology.

"I'm sorry."

Elliot was at the dresser, his back to me and the door, tossing clothes into the duffle bag on the bed. Every muscle in his back tensed up when I spoke. It was several long seconds before I saw him forcibly relax his shoulders.

"Hey, no reason to apologize," he said with a patently false casual tone. "It's not like we have something monogamous going here."

"Please," I wanted him to turn around, to look at me, "let me explain."

He turned his head, looking half over his shoulder but not really seeing me. "I think you already made everything perfectly clear. Message received. My job here is done."

"Job?" What was he talking about?

"You hired me to make the ex jealous, and clearly it

worked." With a handful of socks, he crossed to the duffle, threw them inside, and pulled the zipper shut in one swift movement. "I'll send you a bill when I get home."

He started for the door. Other than tossing my body down in his path, I didn't know how to stop him. So I started talking. Fast.

"You weren't hired to make him jealous, you were hired to keep him away. And I thought—I thought that was all over now." I was babbling, but I couldn't stop. "But I found out that what I thought I knew wasn't right at all and I was all wrong about him and his secretary—Rhonda. You know her."

When he tried to sidestep me, I leaped back and pressed myself up against the door, blocking the handle. Anything to keep him from walking away. Maybe for good.

"So I wanted to see what I was missing—if I had made the wrong decision two years ago because I don't want to spend the rest of my life wondering. It might not work out this time either but what if it did. I'm a different person now than I was then. Yes, I'm spending time with him, but I want to spend time with you too. I have fun with you—the kind of fun I didn't know I needed in my life until I met you, and I don't want to give you up for something that might or might not work out."

I saw a teeny bit of softening in his eyes. Hoping that my inane, rapid-fire explaining was getting through, I stepped forward and pressed my hands to his steel-tense chest.

"I know it's not fair to either of you but I—" This was low. I dropped my eyes. "—I can't choose. Not yet. Either way I would always wonder *what if.*"

Though wouldn't admit it on the record, I had watched a

few—okay *all*—of those shows where a bunch of singles vie for the eye of an eligible bachelor or bachelorette. And I, like the rest of the country, fell victim to the patriarchal view that the bachelors were sour balls, but the bachelorettes were sluts.

Now, finding myself in the position of choosing between two guys and wanting to explore relationships with both of them before having to make my decision, I suddenly sympathized with those women.

"Please, give us a chance," I pleaded. "Stay."

His eyelids fluttered down, shielding his readable blue eyes from view. I could feel him weighing my argument. Weighing his own feelings.

Then, eyes still closed, he lowered his forehead to rest against mine.

"I'll stay," he whispered, "because I'm not strong enough to leave."

His lips pressed softly against mine.

The duffel dropped to the floor with a soft thud.

"Besides," he said against my mouth, "I only packed half my things. I couldn't leave without the trench coat."

"You brought it?" I asked, giggling more in relief that he was staying.

"Of course," his hands dropped to squeeze my backside playfully. "What good is a fantasy if you don't bring the props?"

Noticing the time on the filigree clock on the dresser, I pulled out from his welcome arms and sought my pajamas. The red satin ones. Somehow candy hearts didn't belong in the fashion capitol of the world.

"Good, because it's supposed to rain tomorrow and I

wouldn't want you to get drenched on the moped. I am only attending the first two catwalk shows tomorrow and I expect a full tour to follow." I finally found the shiny red satin in the bottom drawer of the dresser. They slinked along the edge of the drawer as I pulled them out. "It wouldn't do to have my tour guide getting sick and bailing on me."

"No," Elliot's voice was low and slow, "it wouldn't do at all."

Turning, I knew that lustful smile was there before I saw his face. "You, mister, need to get into your jammies and into bed."

"Yes, ma'am," he replied, hurriedly tugging his sweater over his head and kicking his shoes off. "Been wearing my jammies all day just waiting for this occasion."

For several tortuous moments, as I watched him disrobing before my eyes, I thought he was serious. My gaze riveted to every movement of his tan, masculine hands. When he was down to his t-shirt and slacks he hesitated, his fingers gripping his waistband but not undoing the button.

My eyes, anxious and terrified at the same time, flew to his. Those bright blues laughed at my distress.

"Get changed, princess."

Elliot crossed in front of me, scooping his duffel off of the floor instead of stripping the rest of his clothes off—a prospect I was not opposed to on a purely aesthetic level, but if a girl is feeling out a relationship with two guys, It would be pretty sluttish to try either one out all the way.

"I-I'll just be," I stuttered as I backed into the bathroom, "in here. Getting ready. Um, changed. For bed."

My face flamed.

Safely in the bathroom, the door firmly and swiftly shut

behind me, I pressed my palms against the amber colored marble of the countertop. Only the last shreds of dignity saved me from stripping naked and lying on the equally-marble floor in a desperate attempt to cool off my burning body.

Really, a girl's body was not designed to turned on and off like hot and cold running water. Especially not twice in one night.

If it weren't already so late I might have been tempted to run an ice cold bath in the enormous garden tub and chill my libido into submission.

"I don't know how polygamists do it," I said to my flushed reflection. Only one night in the company of two guys and already I felt caught and tugged in two directions like the last roll of Smarties the day after Halloween.

Shaking the wayward thoughts out of my brain, I quickly stepped out of the ruffled tank and black cords I'd been wearing for thirty-six hours straight. After a momentary longing for a cold, refreshing shower, I resigned to a cool, damp washcloth and a quick sponge bath.

"Hurry u-up." Elliot's voice sing-songed beneath the white and gold door. "I've got the bed all warmed up."

If only closing my eyes would make this all go away, leaving the right decision sitting front and center in my mind. But closing my eyes only brought conflicting thoughts of Gavin's hot kisses and Elliot's hot body into a knockdown drag-out for my attention.

Well, at the very least I knew that no easy answers would be forthcoming. I had to make the best of the situation I had gotten myself into and not think about the—likely—naked man in my bed.

What I hadn't counted on was my nightly routine taking so

long that it bored him to sleep.

I emerged from the bathroom—admittedly nearly an hour later—to find him fully clothed in plaid cotton pjs and sleeping peacefully.

Pulling back the covers as quickly and gently as possible, I slipped between the sateen sheets and snuggled into the downy soft bed. The room had chilled, thanks to an open window and dropping temperatures outside, and I found the fluffy duvet inadequate against the cold air.

Soon I was shivering and my teeth chattered so loud I was surprised it didn't wake Elliot up. Then again, if the deep, even rhythm of his breathing were any indication, he was out like a light and wouldn't wake unless the sun was up or Vesuvius erupted again.

Forty-eight hours without sleep and six hours' worth of jetlag could do that to a person.

Casting caution aside in deference to a good eight hours of sleep, I took a deep breath and rolled to the other side of the bed. Just being millimeters from Elliot's radiating warmth, my chills vanished.

When, at somewhere around two a.m., he looped his arm around my waist and tugged me as close as I could get, my internal thermometer shot the opposite direction.

"*CARA MIA*, I am glad you came."

I turned in my seat at the sound of Alberto's voice. With his position at Gucci now filed under *former*, I was surprised to see him at their show.

"Alberto, what are you doing here?"

Before I could rise to give him a hug, he leaned across the row and gave me a quick kiss on either cheek.

"My parting was not so bad that I do not still have friends on the inside." With a wink, he took my hand and lifted me out of my fifth row seat. "Come," he insisted, "sit with me in the first row."

Apparently those were very good friends. While the fifth row seats Janice, Kelly, and I occupied were amongst the local media representatives, the first row was reserved for celebs and VIPs.

I hesitated, feeling guilty for leaving my fr— oh no, was I really going to call them that? Yes. My friends. It hardly seemed fair to leave them in the ranks of the unimportant.

But the instant I started to decline, my friends started shooing me from behind.

"You'll never get another chance like this," Kelly argued.

Janice concurred.

"All right," I acceded, allowing Alberto to lead me to a pair of vacant seats between a rising Hollywood starlet and a royal-by-marriage socialite.

"I understand congratulations are in order," Alberto said when we were comfortably seated. I must have looked confused, because he clarified, "For your knew promotion. It is wonderful that you will become a designer in your own right."

"Oh," I answered quietly.

With the uncanny insight he always had, Alberto saw right through me. "Ah, I see. You have not yet made your decision."

He signaled to the tuxedo-clad waiter attending to the front row, who immediately arrived with a tray of champagne. Alberto handed me a flute and took one for himself before shooing the waiter away.

"To your future, *cara*." He lifted his flute to mine and carefully clinked the crystal. "Whichever path you choose will be the right one for you."

I sipped at the bubbly, lost in thought over both decisions I had to make. At least it was only two decisions. Choosing between two great guys and making a monumental career decision was bad enough. If bad things always came in threes—not that I considered my options *bad*—then I could count myself lucky that another decision hadn't fallen into my lap.

Not yet, anyway.

♥

I EMERGED from the show an hour later, sequins in my eyes and shantung in my heart, full of inspiration and awe. All I could think of was locking myself away for a week and immortalizing all my ideas on paper.

"Your chariot awaits, milady."

Elliot sat on a cherry red moped, a helmet hanging jauntily from each end of the handlebar. In my euphoria I had totally forgotten our date. Again. My face must have dropped, momentary disappointment that my design time would be delayed, because he scowled.

"You aren't coming," he accused.

"No," I argued. His scowl deepened. "I mean yes. I mean I *am* coming. Of course I am."

"Oh. Good." He grabbed one helmet—the white one—and pushed it into my hands. "Then why the long face?"

Handing him my purse so I could buckle the helmet into place, I explained. "The show fed my inspiration and I wanted to get some sketches out of my system. But no big deal. They'll still be there later."

I hoped.

Inspiration had a way of dispersing with increased distance from source.

Oh well. If the ideas were any good I'd remember them. Right?

"Have you got your sketchpad?"

"Yes," I answered, throwing a leg over the moped and taking my place behind him. "Why?"

He pulled on his helmet and started the engine before turning to answer. "Because you've got sketching to do and I've got just the place to do it."

I thought I heard him say, "Hold on," before the moped burst to life and darted out into the narrow cobbled streets.

Elliot navigated the streets like a native, choosing to view the street signs and crosswalks as mere suggestions, rather than traffic law. He merely waved at the American tourists who shouted after us for darting in front of them as they jaywalked between intersections. I half expected him to start pointing out the sights to me in fluent Italian.

"That's the *Teatro alla Scala*," he shouted, indicating a yellow-fronted, Neoclassical building on the right. "Built in 1778 on the site of a Medieval church."

We zipped through the little *piazza* without hesitation, slowing when we merged onto a slightly smaller street.

"This over here," Elliot pointed to the left, "is the *Galleria Vittorio Emanuele II*. One of the first iron and glass constructions in Italy."

I peered down the narrow alleyway, covered from above by a long glass roof. Where that alleyway crossed another at the center of the block, a huge glass dome rose above the intersection. All the little shops buzzed with shoppers despite the light drizzle beginning to fall.

How wonderful. Shoppers could feel like they were shopping outdoors without falling prey to the elements.

"How do you know all this?" I yelled in Elliot's ear, not sure if he could even hear me through the helmet.

He turned his head so I could see his profile and smiled. "I did my homework." Taking his eyes off the road for just a second, he threw me a teasing glance. "Surprised?"

"No," I answered quickly. I had learned early not to be surprised by anything to do with Elliot Phelps. Phelps Elliot. Whoever this enigmatic man was.

"Impressed?"

"Definitely."

With a self-satisfied smile he turned his attention back to the road. "Just wait."

I was about to voice my confusion when the buildings on our left disappeared and the moped pulled to a stop in the center of a clearing.

"*Il dio mia*," I breathed.

"Precisely the point."

I was struck speechless by the towering façade of a massive church. A cathedral, certainly. Shaped like a child might form a gingerbread house. Eight, no, ten Gothic spires topped the ornate limestone, reaching Heavenward.

Dozens of tourists milled around the *piazza* in front of the main entrance, staring, pointing, and taking pictures.

"*Duomo*. Third largest church in the world," Elliot explained. "The lower levels are Baroque, but the rest is Neo-

Gothic. Though construction began in the fourteenth Century, it wasn't finished until Napoleon had the—"

"Can we go in?" I finally managed.

Though I was impressed with Elliot's knowledge, and thankful that he had brought me here, I needed to get inside. To see this beautiful building from the inside out.

He laughed at my desperation. "Of course."

My eyes couldn't leave the façade as Elliot pulled the moped to a designated parking area beside the church. Seconds later we were walking—okay, I was practically running and Elliot had to jog to keep up—through the main entrance.

I fished a ten-euro bill out of my purse and pushed it into the donation box discreetly located as we crossed into the nave.

"This is," I sighed, trying to capture the feeling of the dozens of stained glass windows illuminating the *terrazzo* floor like the light of God, "breathtaking."

"How's your inspiration now?" Elliot asked.

Tearing my gaze from the fine beauty of the church, I met his sincere eyes. "Magnified." I smiled and threw my arms around his neck. "A thousand-fold."

"Well get to sketching, already," he joked, even as his arms slipped around my waist in a friendly hug. "We have about fifty more stops on our tour."

If I wasn't starting to know him so well, I would have thought he was joking. But I had a feeling fifty stops was his bare minimum.

"Yes sir." I saluted him playfully before heading for an unoccupied pew and pulling out my sketch pad.

Rather than explore the rest of the church, as I thought he

would want to do, Elliot slid into the pew in front of me and took up people watching. He seemed content to relax and absorb the energy around him.

As my pencil moved across paper, I managed only a few sketches for jewelry pieces before I found myself sketching the work of art in front of me.

Master sculptors and artisans had nothing on the fine eye of Mother Nature. Any woman would rush to buy a t-shirt with Elliot's beautiful mug on the front. Before I knew it, I had a dozen sketches of every detail of his face.

A girl had to take inspiration where she could.

"DO YOU KNOW," Gavin mused across the dinner table Friday night, "I haven't seen you eat a single piece of candy this entire trip."

I gulped down the last of my minestrone before answering. "I'm—" Dabbing at the corners of my mouth with my napkin bought me a few seconds. "—trying to quit."

I expected shock or teasing or even superioristic advice, but Gavin simply smiled and said, "Good for you."

Like nothing else, that hit the problem home for me.

And it was true, I was *trying* to quit. The gummy bear incident had solidified for me what my mother had been trying to tell me for years. I placed too much emotional value on sweets. Either I needed to find a better outlet or a better dentist.

Actually, my teeth were in perfect condition, but any crutch in a storm was a problem if you brought it out in every slight breeze.

So, I had carefully packed my suitcase candy-free. Even with the dish of Mike&Ikes on the foyer table calling to me as I walked out the door.

Not that I had been entirely on the candy wagon.

I couldn't come to Milan without sampling the *marron glaces* from some quaint, Old World shop on a quaint, Old World street. Giving up my obsession didn't mean giving up on every ounce of edible delight in my life.

Still, my sugar consumption was at an all-time low, and I was—surprisingly—invigorated. I had energy to spare and, with all the fashion shows, must-see sights, and competing dates, plenty to spend it on.

"What is the plan for your birthday?" Gavin asked.

He couched the question with enough nonchalance to fool someone who hadn't known him half his adult life. Me, I saw right through.

I knew my birthday would be difficult to coordinate. Both Gavin and Elliot wanted to claim the day for their own—though I had to contend that it should really be for me, but that seemed a secondary concern.

"Well," I hummed, eying the dessert cart only a few feet away like a junkie with an eye on her next fix, "I've been thinking about that. After a lot of thought, I came up with a schedule that I think will make everyone happy."

Or at least as happy as they can be.

Gavin inclined his head, indicating he was listening.

"Ferrero's show will be the dividing line." Before Gavin could voice the confusion clear in his warm brown eyes, I explained, "Their catwalk show, which I have been waiting for all week, runs from four until five. I will spend the day with one of you from first thing in the morning until four and with the other from five until the night is over."

I consciously avoided saying "until bed," trying to keep any wayward thoughts from surfacing.

"Who gets which half?" Gavin asked, ever the pragmatist.

"That's the best part." For me, anyway. "You two get to choose."

If I made that choice, no matter which way I chose, feelings would be hurt, egos bruised, and assumptions made. Whoever got the morning would say that the night was the more significant part of the day. Whoever got the night would say that the morning was longer.

Much better they figure out a way to assign the schedule themselves.

"Don't you care?"

"Gavin," I said meeting his injured gaze earnestly, "I want to share my birthday with you both. And, since I don't think you'd like to celebrate the whole day as a threesome, I will take what time I can with each of you."

He looked ready to protest, to pout even.

"Now let's get out of here before that *panettone* jumps of that tray and sashays its way onto my plate."

Back at the hotel, Gavin and I parted in the lobby. I went upstairs and sent Elliot down so the pair could work out the schedule for tomorrow. Anxious and excited to celebrate my birthday in Italy—thirty-fourth or not—I hurried to get ready for bed and slipped between the sheets.

I wanted to be asleep before Elliot returned for two reasons. First, I wanted the identity of my morning date to remain a secret until I opened the door. And second, I had a feeling my morning would be starting mighty early.

Whoever got the first shift would want to maximize his time. After all, the night shift had no ending deadline.

Finally sinking into slumber nearly an hour later—and still alone in the room—I dreamt of all the once-in-a-lifetime things I wanted to do on my birthday.

TWENTY

"HAPPY BIRTHDAY, BEAUTIFUL."

Gavin stood in the hallway, a fragrant bouquet of pure white roses in his hand and a beaming grin on his face.

"Thank you," I said, taking the flowers and inhaling their heavy scent. "They're gorgeous. But where will I—"

"Already taken care of." From behind his back, Gavin produced a gilded vase covered in floating cherubs and swirling ivy. "This hotel has everything."

Stepping past me, Gavin set the vase on the dresser and took the bouquet from me to set the flowers in a simple arrangement that coordinated perfectly with the room. If luxury was in the details, *Hotel della Regina* defined the term.

I took one last moment while Gavin's attention was on the flowers to check my appearance. For this very special day, one that would run nonstop from a morning outdoors to a fashion show to a night out, I had selected a very special outfit.

A strapless, A-line dress in a dreamy shade of cream that made my fair complexion look like fine porcelain, decorated at the hem and neckline by black embroidered flowers, and pulled together by a narrow black belt. Add a black cashmere cardigan to ward off the chill, a pair of black peep-toe heels, and a boxy tote that held a pair of black ballet flats for emergency foot relief, and I felt like Audrey Hepburn in *Roman Holiday*.

"Ready for your big day, Cinderella?" Gavin asked as he moved to stand behind me at the mirror.

I tucked one wayward strand of light brown hair back into the neat ponytail sitting low against my neck. "Absolutely," I said, turning. "You ready, Prince Charming?"

Gavin offered his arm and I slipped my fingers into the crook of his elbow. Our eyes met, and I caught a glimpse of intense emotion.

His voice low and intent, he answered, "For anything."

Oh my. And the day hadn't even begun yet.

My legs threatened to go wobbly and send me to the ground—or into Gavin's arms, which might have been their motivation—but I remained on my feet and reasonably stable. Still in my heels, even.

Gavin stood and pulled his jacket off the chair back with a flourish and signaled the waiter for the bill. When we were out of the café, walking down the street with his arm wrapped securely around my waist, he asked, "What's next on the list?"

As if on cue, a bell tower pealed out three loud gongs followed by two smaller chimes. Three thirty.

"Actually," I sighed, though I wasn't sure if I was reluctant or not, "it's time for me to head to the runway."

"Oh."

Without further comment, Gavin hailed a taxi and asked him to take us to the Fiera Pavilion. As the tiny car wove through heavy, Saturday afternoon traffic, we remained silent.

My thoughts swirled around my feelings for Gavin. How was I ever going to survive backstage at Ferrero's show?

"You know," he finally said as we neared our destination, "we could just pick up where we're leaving off after the show."

He said it softly. Quietly. And I knew what he asked.

He was asking me to make my decision now. To choose him over Elliot and spend the rest of the day and night with him.

If I were certain of my feelings, I might have done just that. But deep inside I knew I wasn't ready. To protect my heart, and his as well, I had to say no. Even when a part of me deep down inside wanted desperately to say yes.

"I—"

Gavin waved off my explanation. "That was unfair of me to ask."

The taxi screeched to a halt and Gavin leaped out of the car to open my door. He asked the cab to wait, promising a bigger tip.

"Listen," he said, taking my hands in his, "I know this is a difficult decision for you to make, and I am willing to wait. For a while. But I'm not Job, Lydia. I can't wait forever."

He pressed a soft kiss to my lips, and I pressed back. A warm feeling started at the contact, flowing gradually down my spine and out my limbs to the tips of my fingers and toes. A feeling like coming home.

But was that feeling strong enough on which to wager an entire lifetime?

As Gavin ducked back into the cab and sped away, I knew that was only half the question I needed to ask. And answers were a long time coming.

"CARO," Ferrero's voice cried across the zoo of people bustling around the backstage area, "you have arrived. And just in time. Come. Help me pull delight from disaster."

Models taller than basketball players were everywhere. Several sat in front of a long bank of vanity mirrors, mindlessly enduring the ministrations of the makeup artists. A cluster stood near the pair of garment racks that held the remainder of the collection, chain smoking and speaking in some obscure eastern European language. Another bunch paraded around Ferrero as he fussed over this detail and that.

He looked calm and pulled together on the surface. But his accent, which had grown more heavily Italian with each day of the trip, wavered and died by the end of his speech. This, I knew, was a sign of a frazzled Ferrero.

Tucking my purse into a cubby with several others, I asked, "What can I do?"

"Oh!" he cried as he saw the models smoking near the racks. "Someone get those cigarettes away from the clothes. Sequins are extremely flammable. You there! Smoke somewhere else!"

At his shouting, the offending models looked at him without moving a muscle, dismissed him, and returned to their conversation.

"Oh my," Ferrero breathed, fanning himself with his hands. "I can see it now; the whole collection up in smoke. All because that anorexic Slav, Nadika, has to have her way wi—"

"I'll take care of it," I soothed. A distracted designer was not a great asset at a fashion show. "You finish with the inspections."

He smiled in gratitude before turning back to the impatient Pixy Sticks awaiting his approval, muttering something about lung cancer and karma.

"Nadika?" I approached the models, careful to sound deferential to their exalted status.

In return, I got a scathing glare. At least I had their attention. Maybe a little white chocolate lie was better than an all-out confrontation.

"I'm very sorry to disturb you," I mewed, choking on every honeyed word, "but the stage manager said there was a call for you from—" I raced through a series of high fashion locales before taking a guess on something that might hit closer to home. "—Budapest."

For a moment she, the tallest one with a white platinum bob and ice blue eyes, just looked at me. Weighing my worthiness, I imagined.

Then, in a sudden and startling transformation that sent me back a step, her face softened. She smiled, and sighed, "Gregor."

Without another word she took off in the direction I had vaguely waved to as the location of the phone, running across the concrete floor in four-inch stilettos, the pale blue ruffle of her cocktail dress fluttering behind her.

With the queen bee gone the other models dispersed, stomping out their cigarettes and returning to their assigned stations.

Satisfied, I returned to Ferrero's side.

"Everyone," he called, "everyone please gather around."

Most of the bodies in the backstage area, with the exception of the stage managers—stern-looking women dressed all in black and shouting into headsets—moved into a close circle around Ferrero.

"Before the show begins, I want to thank everyone involved. This is the best collection yet, and it would not be possible without the help of each of you."

Everyone applauded, including Ferrero, who inclined his head at the group as a whole.

He raised a hand to quiet them. "The time approaches. Let the madness begin. And I expect to see every last one of you at the after party tonight."

A huge cheer erupted. The crowd dispersed to their pre-show positions, leaving me alone with Ferrero.

"Thank you, Lydia," he said, his voice heavy with sincerely and without a hint of accent. "For being my inspiration and my sanity."

He waved me off when I started to protest. "Are you ready to experience the reason I became a fashion designer?" When I nodded, he smiled like a guilty little boy. "Brace yourself for the adrenaline rush of a lifetime."

On cue, the stage manager's voice announced over the speaker system, "Places please."

Models lined up on the steel stairway leading to the catwalk. Makeup artists, makeup kits in hand, walked the line of models, touching up porcelain pale skin and cherry red lips. Ferrero moved to the curtained doorway that marked the last step before models emerged on stage.

From beyond the curtain, the announcer's voice welcomed the guests attending the show and gave a brief history of the fashion house. The music started. The stage manager counted down, slapping her hand against her thigh in time to the beat.

"... three ... two ... one ... go!"

The first model stepped through the curtain. Ferrero fussed with the collar on the second.

"Go," the stage manager ordered.

The second model went.

Ferrero aligned the hem on the third.

"Go."

The third model went.

The first model emerged seconds later on the opposite side of the stage, climbing down the steps and heading to the garment racks for her wardrobe change.

Without pause, this procession continued. Ferrero perfected the clothes on one model, she walked the catwalk, she changed her outfit, she lined up to do it all over again.

My head spun.

In all the years I'd worked with him, I had counted Ferrero as a bit of a flake. A gifted and talented designer, without question, but I doubted his reliability. Watching him work every model, assuring perfection time after time for the hour-long duration of the show, erased my doubts.

By the time the stunning shantung and organza wedding gown closed out the show and Ferrero took his walk with the models smiling and the crowd cheering, I was in awe. My mind began imagining what it would be like to have a show of my own. To go through that kind of insanity with my own line of jewelry. Sure, jewelry shows were not nearly as big and overwhelming, but any show would come with a certain amount of pressure and excitement.

The trouble was... I didn't know if I wanted that or not.

Why did it seem like the decisions I had to make got harder every day?

MY HEART WAS STILL RACING with the thrill of the show when I walked out front to meet Elliot. After standing for over an hour in my heels I had changed into the flats, both to save my aching feet and in anticipation of tooting around Milan on a moped again.

But when I got to the sidewalk, all I saw was a row of cars waiting to rush the fashion show guests to their next event. A parade of black sedans led by a white Ferrari. Celebrities. They loved to drive those flashy cars.

When the door to the Ferrari opened, I turned back to the entrance to see which celeb the car belonged to.

"Lydia."

Spinning to the sound of my name, I found Elliot standing next to the white Ferrari, an unsuppressed grin on his face and an ivory orchid corsage in his hand.

He was dressed for an evening of elegance. The black tuxedo—one of Ferrero's own, if I had to guess—fit his frame perfectly. Not a single pucker or stretch. Like it had been tailored to him.

By a tailor with an appreciation of the male body.

"What the—"

"Like it?" he asked as he moved around the car, dragging his fingertips across the gleaming hood, and chivalrously opened the passenger door for me.

"It's, um, wow." And I wasn't just talking about the car.

"Yeah," he agreed as he lowered me into the soft leather seat, "that's kinda how I felt, too."

He knelt on the sidewalk, the knee of his two-grand tux scraping against the concrete, took my right hand in his, and slipped the corsage onto my wrist. The ivory flower matched my dress perfectly.

"Wha—whe—we—wo—" I struggled to find an actual word from my vocabulary, finally coming up with, "Why?"

"Why?" he repeated, rising and not bothering to dust off his knee. "Because it's your birthday. Because I wanted our last night in Italy to be special. Because *you're* special."

I sighed as he shut the door. I didn't think my poor heart could take any more unexpected tugs without giving up on me completely. But, as Elliot slid into the driver's seat and at least a few hundred horses purred to life, I had a feeling I was in for a few more.

"I hope you don't mind," he explained as he navigated the narrow streets, turning at a sign for the A9 motorway, "but I thought we might get out of the city for a while."

He would turn the car around if I wished. Thankfully, I didn't wish. "Sounds great. Where are we going?"

"That," he said, grinning enigmatically, "is a surprise."

If there was one thing I had learned to count on with Elliot, it was surprise.

Sinking back into the plush seat, I watched out the window as city faded into countryside. The flat expanse of Milan gave way to lush green hills. In the distance I could make out the snow-capped peaks of the Italian Alps in the moonlight.

"How has your birthday been so far?"

"Wonderful," I sighed. Then, when I feared he might think I was speaking *only* of my time with Gavin, I hastily added, "Especially the fashion show. I don't know if I could go through that on my own."

"Are you thinking of going it alone?" He asked, apparently picking up on the undertones.

"Not exactly," I explained. "Franco has offered me the chance to design under the umbrella of his name."

"You would give him credit for your designs?"

"No, it would be *Ferrero by Lydia Vanderwalk*." I traced my fingers over the stitching in the leather seat. "Or *Lydia Vanderwalk for Ferrero*."

I looked at Elliot, gauging his reaction. His eyes never left the road, but he squinted like he was concentrating on bending a spoon or something.

"Sounds like a crappy deal to me." He glanced at me, his eyes full of sympathetic concern. "Seems like Ferrero gets all your talent and you get nothing."

"I get security. I get the use of his name. A lot of designers start out within an established house. It gives them instant name recognition." At least until their own name becomes recognizable on its own. "Alleviates some of the risk."

"Why would you want that?"

"What? Reduce the risk?" I asked.

"Risk is what makes life worth living."

Elliot pulled the car to a stop. I looked out the window, pondering his philosophy on risk, to find we had arrived in a small, Medieval village. The buildings, weathered limestone with red tile roofs, stacked around us like children's blocks.

When Elliot opened his door, a rush of cold wind chilled the inside of the car and goosebumps popped up all over my body. I tightened my cardigan around me, struggling to keep my teeth from chattering as he opened my door and I climbed out.

"Welcome," he pushed my door shut and clicked the locks with the remote, "to Bellagio."

"Bellagio? You mean it's a real place. I thought they made that up for Vegas."

"Nope, it's real. And you're in it." He wrapped an arm around my shoulder and I sank into his body heat. "This way, Madame."

I let Elliot lead the way across the narrow, cobblestone street and through the pair of doors beneath a sign proclaiming, *Trattoria del Lago*. The host, a friendly man with a knowing smile, led us down a hall hung with elegant landscapes depicting a beautiful lake surrounded by tree-covered hills.

"How did you find this place?" I asked.

"The concierge at the *Regina* was happy to assist." He leaned close as we emerged in a large room full of guests dining at cozy tables. "Especially when I told him a birthday was involved."

"Oh Elliot," I exclaimed. "It's breathtaking."

The entire far wall of the room consisted of floor-to-ceiling windows overlooking the lake depicted in the landscapes. A gorgeous view from every corner of the room, but the host led us to the central window. The best in the house.

"Just wait until you see what I have planned for dessert."

Sweet Saltwater Taffy. I didn't think things could get better than this.

It was nearly seven when we finished the last bite of *tiramisu*. Though I didn't think food was the dessert Elliot had in mind, I was pretty sure a person couldn't leave Italy without having native *tiramisu* at least once.

"Are you ready?" Elliot asked as he held up my cardigan.

"That depends. Does it involve more food?"

"Definitely not."

I shrugged into the sweater and buttoned up for the chill

night outside. Prepared to return to the car, Elliot surprised me by heading the opposite direction. Toward the lake.

"This," he stated as we descended a length of uneven steps, "is my birthday present to you."

A man bundled up in layers of warm clothes met us at the base of the steps and led us along the lakeside walkway to a small boat dock. He climbed aboard a small tour boat, complete with several rows of seats and a small captain's cabin. Turning, he indicated we should follow him on board.

"Oh no," I argued, already imagining the frigid temperatures that must sweep across the lake itself and shivering harder at the thought. "I'm not going on that. I'll freeze."

"*No. No frio, signorina.* " The little man ducked into the cabin and returned with an armful of blankets. He handed them to Elliot and waved me onto the boat.

"Here, here," he said in nearly indecipherably-accented English, heading to the front of the boat and pointing to a bench seat situated against the front wall of the cabin.

Elliot climbed on board behind me and urged me forward, not letting up until I lowered onto the bench. He set the blankets down next to me and thanked the captain.

"*Grazie.*"

"Sit. See." The captain pointed at Elliot and then the bench. And then waved his hand in a sweep of the lake. He grinned as Elliot moved the pile of blankets and sat by my side. "*Amore.* "

Then the captain disappeared, leaving us alone on a bench on a freezing lake on a freezing night. I was about to complain, but when Elliot hooked one arm around my shoulders and began wrapping us in woolen blankets my body and my heart warmed. I could definitely see the possibilities in this adventure.

"We go." The captain's voice crackled over a tiny speaker above our heads, followed by the romantic strains of a Verdi composition.

"That's your problem," Elliot said as he tucked the last blanket behind my hip, "you need more risk in your life. You're a Marilyn trying to be a Norma Jean."

"What? What does that mean, I'm a Marilyn?"

"You think you're this nice, reserved, *tame* woman who dresses safe, takes the safe job, and keeps her heart safe and locked away. But you're not. You're a firecracker, Lydia Vanderwalk." He leaned in close and whispered in my ear, "You're an Atomic Fireball trying to be a Tic Tac. You just don't know it yet."

It might have been the night air or the brush of his breath against the ear, but when my entire body erupted in shivers I had a feeling it had everything to do with the challenge of his words.

TWENTY-ONE

ELLIOT WHISKED us back to Milan and the hotel in no time—the guy sure got used to driving a quarter million dollars worth of speed in a hurry. As we changed for Ferrero's after party, I considered what he had said about me.

Was I really waiting to explode just beneath the surface? Or was I really just a plain and dull as I always imagined myself to be?

"Did you bring that slinky dress?"

"What dress?" I asked, turning away from my selection of clothes long enough to wonder what he meant.

"The one you wore at that first party. Gray. Shiny." He cocked his eyebrows for emphasis. "Slinky."

Oh, that dress. "Yes I brought it. Why?"

His eyebrows dropped, hooding his lids in a seductive, bedroom-come-hither look. "Wear that."

My cheeks burned and I felt a rush of tingling heat shoot through every vein and nerve in my body. I had thought it too cold to wear such a revealing dress, but I was overheating now.

One look and I was a puddle.

"Oh," I said, breathless, "okay. Good, um, choice."

I swallowed hard, forcing myself to look away. To search through my belongings to find the one dress I now *had* to wear. The thought of wearing anything else evaporated along with my willpower, inhibitions, and capacity for rational thought. It was bad enough he already looked delicious, now I had developed a gnawing hunger.

Finding the dress hanging neatly and unwrinkled in the armoire, I slipped it off the hanger and darted into the bathroom to change.

Dubble Bubble Damn, I forgot to grab the nude, seamless panties I needed to wear underneath. All others either showed in bulges beneath the clinging jersey or cut my flesh into hills and valleys. Neither resulted in a streamlined sexy look.

Thumbs hooked through the waistband, I shimmied out of the black lace bikini I had been wearing with the intention of grabbing the right pair and slipping them on before we left.

When I emerged from the bathroom, slinky dress donned and smoky makeup applied, I found Elliot leaning against the door in a casual-but-ready-to-go pose.

He still wore the tailored black tux, but had replaced the stark white shirt with an unstructured one in a light blue that accentuated his eyes. The first two buttons were undone, displaying a delightful triangle of smooth, tanned skin. His hair was still a windblown mess from the stretch of driving with the windows down, but the disheveled look worked oh-so-well on him.

"Hey hot stuff," he greeted. "Ready to go?"

I could barely breathe. "Yes, just let me grab my clutch."

As I transferred a few essentials from my day bag to my chic black sequined clutch, I knew I was forgetting something.

And it felt important.

"Come on. We don't want to miss all the good champagne."

Oh well. If it was *really* important, I would have remembered.

"I'm ready."

Arm in arm we left, heading for the *Corona Reale* ballroom on the mezzanine level.

It wasn't until the doors closed on the elevator that I remembered what I had forgotten.

💜

"NO, I DON'T RUN MUCH," I heard myself telling an up-and-coming Italian designer who seemed to be trying every possible bad pick up line ever written.

"Well you've been running through my mind all day."

I sighed, which he took as a sign of relent, and glanced around the room for a friendly face.

"Was your father a thief?"

"No," I answered. Momentarily excited to find a flash of platinum blonde until I found it was only that blue-eyed model, Nadika. "He was in advertising."

"Because he stole the stars and put them in your eyes."

Not yet pushed to the edge of being entirely rude, I tried diverting the conversation. "I design jewelry."

"I design ladies undergarments." He moved in closer and whispered in my ear, "Want to see."

I gasped, even as all the blood in my body rushed to my

face. My hand instinctively pulled back to slap him indignantly across the face. "No, I—"

"There you are, angel."

Gavin took my hand and pressed a soft kiss to the warm center of the palm. I positively melted into his side when he swung an arm around my shoulders in a possessive, this-girl-is-mine gesture.

My sleazy, would-be seducer took the hint and slunk away.

My grin couldn't have been brighter.

"Thank you," I offered as soon as he was out of hearing. "I never knew Italians were so fluent in bad pickup lines."

"Your salvation is my greatest pleasure."

Gavin bowed chivalrously, looking quite pleasurable himself in a scrumptious suit just a little lighter in color than my dress with a slight green tint that made his eyes glow. Blonde hair neatly combed and not a lock out of place. Cheeks flushed with little boy excitement. He looked just like his *GQ* cover shot.

"What all goes on at these fashionable after parties?" he asked.

"Well..." I glanced around the room, at a sea of the fashionable and fawning. "Some mingling. Some networking—like over there," I indicated a pair in deep discussion in the near corner, "they might be closing a deal on a big order."

"Or they might be arranging the time and place for their romantic rendezvous."

"Or that," I laughed. "If you hadn't interrupted, I might be doing that myself right now."

We exchanged meaningful looks. I exploded in laughter. Different from the kind I had with Elliot—those laughs usually bubbled out of me despite my best efforts to keep them in. This was a mutual laugh.

"And what about that?" Gavin asked, motioning to the center of the room. "What's going on there?"

"That," I whispered, leaning in conspiratorially, "is the most important aspect of a party like this."

A circle of guests surrounded Ferrero, each vying to congratulate him on the successful show. Ferrero stood in the middle, pretending to be humble and waving off their compliments. But even those untrained in the art of social modesty could see he was enjoying every second of it.

I looked away, unable to stare into the light too long without risking blindness. "The fawning."

"Aaah..." Gavin nodded in understanding. "In business we call it brown-nosing."

"Hey you two!" Janice's voice called to us like the whine of an airplane. Or a Long Islander reverting to her native, nasal accent. "Hi there lovebirds!"

She appeared in front of us, platinum tresses loose and flowing to her waist. Dressed in muted gold palazzo pants and a matching cowl-neck sweater, she looked more elegant than I had ever seen her. If not for the unfocused glint in her eyes. The unsteady sway in her walk. The half-empty tumbler in her left hand.

After the week-and-a-half she'd had, I guessed she was due a little alcoholic respite.

"Is the wedding back on yet?" she asked.

My jaw clenched and I positively felt Gavin scowl. I knew that Gavin-and-me-and-Elliot was a prime topic of conversation between Janice and Kelly, but that didn't mean she had to bring it out in public. Drunk or not.

"Hello, Janice." I spoke a little louder than normal, making sure my voice penetrated. Hoping to successfully change the subject. "Isn't this fun?"

She beamed like a little girl, eyes closed and chin thrust forward. "It's wonderful." *Hic.* "Ferrero deserves such a celebration for his homecoming."

"His homecoming?" Gavin asked.

I rolled my eyes. Not once had I heard Ferrero himself say that he was Italian-born—probably because it wasn't true—but nearly everyone involved in fashion week believed him a native. I could pretty much handle the world at large thinking that, but Janice must have known the truth.

A woman couldn't work with him for nearly twenty years and not realize the accent faded in and out. That he ate more Coney dogs than *cannoli.*

"Don't you know?" Janice jabbed an accusatory finger at his chest, missing by several inches. "Ferrero is from Milan. Originally."

"Oh," Gavin acknowledged, "I didn't know that."

"Yep. Well, from a little village just to the north. He moved to New York in his twenties to pursue his passion, but at heart he's always an Italian."

Some of her words slurred together and while she spoke she turned her head to make goo-goo eyes at the subject of her little fantasy. Not only was this not healthy, it was darn annoying.

"No, he's not," I interjected.

Both pairs of eyes turned on me.

"What do you mean?" Janice stepped closer.

There was a tremor of threat in her voice. She dared me to explain. To finish my thought.

"You know that Ferrero isn't from Italy," I said quietly.

Janice blinked several times, as if that speeded up her comprehension. "Of course he is," she argued. "He's from Milan."

"No," I said a little louder, "he's not."

She looked blank. Then started laughing. "You are such a kidder," she wailed. She turned to Gavin, "Always joking, this one."

I didn't know what was more appalling: her misconception about my personality or her drunken dogmatic insistence that Ferrero was Italian. "He is not Italian."

"Yes, he is."

"No, he isn't."

"Yes, he is."

"No, he—"

"Yes!" she shouted, sloshing her drink onto the carpet with a grand gesture. "He's from Milan!"

"No he's not!" I shouted back.

She shoved her glassed at Gavin and, as he caught it before it fell, stuck her fingers in her ears and starting humming. "La la la. I can't hear you."

My frustration and determination met in a combustible mixture. "Franco Ferrero is not Italian! He's from South Jersey!"

Oh no. That had been louder than I'd intended.

An instant hush fell across the crowded ballroom. All eyes were on me. A quiet wave of whispered gossip began near me and spread from guest to guest in a building wave. I watched, helpless, as the wave circled and neared the center of the room.

My eyes locked on Ferrero, I saw the brief moment of disappointment in his face as he heard the news.

The center of sudden and unwanted attention, Ferrero did the only thing he could in a situation like that. He laughed. He laughed, and the laughter spread. Following the same path of the gossip wave, the laughter swept the room and finally reached me.

I, too, laughed, knowing it was the only way to save face. Both mine and Ferrero's.

Before his attention returned to the nearest fawning fan, I caught a trace of pain in his eyes.

The look in Janice's eyes was closer to fury. She looked ready to scalp me. Maybe if Kelly had been close by she could have used those acrylic nails to do the job.

I expected her to scream, maybe yell, definitely launch herself at me with claws flying. Instead, she turned her back on me and walked away. As if I was so beneath her notice that she didn't even bother telling me off. Like an M&M Mini squashed to the bottom of your shoe; not the most pleasant thing on the planet, but definitely not worth the hassle of taking off your shoe and cleaning it.

Gavin, still at my side, looked confused. "What just happened?"

"Can we get out of here?" I needed to be far, far away.

"Sure," he agreed immediately. "But will you tell me what's going on?"

I let him take me by the elbow and lead me through the crowd. "I just ruined a career."

Breaking into the less populated hallway and making for the stairwell, Gavin asked, "Whose?"

Sighing, I click-clacked down the stairs in my heels.

"Everyone's."

♥

"YOU'RE DRUNK," Gavin declared.

Lifting my head off the table in the hotel bar, I winced as the walnut and gold interior swirled unsteadily before my eyes.

"Yup." Letting my head drop back onto the table, I smiled as the images in my brain stopped moved. "Def'nily dunk."

"Come on." He took my arm, pulling me to my feet despite my protest. "You need to get to bed."

No, I needed to go back in time and undo, oh, the last six weeks. From the moment I invented the non-existent boyfriend and until I opened my big mouth about Ferrero's nation of origin.

"Hey, how'd we get on th'elevator?"

Come to think of it, how'd I end up cradled in Gavin's arms? That's what I got for drowning my sorrows in sweet-tasting brandy. *Stick to vodka, Lyd. At least you feel it going down.*

"Your room or mine?" Gavin asked.

As he strode into the hallway, carrying me like a baby, my stomach turned. "Ungh. Mine. Def'nily mine."

The porcelain was calling me. And I was listening.

"Fine," he grunted and dropped me unceremoniously on my feet.

"Wha? Why'd you do that?"

"Go on to your boy toy. I'm not carrying you into his arms."

"Boy t—" Did he mean Elliot? "Elliot's not my— He's— Nothing's happened between us."

"Sure." The venom in his voice penetrated my brandy fog. "Men and women share beds all the time purely platonic-y."

Platonic-y?

"You're drunk, too."

"Maybe, but I'm thinking clearer and clearer." By now he was practically shouting. "If you want to climb into bed for some nookie then you have to choose. His bed or mine."

I didn't understand. All I wanted was to get into the bathroom and hug the toilet. And maybe bed. Much, much later. If I didn't wind up on the marble bathroom floor.

I glanced longingly at my room door. "Gavin, I just—"

"Fine." He turned and marched towards the stairs. "I'm going back to the bar."

"Wait." The stairwell door clicked shut. "We're on the eleventh floor," I finished lamely.

My stomach lurched. Fishing the room key out of my clutch—miraculously still hanging from my wrist—I dipped it in and out of the card reader and ducked into the room.

"Welcome back," Elliot called out as the door closed behind me. "Where've you been?"

A quick search found him digging through his duffle bag.

"Are you leaving?" I asked.

"Nope. Ah, here they are." He pulled a small box out of the bag. "Just finding my business cards. Met an editor of Italian GQ who wants me to do a spread devoted to male muses."

I dropped my clutch on the floor. Everything that had happened that night built up right behind my eyes and suddenly it all poured out. Tears burst out.

"Honey," Elliot dropped the box and appeared at my side. "Honey, what's wrong?"

Looking into his concerned blue eyes my despair doubled. "Everything!" I wailed.

Taking me in his arms, he rubbed soothing circles on my back and whispered calming words in my ear. "It's okay. Everything will be fine. Tell me about it."

In garbled and sob-wracked words I explained all about the party and getting drunk and the argument with Gavin and my confusion about just about everything in my life.

"You're fine," he assured me. "What you need is sleep and plenty of it. Let's get you into bed."

He swung me up in his muscular arms with little effort and carried me to the bed. Securing me with one arm, he grabbed the covers and flung them across the bed. As he lowered me to the sateen sheets, I clung to his neck.

When he chuckled and tried to unwrap my arms, I pleaded.

"Stay."

He froze.

For about ten seconds he stood motionless.

His answer was unequivocal. "No."

"Please," I begged.

Releasing him, I ran one palm over his chest. His pecs tensed beneath my touch. I needed to touch him, to feel him all over. I needed to be close to someone. To him. To forget all about my horrible night.

"Please stay." I cupped his jaw in my hand and lifted my mouth, seeking his.

"No." He pulled back, leaving me reaching for air.

"Stay," I persisted, smoothing my hands over my body and wishing they were his hands exploring me. "I want you. I need you. Make love to me."

"You're drunk and you're upset." He grabbed the box off

the floor and headed for the door. "You don't know what you want."

As my hand skimmed my hip, a memory surfaced.

"I'm not wearing any underwear."

He stopped, hand on the doorknob, back to the room.

"Goodnight, Lydia."

Angry and frustrated, and hurt by his rejection, I shouted out the one thing guaranteed to earn me a reaction. "I'll pay you extra."

"What did you say?" He still didn't turn around, but I could hear the dangerous warning in his voice.

Sitting up in bed, I pushed further. "What was your fee again? $200 an hour? I'll double it."

I watched the muscles in his back tense and release several times, but he didn't speak again.

"Four-hundred an hour," I offered. "Five if you satisfy me."

The silence rang in my ears.

"You're drunk, so I'll forgive you in the morning." He jerked the door open and looked back over his shoulder. "But you'd better think about what you just said. Right now I can't stand the sight of you."

He disappeared into the hall and the door swung shut behind him. Realization hit with a resounding smack.

I bolted out of the bed and rushed to the door. On the way, the halter tie on my dress unknotted and the top of the dress fluttered to my waist. Haphazardly holding the bodice up over my chest, I pulled the door open and stepped into the hall.

"Elliot, wait!" I shouted, looking both ways down the hallway and finding him approaching the elevator.

Without hesitation, he kept walking.

The elevator arrived at the same time he reached it.

When the doors slid open, Gavin stepped off, running directly into Elliot. As he apologized he caught sight of me, nearly topless and calling for Elliot. His eyes narrowed and he turned and stepped back onto the elevator, taking his place as far from Elliot as possible.

Nausea hit me full force. Turning back to sprint for the toilet, I ran into the locked door.

"Damn!" I shouted to no one but myself.

Deep breathing and a steady refrain of *I Will Not Puke* kept my stomach contents in place. But nothing could dampen the realization that everything in my life that could go wrong, had.

My despair was complete.

Mental Post-It: next time you tell yourself that nothing worse could happen, punch self in gut before the world has a chance.

❤

WHEN I FINALLY MANAGED THE physical and mental capacity to re-tie my dress and travel to the lobby to get a new key—I must have spent a good twenty minutes sitting on the floor and another twenty trying to manage the stairwell because the elevator did *not* sound like a fun idea—I found Gavin and Elliot sitting in the hotel bar like old drinking buddies. Huddled together at a small table in the corner and gesticulating wildly. An empty bottle of whiskey between them.

My haze was wearing off, but clearly they were just getting starting.

Not wanting to add *very public scene-making* to my expanding resume of social *faux-pas*, I moved as stealthily as possible through the lobby to the front desk. And tried to retreat just as unseen to the elevator after receiving my key.

"There she is." Elliot's voice echoed across the marble space.

"Yup," Gavin concurred, "the lady in—lady in—uh —question."

Their voices grew louder with every word.

"Speak of the devil," Elliot shouted to anyone within hearing, "and she appears before your eyes."

I jabbed at the call button, willing the elevator to arrive and take me away before things got worse.

A tap on the shoulder told me it was too late.

Dubble Bubble Damn, why hadn't I erased the word *worse* from my vocabulary. It always made things, well, *worse*.

Elliot and Gavin had left the bar—but not their bottle—and staggered to the elevator. Gavin, who had been drinking longer and was ten times worse than when he left me in the hall, glared at me through hooded, bloodshot eyes. By his side, hand on his shoulder for support, Elliot was fast behind. Sober when he left the room, he was now as drunk as Gavin appeared to be.

Stifling a groan of distress, I schooled my face into a look of neutral curiosity.

"Yes?" I asked, my heart racing even as I maintained my nonchalance. "Did you need something?"

"You," Elliot barked, swaying with the momentum of jabbing a finger at me, "are a tease."

"And," Gavin added, "a two-timer."

Eyes closed, I wished them both away. Not forever. Just for

the night. For the next two minutes, even. Long enough for the elevator to show and whisk me away.

"We be'n talkin' an' we thunk—" Gavin, the usually faint traces of his West Virginia upbringing coloring his speech, shook his head at the misspoken word. "We think you stink."

Elliot laughed out loud. "We think you stink." *Ha ha ha.* "You rhymed."

"I'm a poet and I—"

"I'm leaving," I interjected.

Surprising enough, considering the day I'd had, the elevator chose that moment to ding its arrival. I turned and marched inside the moment the doors opened, spinning to face my accusers in triumph as the doors shut on them.

Only the doors didn't shut.

I stood there, blankly waiting for the shiny gold panels to glide together, closing out Gavin and Elliot's equally confused faces. Nothing. Not even a warning bell or an apologetic ding.

Ten seconds. Twenty. Thirty.

Clearly, the elevator had no plans to leave.

Opportunity presented itself and the rhyming twins stepped on board, grinning drunkenly at their good fortune.

"We gotcha now," Gavin gloated.

Elliot nodded his approval. "You have to listen."

They stood on either side of me, sandwiching me between them so I had nowhere to turn. Deep breath. *Dee-eep* breath.

"Fine. Say what you have to say."

I did a quick mental evaluation. My nausea was gone, at least for the moment, and nothing they said could possibly make me feel worse than I already did. Of the two men I cared about, I had treated one like a cast-off and the other like a whore. Let them do their worse. At least it would soon be over and they would probably feel better for berating me.

"We know," Elliot explained, leaning close and speaking softly, "that you care about us both."

"We don't blame you for that," Gavin added from the other side. "We know you can't choose who you love. Of all people, we know that best."

"We certainly didn't choose to love you."

"But we do."

My eyes shot from Gavin to Elliot and back again.

"It's true." Elliot tucked a strand of hair behind my ear, pressing a kiss to my temple when I looked shocked. "I love you."

My heart raced. Elliot loved me? This was—I mean—I knew he—Holy Hot Tamales, *love*?

"And," Gavin whispered in my other ear before my brain had fully processed Elliot's confession, "I love you, too. Still."

Gavin loved me, too? Still? Our eyes met and I knew he had never stopped loving me. Not when I disappeared from his life without explanation. Not when I reappeared with a male model on my arm. Not when I came to Italy with said model and wanted to date them both. He loved me.

They both loved me.

I looked back and forth at the two of them. Each looked happy and expectant. Genuine.

In the end, I couldn't keep darting looks between the two eager faces like a courtside spectator at Wimbledon. I stared straight ahead, not seeing the ornate gold and marble lobby, the front desk, the bar, or the pair of guests waiting for us to decide whether we were coming or going from the elevator.

"The thing is," Elliot stepped out into the lobby as he spoke, "neither of us wants half of you."

Gavin joined him, leaving me alone in the elevator car. "We would rather have none of you than that." His green eyes met mine, imploring. "It hurts too much."

My heart broke.

In four short words, I could see how much my indecision was unfair to the two men I loved. Because I knew that I loved them both, each in their own way. And it killed me that I had caused them both pain.

But what could I do?

"We've come to an agreement."

Gavin nodded. "Whichever man you choose, the other will walk away uncontested."

I frowned. What did that—

"But the crux of the thing is, Lyd—" Elliot smiled weakly.

"—the bottom line, Lydia—"

"—you have to make the choice."

"And neither of us will see you until you do," Gavin declared with inarguable finality.

The couple in the lobby, deciding not to wait any longer, stepped into the elevator and pressed the button for their floor. Instantly, the doors slid shut.

At a loss, I watched Gavin and Elliot disappear behind a wall of shiny gold and I silently cursed the word *worse* out of existence.

Happy Birthday to me.

TWENTY-TWO

NO ONE SPOKE to me on the flight back to New York. Not that I was much up for conversation anyway. Ferrero was, understandably, not speaking to me. Janice and Kelly were mad at me on Ferrero's behalf.

Gavin and Elliot were standing by their ultimatum and avoiding me until I made my decision.

Since I had only myself for company, and I was pretty miserable company at that, I popped a pair of sleep aids, found an empty row of seats in coach, and slept the entire flight.

I didn't wake up until a flight attendant shook me and asked me to prepare for landing. I just buckled in where I was and, by the time all the rows in front of me had disembarked and I got up to first class to grab my carry-on, all of my traveling companions were gone.

The only person I recognized at the baggage carousel was Ferrero's driver. He gave me a sympathetic smile as he shook his head and told me that I was instructed to find my own transport home.

Way to round out a perfect week, Vanderwalk.

Things couldn't possibly get—

No. Nope, nuh-uh, I wasn't saying this time. Because time had taught me that things could always get... yeah, that.

"YOU ARE A GENIUS, LYDIA."

I stared at the phone in my hand, wondering if I'd downloaded some fancy new app that reversed what the caller was saying.

"Ferrero?" I asked, incredulous that he would be calling me at all, let alone phoning to call me a genius.

"Pre-sales on the Fall collection are through the roof." His Italian accent was gone, South Jersey coming through loud and clear. "Thanks to you."

"What do you mean?"

Rubbing the sleep out of my eyes, I crawled out of bed and headed for the kitchen and a mind-clearing cup of peppermint tea.

"Your publicity stunt worked," he continued. "The press ate it up like Godiva, plastering my name on every rag sheet from here to Tokyo."

"Publicity stunt?"

"Denouncing my Italian identity at the after party in front of everyone." He sounded delighted. "Brilliant!"

I squinted at the clock on my stove. *6:15.* Maybe I needed to unplug my phone at night. None of these early morning conversations ever made sense. I set a cup of hot water in the microwave and punched it on for ninety seconds.

"Ferrero, it's too early for this kind of confusion. What are you talking about?"

"Lydia, darling, every newspaper in the world covered my party—and my collection—because you outed me in public. There is no such thing as bad press. Our value doubled over the weekend."

"Oh."

The microwave beeped and I rushed to pour the boiling water over the tea bag in my coffee mug. While it steeped I inhaled the wakening aroma of peppermint, praying it notched my alertness up a level.

"And it's not early," he added, "it's late."

Bent over the counter to sniff my tea, I had a closer view of the clock and made out the tiny *P* next to the time. Jetlag must have hit harder than I thought.

"So you're not mad at me anymore?" I deduced.

"Mad?" Ferrero squealed. "I adore you!"

If I weren't so exhausted I might have been happy about that. "That's good."

Deeming my tea steeped enough to drink—and my brain desperate enough to endure weak tea—I swallowed a tingling gulp.

"Have you decided about my offer?"

"I didn't know the position was still available."

"Of course it is."

Though peppermint was supposed to calm upset stomachs, mine clenched. Yet another decision to make.

"I'll let you know by Friday," I offered. By then my brain might have stopped spinning.

"SO FERRERO LOVES YOU AGAIN?" Bethany asked.

When my enthusiasm level upon returning from Italy hadn't measured up, she and Fiona called an emergency Wednesday night meeting at Sweet Spot.

"Yes. He even wants me to become his accessories designer."

"And Gavin still loves you?" Fiona tapped the stainless steel tabletop with a matching silver fingernail.

"Yes," I moaned. This was nothing I hadn't been over a billion times in the last two days. "He always has."

"Phelps too?" Bethany made a note on the rose-colored notepad in front of her.

"It's Elliot, actually."

"You call him by his last name?"

"No," I explained, throwing a scowl Fiona's way for not telling me in the first place, "his real name is Elliot Phelps. Phelps Elliot is apparently his professional name."

"Hey," Fiona returned, hands raised is a defensive gesture, "I didn't think it'd come up. How was I to know he would fall in love with you?"

"Anyway," Bethany interrupted, "he loves you too?"

I nodded. My eyes blurred as I stared at the untouched Lemon Drop on the table. Fiona was certain my problem could be solved by a girls night out and buckets of vodka. Noticing that my ice had melted, she grabbed the drink and headed for the bar.

"You love them both?" Beth's voice softened. "You're in love with them both?"

I nodded again.

"But they're so different."

"I know." My heart thudded in despair. "That's why I can't choose."

"Here's the deal," she asserted, laying it all out for me. "Either you choose one or you lose them both. So let's figure this out."

Fiona returned to the table and set down the glass as she sat. "Start with pros and cons. What's good about Gavin?"

"He's kind, considerate, and reliable. Established and successful. Ready to settle down." I watched Bethany take copious notes on a cocktail napkin as I evaluated Gavin like a prize pig. I remembered the special order lemon *semifreddo* and taking me to see *The Kiss*. "He remembers all the little things and he makes me feel warm and fuzzy inside."

"Okay." Beth scribbled the last of the pros in Gavin's column. "What stinks about him?"

"Well..." I opened my mind to an objective imagination of what life would be like with him. "He likes to plan. Likes to have things go his way. And he lives by routine. Things could get dull. And most of the time he's emotionally reserved."

"Not in touch with his feminine side, huh?" Fiona appeared to ponder my two lists, absently raising my drink to her lips and guzzling.

"Phelps?" Bethany prodded.

"Elliot," I corrected.

"Pros," Fiona gasped as she choked on the sour vodka.

"He's exciting. Surprising. Spontaneous." I smiled at the thought of seeing Southampton and Milan via scooter and cruising Lake Como after dark. "He's always up for fun and adventure. He shakes things up."

And when I thought about his kisses, my entire body burned.

Bethany grinned. "Not to mention he obviously lights your fire. Does he have any cons?"

"Oh yes," I hastily answered. "He's reckless. Has no ambition or definitive plans for the future. And," I added, drawing out the word with extra importance, "he's younger than me."

"That should be a pro." Fiona grinned wickedly.

"Where does this list get us, sugar?"

Bethany pushed the pink pad across the table. Her feminine script outlined Gavin and Elliot in all their glories and flaws. The truth was, none of it made a difference. Feelings weren't something you could define on a sheet of paper. They came from deep inside. That was where I would find my answer.

In the background I heard Fiona order another drink and sensed Bethany take the list and tuck it back into her purse.

Despondency sank its teeth into me, right into my heart.

Tears filled my eyes.

Fiona pushed the fresh Lemon Drop in front of me. "What are you going to do?"

I stared at the drink as if I could find my answer there.

If only I could read ice cubes like fortunetellers read tea leaves. But in the end, all I saw was frozen water and vodka. And more problems than answers.

This was the hardest decision I had ever faced. In a perfect world, I'd get to choose them both.

"Honestly," I said as I pushed the drink away, "I just don't know."

But even as I said the words, a small voice in the back of my mind said, *Of course you do*. I just had to be courageous enough to make the choice.

TWENTY-THREE

THE WAREHOUSE WAS full of rich people, beautiful people, and the lucky few who were both. From across the sea of highlights and updos, tuxes and tiaras, he stood like a mannequin. Somewhat in the crowd, but also apart from it.

I saw him, and my entire self—body, mind, and soul—leaped. Elliot.

I knew he hated society events like this. Everyone dressed in clothes that cost enough to feed starving families for a generation, all in the name of raising money for some trendy cause on another. The choking stench of hypocrisy was overwhelming.

Fiona had told me about the gig. Some young, up-and-coming designer had hired a dozen professionals to model his wares at the event to show everyone how beautiful people looked in his clothes and to start the buzz about his new collection.

Fi had convinced him to take the job.

I watched as a rich, bored housewife walked up to him.

"Goo-ood evening," she drawled, just before a pair of over-manicured fingers reached for his left cheek. "Who are you wearing tonight? Me?"

He stiffened as he turned to face his latest molester. "Good evening, ma'am. This is from Mario Max's new collection."

I swallowed a laugh. That wasn't what she asked, and calling her *ma'am* would send her into a middle-aged crisis call to her plastic surgeon.

He groaned and rubbed his face as she stormed away. He looked miserable.

I couldn't wait any longer.

"Something wrong, Sweet Tooth?"

He spun at the sound of my voice, eyes wide like he couldn't believe I was there. His eyes devoured me, scanning first over my face then my body, as if he had to reassure himself that I was really there.

When he saw what I was wearing, his jaw dropped.

"Like what you see?" I asked.

He took it all in. I stood at least four inches taller than usual in a pair of black stilettos. My legs were encased in silky black stockings. The rest of my attire was concealed by the tan trench coat knotted tightly around my waist and buttoned all the way up to my neck.

It had taken all my courage to walk out of the house like that.

His gaze stuck on my hair. Well, not *my* hair. On the platinum blonde, Marilyn Monroe sex kitten wig.

He stood silent, mouth agape and apparently unable to form words. Just as I had hoped.

"I'll take that as a yes," I said. One slow, seductive step at a time, I moved closer. "Wanna get out of here?"

He nodded, mumbling something that sounded like, "Yuh-hun."

"Good." I dropped to a confessional whisper. "I can barely remain upright in these shoes."

That spurred him into action. In a flash, he took me by the hand and headed an emergency exit that had been blocked open in the back, navigating the overwhelming crowd. I ignored the jealous stares of women who wondered why *I* got to take him home. He was mine. All mine.

The exit led into a back alley illuminated by a million white Christmas lights. Several guests, needing their nicotine fix but not allowed to smoke inside, stood around looking fashionably rebellious.

I was about to ask him to find somewhere less crowded when he squeezed my hand and headed down the alley, around the corner, and into the connecting side alley that happened to be miraculously empty.

Not willing to take a chance, I double- and triple-checked the area.

"Are you sure this is safe?" I asked.

"Absolutely," he said. "This is a perfectly safe neighborhood. Cops patrol it twelve-hundred times an hour."

I laughed. "If you're sure..."

My hands shook as I walked over to the brick wall and relaxed back against it.

"I'm sure." He stepped toward me, his feet on either side of mine, trapping me between his body and the building, and cupped my face in his hands. "God, I've missed you, Lyd."

"I've missed you, too."

"It's been over a week," he said. "I was starting to think you'd chosen..."

He couldn't even say Gavin's name, but he didn't have to. I'd made my choice. No one would come between us again.

"I had a lot of thinking to do," I explained. "I thought a lot about what you said, about me being a Marilyn, not a Norma Jean. And I finally realized that you're right. I am an atomic fireball."

To emphasize my point, I slid my hands into his hair and pulled him down into a searing kiss. My lips opened over his and he groaned into my mouth, welcoming my exploring tongue. He leaned more fully into me, pressing me deeper into the wall and kicking his feet between mine so he could step into the vee of my thighs.

I almost got lost in the kiss. But I wasn't done.

Pulling back, Elliot tried to follow me with his mouth. I placed a hand on his chest and held him back. "See." One more quick kiss. "Firecracker."

"Good thing I used to be a Boy Scout," he teased. "I know how to start all kinds of fires."

Our eyes met, and for several long seconds we just looked at each other.

Finally, in a low, serious voice, I confessed, "I love you, Elliot Phelps."

"Yeah?" His mouth kicked up in that cocky smile. "Why is that?"

"Because you inspire me. You make me feel like I can be so much more than I am. You make me believe I can strike out on my own and make a go at having my own jewelry and accessories line."

"Really?" He looked awestruck. "You're not taking either job."

"Nope," I answered, excitement bubbling up in my chest. "I am currently unemployed."

It was terrifying, but also thrilling. Just like life with Elliot would be.

"Not unemployed," he insisted, picking me up by the waist and spinning me around. "You're an entrepreneur."

I giggled as he set me back down against the wall. "I guess I am."

"I'm very proud of you."

"Thank you." I pressed a soft kiss on his mouth. "I wouldn't have the courage to do this without you."

"I like that kind of thank you," he teased, kissing me back. "In fact, I could think of a few other ways you could thank me if you were so inspired. At least a dozen involving this trench coat."

Placing my hands on his chest, I held him back again when he tried to steal another kiss.

"Actually, I came up with one on my own."

"Really?" he growled.

"Hidden somewhere on my person is a symbol of how I feel for you." I pushed him back a step, looked both ways down the alleyway, and tightened the belt on the coat. "Find it."

With a primal growl, he lunged for me, his hands roaming every inch of my body.

"Sir," a booming voice ordered, accompanied by the bright glare of a flashlight, "please step away from the lady."

A patrolman stood at the mouth of the alley, a stern look of disapproval on his face. Elliot took a step back while I made sure I was fully covered. My attire was not meant to be seen by the NYPD.

"Is he bothering you, Miss?"

"N-no, officer," I stammered as I clutched the trench coat over my chest. "He, um, is... his advances are welcome, if you know what I mean."

"Yes, Miss." The fatherly officer actually blushed. "Then you should take this somewhere private before you get an indecent exposure rap."

"Right away, sir."

When the officer didn't move, Elliot took me by the hand and walked out of the alley. Within seconds he had hailed a cab and given the driver directions.

I yanked off the wig—it was itchy as hell—and flopped back against the seat.

"That was the most excitement I've had since..." She pondered, still grinning. "Well, since that boat ride in Italy."

"I'm happy to be of service." He reached for the trench coat. "Hey, where's that thing hidden, anyway?"

Oh yeah. I checked the driver's attention. Finding it on the road, I reached inside the coat, into my cleavage, and pulled out a small, round, shiny green ball. I reached forward and placed it against his lips, and he obligingly opened and let me drop it on his tongue.

"Mmm," he hummed as he sucked on the ball. "Sweet. Whad ith it?"

"An Everlasting Gobstopper."

This was a symbol of my feelings for him, that they were everlasting.

He grinned and spit the candy into his palm, depositing it in his jacket pocket before leaning in to kiss her confused mouth. "Then I'll just make sure it lasts longer than Ever."

I sighed and sank into his side. "I'll hold you to that. Verbal contract."

The cab pulled to a stop in front of Elliot's building. We climbed out and while he paid the cabbie I reknotting the belt on the trench coat. I hadn't even noticed him untying it. Sneaky, sneaky.

"Did I tell you my first name isn't Elliot anymore?" he teased, taking my arm and leading the way into the building. "I've changed it to Gobstopper."

"Why is that?"

"Because I'm Everlasting."

I laughed at his stupid joke, I couldn't help it.

"I hope so," I replied. "I expect to love you for a very long time."

"Oh yeah," he replied. "In love, too."

He waggled his eyebrows and I smacked him with the wig. "Ha, ha, very funny."

"That's why you love me," he teased.

"Yes," I sighed in mock resignation, "I suppose it is."

"Now we need to come up with a new name for you, Miss Vanderwalk." As we crossed the lobby, he pretended to consider. "What goes with Gobstopper?"

"How about..." I whispered a suggestion in his ear.

His gaze melted me. Neither of us would ever look at Licorice Laces the same again.

"Naughty, naughty girl." Elliot swung me into his arms and bounded up the stairs to his apartment. "I love candy."

Dear reader,

Eye Candy was the second book I ever wrote, way way back in 2005, and the first book I self-published, way back in 2011. It's been through some changes since then (as have I) but Lydia and Elliot still hold a special place in my heart.

I hope you loved their story! Even if you didn't, please take a moment to leave a **review**.

The City Chicks series continues with Southern belle Bethany's story in *Straight Stalk*. Turn the page for a sneak peek…

To get insider extras, exclusive giveaways, and breaking news, visit teralynnchilds.com/subscribe to join my mailing list.

Tera L. Childs

STRAIGHT STALK
Prologue

"You're a turner," Lydia declared, her voice carrying crisply despite the noisy crowd in *Cafe Frais*, my favorite SoHo teahouse.

Intrigued, I regarded her over the gold rim of my teacup.

Next to me Fiona choked on her Earl Grey. "Is that anything like a spinner?" she sputtered as she dabbed a napkin to her chin.

I wasn't sure what Fiona meant, but odds were it was obscene. Her mind lived forever in the gutter.

Carefully setting my own teacup on its waiting saucer without a clatter—some Southern manners were hard to lose—I considered the conversation leading up to Lydia's odd statement.

We had been discussing my romantic past. Not exactly my favorite subject, but with new beau Evan on his way to join us for brunch—meeting the girls for the first time—they seemed intent on rehashing history. I had just finished telling them about seeing my latest ex shopping at Gracious Home with his new boyfriend.

Sad, but true.

Which did not explain Lydia's bizarre declaration.

"What precisely do you mean?" I asked.

"Well," she began, resting her elbows gently on the floral tablecloth. "David is gay."

I nodded politely at her statement of the obvious. "Yes."

"And before David there was Jon. He's gay, too."

Also true. Two for two. With a sinking feeling about the direction of this conversation, I nodded again.

"Tell me, Bethany. How many of your ex-boyfriends are gay?"

"Just the—" *two*, I started to say. Then I remembered Tad. But that was all—oh. And Richard.

Four?

How was it possible that I had blocked out the glaring reality that my last four beaux had since burst forth from the closet? That was the sort of pattern a girl really ought to notice.

What did this say about me? Was I the kind of girl who only attracted men of uncertain sexuality and repressed urges? Was I a ... closet cleaner?

My face must have fallen, because Lydia leaned even closer and smiled sympathetically. "A turner," she repeated. "See what I mean?"

Yes, I did. All too well.

This was probably all my fault. How depressing. Oh, not that I made a conscious decision to only date un-outed gay men, but must have been signs. Little indications—or big ones, as in the case of Tad's "roommate" in his West Village studio apartment—about a man's true sexuality.

That I had overlooked these signs in the past might mean I was only looking for unavailable guys. I couldn't get hurt if rejection was beyond my control, right?

Sounded like something a therapist would say.

Deeply psychological.

I read once that girls only sought out men either similar to or the opposite of their fathers. Since none of my exes were the strict, overbearing, ultimatum-giving type, I had to assume I was seeking out the latter.

I sighed, lifted the teacup of English Breakfast with two sugars, and took a fortifying sip. Over the porcelain edge I caught sight of Evan making his way through the crowded café.

A welcome sight.

"Evan's here," I announced as I set my cup back on its saucer. "He's different. Not a gay bone in his body."

Fiona snorted again, but turned with Lydia to get their first look at the new man in my life. Well, he wasn't new to me. We'd been dating for almost six months, but I kept him tightly under wraps. After my previous disasters I'd wanted to wait until I was sure before introducing him to the closest thing to family I had in the city.

Seeing me, Evan waved enthusiastically.

He dressed so well. In a non-gay, purely heterosexual way, of course.

Simple black leather jacket. Flat-front black trousers. Shiny black loafers. Lavender paisley shirt?

I scowled.

Fiona and Lydia exchanged a less-than-inscrutable look before turning back to me.

"Good luck with that," Fiona said.

Lydia added, "I'm so sorry."

I did not need sympathy. Evan wasn't like the others. Lydia had already found her Mr. Perfect. Fiona was working her way through the entire male population of New York before settling on a favorite. And I, despite my questionable track record and my friends' initial impressions, had found mine.

I was certain.

We talked about everything. He made little romantic gestures like leaving a single red rose on my pillow and sending me chocolates at work. The sex was—well, the sex was mediocre at best, but the rest of the relationship more than made up for that lack.

Just as I had that affirming thought Evan reached our table. He came immediately to my side and bowed down to kiss me on the cheek. As he leaned in I noticed the silver and leather jewelry adorning his neck and wrist.

"Evan, I've put a lot of time and effort into you," I said before I could stop myself. "If you turn out gay, I'll castrate you."

Chapter 1

Walk-In Closet was doing okay. Not great. Not fantastic. Not an overnight success. But for a relatively new SoHo boutique it was doing okay.

Two years in business and going strong.

Still, it could be better.

Things could always be better.

If a great windfall fell my direction, I wouldn't step out of the way.

The bell over the front door tinkled just as I finally found a home for a box of shantung neckties in the overcrowded back room. Quickly dusting off my *toile* skirt, I pushed through the sage green damask curtain separating the showroom from the storage to find my mail carrier walking to the counter.

"Good morning, Fred." I smiled even as I cringed at the thought of another delivery. If he had anything bigger than a clutch purse I would have to start turning the boxes into displays.

Or he might have bills. Bills would be worse.

"How was your weekend?" I asked.

Fred answered with a terse, "Fine."

One word responses were his forte.

He was never much for conversation. In fact, in the two years since Walk-In Closet opened I couldn't think of a single time he had actually spoken more than two words to me. And those were usually, "Sign here."

I only knew his Christian name because Albert, the Saturday mail carrier, was a friendly older gentleman who loved taking the time for a chat. Fred seemed to resent the fact that I had learned and called him by his name, but I took a perverse pleasure in being friendlier than his behavior warranted.

Eventually the honey would sweeten him up.

Without another syllable, he handed over the small stack of envelopes—all disgustingly bill-shaped—and walked back out the door.

Sometimes I felt he would prefer my absence so he could leave my mail on the counter. But I was convinced I must be the only pleasant interaction he got all day and that he needed all the help he could get. One day I would break through that gruff veneer. One day he might even say, golly, *three* words.

A girl can dream.

Quickly flipping through the pile, I saw two bills that absolutely had to be paid by Friday and several more that could be put off another week.

This was not how I had imagined running the store. A financial balancing act between downright necessities and necessary improvements. I downright *needed* to pay the rent. But I also needed to order better quality padded hangers before another careless shopper left the floor around the lingerie display littered with slinky camisoles and lace garter belts.

Footprints didn't wash out of pastel silk.

The SBA loan that jump-started the shop had gotten me the lease and the décor and the initial stock with a little left over for advertising. But that was gone. Now that I *knew* what I needed.

Too soon old, too late wise.

I pulled the portable file tote from beneath the register and filed the vital bills in the "Pay Now" file and the rest under "Pay Someday." The "Pay Now" file was a little plumper in the pants than I last remembered.

With the business bank account hovering precariously above the red, I had to bring in some bill-paying cash soon.

Whenever I needed extra cash flow there was one easy answer. Well, two, but I wasn't about to call and ask my father for help. His opinions on my choice to stay in the city and start my own business rather than return home and marry a nice, successful Southern boy were unequivocal: he would neither forgive nor assist me.

So, it was time to hold another trunk show.

They always brought in a crowd of fashion hunters desperate to get the newest, hottest couture. When they found the perfect piece, they usually bought an item or two from the shop to go with. When they didn't, they usually bought *something* from the shop so they didn't leave empty-handed.

Thanks to Lydia's connections, I could always get a Ferrero Couture trunk show when I needed one—occasionally with an appearance by Ferrero himself. And the last one had been nearly four months ago.

Right around the time Evan and I broke up. *Le sigh*.

At least that relationship had dissolved over another woman—not another man.

I had the card for the Tri-State sales rep tacked up in the storeroom. Pushing back through the damask curtain, I hadn't taken two steps into the cardboard maze when the doorbell tinkled again.

I groaned.

At least it couldn't be more bills. Unless one of my creditors had resorted to couriered delivery or repo men.

Maybe it was a customer.

Actually, I noted as I stepped into the showroom, it was two.

A pair of well-dressed-if-a-little-on-the-West-Village-artistic-side men stood inside the doorway, scrutinizing the store. Though Walk-In Closet carried both full men's and women's wear, most of the men's wear was bought by women shopping for men. Hiding my surprise, I stepped forward and greeted them.

"Welcome to Walk-In Closet, gentlemen."

Their attention turned to me, assessing me as avidly as they had the shop.

"My name is Bethany. How can I help you?"

One man, the taller of the two, stepped forward and asked, "You're the owner?"

Not usually the first question out of a customer's mouth.

If not for their generally professional appearances, I might have reconsidered them for repo men.

"Yes," I answered.

They smiled. The tall one nudged the blond one in the ribs.

"I need a shirt," the blond announced.

The other two nodded in enthusiastic agreement. A pair of bobbleheads.

"Wonderful," I cooed. Clapping my hands together, I led them to the men's shirts. "What kind of shirt are you looking for?"

"Oh dear," the blond said, "I hadn't thought of that."

This seemed an odd comment from a man who had presumably entered the shop with a purpose. But after two years, very little walked through that door that still surprised me. I'd seen much, *much* stranger things.

"All right. Let's start with type. Dress shirt, sport shirt, or t-shirt?"

The three men looked at each other, conferred for a moment, before deciding on a dress shirt. Making a mental evaluation of the blond's style—youthful, energetic, a little flamboyant—I headed for the latest shirts from Vanny-O, a talented young designer who lived in my building.

I took every opportunity to promote local designers. It had to be good karma to help someone on the way up.

Pulling three of the more colorful designs off the rack, I wagered with myself that he would choose the one with bright yellow, purple, and lilac variegated stripes. I was rarely wrong.

For a moment, when I held the shirts up, his eyes brightened like a schoolboy. Then the thrill banked and he approached my outstretched hand cautiously.

"I'm not sure," he mused, taking the pale green shirt covered with bright turquoise pinwheels and holding it up to his chin. "This seems awfully bold for the office. I'm not sure I could carry it off."

The tall man stifled a snicker.

"Nonsense, of course you can... I'm sorry, what was your name?"

Small business success hinged on relationships. The first step to creating a relationship with a customer was an open, friendly atmosphere. That was why I always introduced myself by name to new customers, and asked their name at the first opportunity.

That was how I had regular customers today who had first walked through my doors two years ago.

"Steven," he answered with a grin.

And that was how I would get and keep Steven as a customer.

"Pleasure to meet you, Steven." I took the pinwheel shirt out of his hands and handed him my choice. "Office fashion is overwhelmingly relaxed these days. Even many professional workplaces have eliminated ties from the dress code. That leaves a man little room for color in his wardrobe. The dress shirt, whether worn with cargo pants, dress cords, or a pinstripe suit, is your canvas. You don't look like a man who's afraid of a little color, now are you, honey?"

Steven beamed. Nearly ripping the hanger from my grasp, he held it beneath his chin and turned to admire himself in the full-length mirror. "What do you think, Trevor?"

The tall one, Trevor, nodded in considered approval. "I think we have a winner, Steven."

Steven clapped his hands in unrestrained glee. "Wonderful." He grabbed Trevor's wrist, pulling him to the mirror. "Now do him!"

Between them, they tried on nearly every item in the shop —including some pieces from the women's collection. By the time Steven and Trevor left, their purchases rang up at nearly three-thousand dollars.

What a way to start a Monday.

Looked like new padded hangers might make the cut. One more sale like that and the new mannequins for the storefront would have a chance, too.

Coming down from the euphoria of an excellent sale, I knew not to let one successful sale eclipse a thin bank account. I still needed an influx of cash if I wanted to pay the bills *and* make all the improvements on my list. Heading once again through the damask drape, I wound my way through the maze of boxes. I finally reached the bulletin board next to the restroom. Just as the doorbell tinkled.

Another customer, I hoped.

Determined not to navigate the maze again, I quickly snagged the business card and tucked it in my only available pocket. My bra.

Back through the boxes and the curtain.

I found the shop empty.

That was strange. I knew I'd heard the bell.

I stepped into the shop, the periwinkle heels of my peep-toe slingbacks clicking on the parquet floor. To my right, a head of tight black curls popped up from behind my display of men's shoes. Followed by a cheery round face I recognized instantly.

"Cassie!" I cried.

"Bethany!"

She darted around the display, throwing her arms around me with abandon when I met her halfway. I returned the hug with equal enthusiasm—though perhaps a bit less abandon. Southern women always show a little restraint.

"Cassie, good Lord," I exclaimed. "What are you doing in New York?"

"Didn't you hear?" she gasped. "I've got a new job."

No, I hadn't heard. And why hadn't she called me?

"In the city?"

She nodded emphatically. "I've been back nearly a week, but haven't had a spare moment outside work. This job is keeping me on my toes."

"I'm glad you found time today."

She bit her lip, the pencil she habitually chewed on noticeably absent. "Actually, this is work, too."

"What do you mean?" I asked.

The last time I saw Cassie Bishop was graduation day at Columbia. Ten years ago. I'd stayed in New York and laid the groundwork for opening Walk-In Closet. She'd headed for California and a career in television.

Over the years she had risen through the ranks from coffee gopher to second assistant production manager to assistant production manager, mostly on soon-canceled TV shows and movies of the week. The jobs weren't always the greatest, but by Hollywood standards she was a resounding success.

Seeing her again made me feel a decade younger than my thirty-two years.

She hadn't changed. Still the same riot of black curls framing her fair, heart-shaped face. Still cherub-cheek-popping bright smile and light blue eyes that sparkled with possibility. Still dressed entirely in black—I had hoped the bright colors of California style might have rubbed off on her just a little bit— not even a pastel accent piece.

At least Hollywood hadn't changed her.

Though we hadn't seen each other in all that time, we had worked hard to keep in touch with more than the occasional email. We spoke on the phone at least once a month.

It felt like we had never been apart.

"What I mean is," she explained as she headed for the floral chintz settee in the corner, "I'm not here for social purposes. This is business."

She collapsed on the settee, grabbing my hand and pulling at me to sit next to her.

"I'm here to offer you a job."

With my legs crossed at the ankles, knees held chastely together, and skirt smoothed into place, I let her guide me down onto the settee.

"A job?" I shook my head at the nonsensical notion. "Cass, I don't know anything about television."

"Of course not, silly," she admonished. "But you *do* know about fashion."

I couldn't argue that point. For the better part of ten years I had been working in fashion retail, even before opening the shop. My resume included a stint as a buyer at Bradford's, a display designer at Louis Jewelers, and a sales associate at more than half a dozen clothing stores.

Since the shop opened I'd kept on top of all the latest, subscribed to all the trade and fashion magazines, even got interviewed once for a small feature in *Lucky* titled "Southern Gals in the City."

But what did that have to do with television?

Cassie tucked one foot behind the opposite knee and turned to face me. Her eyes widened as she settled into a more serious pose.

"Have you heard of *One Straight Guy at a Time*?"

I shook my head.

"It's a new makeover reality show. A cast of five gay guys with various specialties—culture, fashion, cuisine, grooming, decorating—take a disaster dude and turn him into the perfect man. A whole life make-better." She leaned back with a self-satisfied smile. "I'm the production manager."

"How wonderful! Very impressive title."

"It is," she agreed without modesty. "And as production manager I'm in on all the creative meetings. At the last one the producers and director were talking about outside consultants we need on the show."

I listened carefully, still not sure how this related to me, but happy to see Cassie so enthusiastic about this new job.

"When they said they needed a fashion consultant with loads of real world experience, I recommended you." She leaned in close. Placing a hand on my shoulder, she explained, "Bethany, they love you. They love your shop. The job is yours. If you want it."

"A job?" I repeated. "As a fashion consultant? What does that mean?"

"It means, babe, that the show pays you for your expertise. For your advice. And, if the contractual agreements with the other consultants are any indication, they'll dress the cast in clothes from your shop whenever you want, list your shop in the opening and closing credits, and use your shop on the show a minimum of four episodes every season."

After the full sixty seconds it took for this information to sink in my lungs failed. I couldn't breathe. Couldn't speak.

This was everything my shop needed. Exposure. Advertising. Customers. *Income.*

This was my windfall, and it fell right in my lap.

My ecstatic shock must have shown on my face because Cassie hugged me close and exclaimed, "We'll have so much fun working together!"

When the doorbell tinkled I barely noticed the UPS man prop the door open and load up his hand truck with boxes.

Ready to read the rest? Get *Straight Stalk* now.

DON'T MISS THE REST OF THE SERIES!

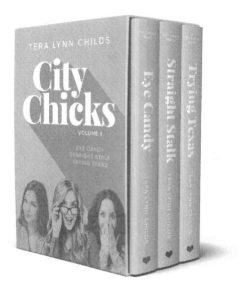

Three feisty city chicks. Three swoon-worthy guys. Three romantic adventures they'll never forget.

Eye Candy

Straight Stalk

Trying Texas

Get all three books in the ebook box set!

City Chicks (Volume 1)

ABOUT THE AUTHOR

TERA LYNN CHILDS is the RITA-award-winning young adult author of the mythology-based Oh. My. Gods. series, the Forgive My Fins mermaid romance series, the kick-butt monster-hunting Sweet Venom trilogy, and the Darkly Fae series. She also wrote the City Chicks chick lit romance series and co-wrote the Hero Agenda and Creative HeArts series. Tera lives nowhere in particular and spends her time writing wherever she can find a comfy chair and a steady stream of caffeinated beverages. Find her online at *teralynnchilds.com*.

MORE BY TLC

the City Chicks series

Eye Candy

Straight Stalk

Trying Texas

City Chicks (Volume 1)

the Creative HeArts series

Ten Things Sloane Hates About Tru

Falling for the Girl Next Door

the Darkly Fae series

When Magic Sleeps

When Magic Dares

When Magic Burns

When Magic Falls

When Magic Wakes

the Oh. My. Gods. series

Oh. My. Gods.

Goddess Boot Camp

Goddess in Time

the Forgive My Fins series

Forgive My Fins

Fins Are Forever

Just For Fins

Pretty in Pearls

the Sweet Venom trilogy

Sweet Venom

Sweet Shadows

Sweet Legacy

the Hero Agenda series

w/ Tracy Deebs

Powerless

Relentless

Printed in Great Britain
by Amazon